THE ROAD
TO NOWHERE

by Maurice Walsh

THE ROAD TO NOWHERE

Maurice Walsh

CHAMBERS

This edition

© Maurice Walsh, Ian Walsh and Neil Walsh 1980

Printed in Singapore
by Tien Wah Press (Pte) Ltd

ISBN 0 550 20417 2

PART I: ROGAN STUART, ADRIFT

CHAPTER I

I

Sоuтн by east the early June sun was slowly climbing the long shoulder of Slievemaol.

The bell-tent, brown and shabby and patched, cowering under the great sweep of hill, stood on the only level plot of ground on the south side of the bay, and that unique plot was not more than fifteen yards square. In front it shelved down to a tilted slab of basalt wherefrom a swimmer might dive into five fathoms of brisk sea-water; behind, it sloped, slowly at first and then ever more hurriedly, into the craggy breast of Slievemaol, whose bald head looked steeply down from eighteen hundred feet. As far as the eye might see, all down the long winding south side of the bay, that insignificant brown cone of canvas was the only evidence of man and his handiworks. But on the north side, across a mile of water, where a wide green valley sloped gently back between the mountains, an ugly, red-brick, turreted mansion was mercifully screened by full-foliaged trees.

On the narrow level between tent and hillside a huge bacon-box rested on its side and was roughly fitted with shelves holding the nucleus of a camping outfit and several cartons of vegetarian dietary. Facing the shelves a long-backed, bronzed young fellow sat cross-legged in the heather, and, with a table-spoon, ate a golden confection out of a glass jar. His plentiful black hair was still tousled and damp after his morning plunge, and his unbuttoned pyjama jacket showed a firm neck and a muscular chest. He was using the spoon so deftly that it made no clink against the glass, and was wolfing the golden confection as hastily and criminally as a small boy in his mother's preserve cupboard.

Back to back with this young cupboard-snatcher sat another man, just as long but many years older—long-chinned, long-nosed, with a humorous, sardonically-lined mouth, and grey-flecked dark hair receding on a white brow. He was simply attired in flannel trousers and nothing more, and the long muscles rippled under his velvet, cream-tinted skin. He sat on his heels before a small but active fire of sticks, and, with a steel fork, carefully turned over three medium-sized sea-trout that sizzled odorously on a long-handled frying-pan. At the side of the fire a tin kettle, not quite as black as the pan, sent out small breaths of steam. He watched the trout intently for half a minute, then sat back on his heels, ran the fork handle through his hair, and lifted up a big baritone bellow with a modicum of tune:

> " I likes my grub, it pleases me
> Better than love or amity :
> Eggs-and-ham, bacon-liver,
> An Easter lamb, trout of the river.
>
> I dream of tart instead of Cupid ;
> A broken heart is very stupid—
> Except the heart of sheep in gravy ;
> Give me that, and Heaven save ye !

"That, Alistair MacIan, my American Highlandman, is the morning hymn of us Anglo-Saxons. All the same, who is going to demolish and devour this third white trout?"

Alistair MacIan swallowed hastily, "One'll crowd my capacity this morning, Paddy Joe."

"Time we tried that vegetarian ham-and-egg on the shelf there. A nourishing food by all accounts?"

8

"Hmn-hmn!" agreed Alistair readily, and his mouth was so unmistakably full that Paddy Joe Long turned on him a slow but suspicious eye.

"What's choking you, tinker?"

"Nothing," gulped the culprit.

"You're hiding something in front of you."

"An empty jar I found—just scraping the bottom of it." He held up the glass jar—and it was empty.

Paddy Joe emitted an anguished yell and started to his long length. He poised the iron fork dagger-wise over Alistair's hunched shoulders and his chin jutted out like the ram of a battleship.

"Yankee robber! King of thieves! Stealer of dead mice from blind kittens! Incontinent, bear-mouthed, sweet-toothed glutton! Oh high heaven! my last jar of nectaire honey that I was cherishing against hard times! On the prongs of this fork I will feed you with your own gizzard, you—you——"

"'Ware trout!" warned Alistair from under shielding arms. "Smell 'em!"

Paddy Joe turned hastily, grasped the long handle of the pan, and shook and tossed the trout with practised deftness. Then he sank back on his heels and laughed.

"Well-oh-well! such is luck. Last night and the night before I toyed happily with the idea of getting outside that jar sort of unbeknownst—but what chance had I against an up-and-comer?"

"Anticipation has its pleasures," philosophised Alistair, tossing the empty jar into the air and cleverly catching it, mouth down, on the iron spoon.

"Ay! and may realisation torment you. 'One will crowd my capacity,' says he. Not as much as a tail if I had any one——"

"Here comes one now," Alistair stopped him, "who grubbed early or went without."

9

Along the pony-track, not more than a score of yards above the tent, came a tramper—not a tramp—a middle-sized youngish man in well-worn flannels, with a light knapsack slung on his shoulders, and a silk oil-coat slipped under the straps. But he was not hasting. His head was doggedly down, his hands deep in his pockets; his slow long stride had something purposeful yet aimless about it—as if he were gloomily determined to get somewhere, yet had no interest in the end of the road.

Level with the tent the odour of the frying fish pierced his concentration, and his slow stride halted of itself. He turned and looked down at the camp and smiled contemplatively. He stood there very still for a matter of seconds, feet apart and head forward, and then brought right hand out of pocket and up to the level of an ancient felt hat.

"God save the good work!" he saluted quietly.

"God save you kindly!" Paddy Joe Long gave back the ritual. He liked the way that lad smiled. A pleasant, reserved smile with a touch of wistfulness in it, the mouth scarcely moving, but a crinkling about the deep eye-sockets and a narrowing of the full eye. And at the same moment Paddy Joe felt a queer psychic impulse flow into him. He smiled back, and swung to his frying-pan, gave the trout a final turn, moved one away from the others, and tapped it lightly with the iron fork.

Alastair was speaking in his easy American drawl with its quaint touch of Highland.

"Plenty early on top of the road this morn—all the way from Corullish?"

"Not this morn. I bedded in the bracken last night." And there was the real Highland note.

"Wow! Cold?"

"As charity—but no, sir!" Again he smiled. "Charity is not cold, nor my breakfast far in front of me. The Red-Indian gentleman has already chosen me a trout."

Alistair laughed. "I saw him. Come away down, travelling man."

In that simple way was this man drawn fatefully into this company. He came down through the thin and worn heather, seated himself on a convenient boss of lichened stone, and slipped the strap of his knapsack loose. "I am extremely grateful to you, gentlemen," he said apologetically. "Hope you don't mind me butting in?"

"Sure, we're all Christians," said Paddy Joe, "and every man is entitled to his bite and sup. Reach me that tin platter, Alistair."

Alistair was measuring spoons of ground coffee from a rusty canister into a steaming kettle. "Just a moment, and I'll slice you some bread and butter. You haven't the barbarous taste for morning tea, Mr——?"

"Stuart—Rogan Stuart." His voice hardened as in momentary challenge, and then: "No, I like coffee."

At that name—Rogan Stuart—Paddy Joe looked up quickly and closely, and looked away again. His jaw muscles tightened, as if a stab of memory, not pleasant, had pierced him, but his voice was carelessly easy.

"Alistair MacIan making coffee *Américaine*!" he introduced with a hand gesture. "My name is Long—Patrick Joseph Stanislaus Long——"

"Paddy Joe for short," the other finished for him. "I have heard of you, Mr Long—and read your last book."

"Why wouldn't you?" said Paddy Joe. "I won't hold it against you. Two years ago I saw Rogan Stuart play stand-off half for Scotland at Lansdowne Road."

The other looked at him steadily out of deep-set eyes.

"I no longer play rugby, Mr Long." He paused, and then: "Two years is a long time."

"A hell of a long time, often," agreed Paddy Joe gloomily.

Alistair MacIan sensed some undercurrent of meaning between the two, something to be avoided, something unpleasant—yet something not shameful.

"Grub-pile!" he cried, beating two tin platters together. "Come and get it."

Like practised outdoor men, they used their iron forks handily and made no crumbs. The soft morning air flowed softly about them; the sun, not yet done climbing Slievemaol, poured its young brilliance on them; below them the green waters of the bay rippled and dazzled between the green-draped breasts of the hills.

"You are old hands at this game," said Rogan Stuart, his eyes admiring the rigid economy of the camp.

"A pan and a tin kettle," said Paddy Joe, "and the width of Ireland to forage in—enough! Anything more, and one might as well stay safe home with one's wife—" He stopped suddenly, but Rogan Stuart ignored the pause and went on making small talk.

"I was lucky this morning."

"Luckier than you knew, Mr Stuart," said Alistair blandly. "You very nearly ran into a vegetarian breakfast. We are trying out that stunt——"

Paddy Joe swallowed hastily and lifted up his long neck. "Ho, ho, ho! Vegetarian stunt, be Japers! Three days ago he ate two pounds of mountain mutton at Corullish Inn ; and yesterday, Mary Whelan at the head of the bay roasted a chicken for him. Look at the elegant cartons in our pantry, and only one seal broken —a thing that with a spoonful of water and a lump of dripping turns into a beefsteak in the pan."

Breakfast over, they filled leisurely pipes, and the two campers, waiving Rogan's offer to help, did a practised clean-up. When finished the camp was housewifely tidy. The morning air flowed under the looped-up fall of the tent, and the closed lid of the big box, draped with a ground-sheet, hid away the few utensils.

While the campers were completing their toilet within the tent, Rogan Stuart sat leaning forward on his boss of lichened stone and smoked contemplatively. His half-closed eyes were on the sheening waters of the bay, and he was feeling comfortable, lazy, a little somnolent. Yes, he was lucky this morning. These were two real men. MacIan—probably Scots with American experience—or the other way about! And all Ireland knew Long—Paddy Joe Long, the rising novelist, married rather romantically to Norrey Carr, the famous actress. A wise bird Paddy Joe! He knew. The twitch of nostril, the flicker of eyelids had shown that he had not forgotten Rogan Stuart's tragedy. Queer—most men had. Self-centred beasts men were—and none more so than himself. Yes! but no one—except one black hound—could know the completeness of the tragedy—the completeness that made this seeming entity that was Rogan Stuart nothing more than—than an empty husk, the trammels of life loose about him, and yet some spirit in him refusing to take the easy road. Never more would he be eager, or hungry—or even sorrowful. He would just drift and drift and drift for a little while by this serene, sea-washed Irish shore, and after that—go on drifting. Nothing—nothing—nothing—that was life.

Alistair and Paddy Joe came from the tent, and Rogan lifted his head, and his eyes, deep under brow, smiled. Oh, my fine, tall, easy-going men with life in your clear eyes and a joyful appreciation of life flowing from you!

"On top of the road?" he enquired, rising to his feet.

"No hurry," said Paddy Joe carelessly.

There followed a little waiting pause, and then Alistair grinned happily. "We have a sort of nefarious date this morning with the harbour-master round the corner at the pier jump," he said tentatively.

"Nefarious is right," said Paddy Joe. "This fellow suggests that a salmon may be caught in more ways than one."

"There's a dandy way we used try—in Canada," said Alistair.

"With a net," amplified Paddy Joe, "and the night not too dark."

"And Tom Whelan, the harbour-master, is a mine of information."

"So we are going up to interview him. Care for a lift?—the coracle below holds three."

Rogan looked down at the cockle-shell moored at the foot of the sloping boulder. The framework was of fragile lath and the skin of tarred canvas; it would carry three in smooth water, but the fit would be a tight one.

"Thank you. I think I'll stroll round."

"Look in at the harbour-master's office," invited Alistair, "and if no one is there, try the bar at the Harty Arms."

"Where one MacIan will be standing us a seldom drink," added Paddy Joe.

"I'll try the Harty Arms first," smiled Rogan.

He sat on his boss of stone and watched the two clamber down to water-level and gingerly board the swaying little craft. Alistair took the narrow-bladed oars, Paddy Joe cast off the line from an empty petrol-tin that served as a mooring buoy, and the coracle slid and dipped with the lightness and security of an egg-shell.

14

Paddy Joe sat in the stern, elbows on knees, and smoked steadily for a while, his shoulders swaying easily to the slow kick of the oars.

"A nice lad yon?" suggested Alistair presently.

"He was in my thoughts," said Paddy Joe.

"The look—something back of the eyes—deep in head —like ice-water down your back. What was it, Paddy Joe? You know?"

"I do, God help me. That damned writer's memory of mine!"

"No weakling either—wine, woman——?"

"Not ever! Two years ago he was as vigorous a man as ever donned the blue jersey of Scotland, and that's saying a mouthful. I saw him stop big Con Dolan flat as a flounder five yards from the line, and Con's fifteen stone like a fifteen-inch shell."

"Two years is a hell of a long time—you said that like a funeral."

"So I did. Think! Rogan Stuart! Does the name stir a memory?"

"Rogan Stuart! No-o! I'm not a rugby fan."

Paddy Joe looked down at the chess-board framework of the coracle and frowned. "My Norrey—your red-head," he half-mused, "and the young ones—God guard them——!"

"What are you driving at?"

"Suppose something happened—some accident——?"

Alistair lunged at the oars. "Drop that, Paddy Joe! Blast you, what a hellish thought! Do you want me to go tearing across Ireland and all Scotland——"

"That is what happened to Rogan Stuart."

"When—how?"

"Not so long ago. He lives in Dublin—or did. His wife and two-year-old daughter left the North Wall by the night-boat last winter and the boat sank in a collision in a Mersey fog."

"Both of them?"

"Trapped in their berth. There was some rumour of scandal too—there always is. Some said the wife was running away from her husband, and others added that she was fleeing to the arms of another man— By the Powers! that's queer."

"What is?"

"We saw that man in the village yesterday."

"That tall good-looker you pointed out to me?"

"Yes—Eudmon Butler, known as the Black Captain— a terror on two feet in love or war."

"Perhaps Stuart is on his trail?"

"It could be—and what a hell of a fight at the end of it! But leave it, lad, leave it! Let the dead rest. Rogan Stuart must dree his own weird. Watch what you're at! Pull your right, or you'll bump the point."

CHAPTER II

I

THE breeze of morning died, and the sun, poised on the shoulder of Slievemaol, grew ardent, too ardent for Rogan Stuart, somnolently abstracted on his lump of stone. Through his abstraction he felt the dry heat beat on the back of his neck, and looked lazily around for a patch of shelter. On the near side of the bridle-path a jag of basalt stood a man's height out of the ground and cast a few feet of shadow on the heather. He lifted slowly to his feet and climbed leisurely towards it.

"O shadow of a rock in a thirsty land!" he murmured deeply, and sank down in the heather; he snuggled his shoulders between the two bumps on the stone and sighed comfortably. From the thighs down his legs were in the blaze of the sun, but the warmth, through the grey flannels, was not unpleasant. He clasped his hands across his flat stomach and receded into his somnolence.

Turning head to left, he could see along the bridle-path to where it curved round a buttress of the hill a hundred yards away; to the right he looked down the length of Dounbeg Bay as far as the narrows of Corullish, four miles distant. The tide was running out through the narrows, and some trick of refraction down there seemed to make the waters run uphill, a canal of shimmering pale gold curving over into the sky. All the rest of the bay was smoothing out into a level floor, and little crinkles of silver ran and spent themselves on the surface of it. Across near the other shore, which was sandy and shelving, the water was a translucent green, but under the basalt bluffs on the near side it was dark-blue, deepening to slate purple.

"I'll be asleep in a minute," thought Rogan Stuart.

Last night he had not slept well in his bracken bed, but that was not unusual; sleep had been an unsafe harbourage for him many and many a night. The sea air had had a bite, and years of city life had thinned his Scots blood. He had been roused by the chill dawn and had looked, with a strange desolation of spirit, at the panorama of mountains outlined starkly against a wan sky; and the floor of the bay was a cold steel mirror wherein the peaks stood head downwards. Then the tall bens were blacker than purple, darker than any blue, and a thick band of mist, softer than pearl, bridged Glounagrianaan and made a scarf for the shoulder of tall Leaccamore. Now the hills were less starkly outlined and more far-away, and looked bigger; green pastures, hazed by the sun, lapped the slopes between the rocky scarps ; high up, basalt flashed yellow and pink and rust-brown; smoked shadows lay in fold and hollow; and the corries hid their ruggedness under a soft veil.

He liked the green over there across the water. It was lovely in the wide opening of the valley, and the trees were dark and restful. But what Fomorian had raised those red turrets? Some foreign man coming into these Irish glens and aping baronial architecture in red brick ! Some idea, probably, of warming the ruggedness of the hills. Could it be that here, too, as in the High-lands, strangers were stealing the lovely places from the old breed? And here was Rogan Stuart, of no stranger blood—out of Appin, like the great Alan Breck whom Stevenson had marvellously created without quite under-standing—sleeping in the heather and the bracken—same as poor lost Davy Balfour—and ready to sleep at this instant—now—in one minute. . . . He was asleep in half that minute.

II

The clink of iron on gravel waked him. Rogan did not wake with a start, but carefully, guardedly, as one who has come out of quiet dreams to many a desperate dawn. His half-shut eyes, under the brim of old felt, looked along the bridle-path to the left. Two ponies, one behind the other, were coming round the curve of the track at a fast smooth walk. It was a pace he had not before noticed in ponies—a walk that was almost an amble. And they were not quite ponies either—topping fifteen hands and wirily built, with manes and tails uncut but well groomed. The first was a smoke-blue, the second a colorado red with white stockings. Not native stock these. Their eyes were set too far forward and were too small—as if they were a throw-back to some ancient and feral breed.

He was so carelessly intent on observing the horses that, for a space, he did not particularly notice the riders. The smoke was ridden by a woman; white stockings by a tall, slimly built man. The man sat loosely in the saddle, his shoulders asway to the gait of his mount; he sported a big black Stetson hat, and his long legs were hidden below loose, yellow leather coverings. The woman wore the same sort of hat, but her legs were cased in the orthodox riding-breeches, and a red neckerchief was tied loosely above a white blouse. No, he did not care for women riding astride. He had seen plenty of them at the Dublin Horse Show, and many of them rode like a sack of flour—too heavy in the haunch and too much fat behind the knee. This young woman— she was young—rode, however, with full-length stirrups, and from saddle to crown she was straight as a lance,

19

and carried herself like a lance, leaning a little forward, so that the firmness of her breasts was outlined against the thin silk. Joan of Arc would ride just like that, with all her iron fighting men behind and watching her straight back out of hard and adoring eyes.

Rogan had somewhere seen horses and riders and high-peaked saddles like these. Where? Of course! That time the cowboy rodeo visited Dublin. What was the name of that laughing plumpish girl who rode the pitching broncho? He remembered how she swung her big hat above her head while she stayed glued to the saddle and loosed a keen and melodious ky-yi-yi. This girl here was not that one. This girl was slim and unsmiling.

The ponies came on. American cow-ponies they would be—imported for the whim of some Western visitors—with a Spanish strain in them. Perhaps all this country-side was being turned into some sort of rodeo film, some soul-destroying unreal reality where the native, himself included, was a mere aborigine sitting stoically on his hunkers.

Rogan was far too lazy or not interested enough even to raise his head, and the drooping leaf of his hat hid all but the riders' boots. The woman's boot was of soft fawn leather, with long straight heels and fancy stitching up the front—size five about and a good instep. Now he could see only the pony's legs, clean and fine and moving with a nice flip from the fetlock. And then the forefeet came together and stiffened, and the hind hoofs slithered an inch forward and stopped.

Rogan pushed back his old hat and looked up. The rear pony stopped short at the other's tail, and the tall young rider swayed lazily forward and back.

The young woman looked moodily down at Rogan from under her big Stetson, and a queer thought came into his mind: a bad-tempered bonny bit vixen under her own weight of misery. Blue—dark blue—her eyes, and her skin had a nice brown. And those eyes, surely made for smiling between dark lashes, were sullen, and a mouth made for laughter had the down-droop of pride and weariness of spirit.

Her lips moved. "This your camp?" Crisp the question, her voice running up resonantly to "camp."

Old and useless conventions have a habit of sticking. Rogan thrust an elbow against the rock behind and drew up a knee, for one was accustomed to rise to one's feet when addressed by a lady. And there he paused. An odd feeling that this was some kind of unreal film work made his mouth quirk. If this lady-star was merely playing a part, then he must play his; he was the aborigine sitting on his hunkers, older and wiser in breed, hiding his scorn, knowing that life, of no value, so brittle and so liable to disaster, was not worth burdening with small conventions. Let her eyes frown and grow imperious. He would relax and resettle shoulders against boulder. He did that.

"Have you a permit to camp here?" Sharp the query and sharply she smacked her long boot with riding-quirt.

Rogan Stuart shook his head, and a small guttural sound rumbled in his throat.

"You cannot camp here without a permit. You ought to know that. This land is mine." There was no doubt of the emphasis on her possession.

Her land! An American woman this, and claiming the ancient soil of Ireland! His forefathers, men of his race, had grown out of this soil, blood and bone, and sunk back into it again, generation after generation—countless generations. And here was this film star insisting imperiously that he must play his part.

"You do not own a foot of this land," he said deeply. "This land is mine."

"What?" That word seemed to lift her out of the saddle. Her off-leg came over the forepeak, her hips twisted, and there she was on the ground, featly as a boy. And all in the same motion she tossed the reins over the pony's head to trail on the path. So! Was it not thus cowmen tied their mounts to the ground? Where was the camera?

She took a stride down to him, and her well-fitting riding-breeches showed that she did not carry any heaviness behind the knee.

"You are being insolent," she cried. "On your feet!"

She would teach the aborigine manners, and at once Rogan's impish memory recalled some incident in filmdom where the misjudged native chief is slashed over the face by the angry heroine. That quirt would hurt like billy-o—and it might be in his part to give the vixen a good shaking in return—and get heaved into the water by the tall horseman. But she did not use the quirt. She halted close above him, and one high-heeled riding-boot tapped the ground impatiently. Out of sheer instinct he reacted on the instant. For years he had been used to going down to forward rushes, his eyes watchful for the football boots that were not in the least particular; so now, in one motion, he twisted, rolled, and was on his feet.

"Referee! Now then, referee!" he demanded, and looked up at the slender horseman. "Have you no control of the game?"

The horseman grinned. "Kick and carry out—let her rip!" The voice was unmistakably English or Irish-English, though the slang was Americanese and the speaker an elegant-seeming cowboy. His three-gallon

Stetson was back off his brow and showed his sleek black hair; he sat aside on the big stock saddle, one knee hooked carelessly over the peak, and already he had started to roll a cigarette. A careless, slouching, handsome fellow—and yet, there was something unsatisfactory about him; perhaps it was the dull, almost melancholic haze in or over his dark eyes, or the peculiar fish-belly pallor of the skin round his mouth in contrast to the delicate flush high up on the cheekbones.

The young woman reclaimed Rogan's attention urgently. Handsome she was, too, but not careless, not slouching — and the very devil blazed in her blue eyes. She was pointing a tense arm at the tent below them.

"Produce your permit—or move that tent right out of here."

Oh, blow it! This was ridiculous—this film was encroaching on reality. Better get right down to reality then.

"Be sensible!" he advised her calmly. "How do I know you have any authority to order that tent out of here?"

"Just watch me!" she said briefly.

She did not look to her companion for help. From the beginning she had acted as if he did not exist; the land was hers, the order she gave was hers; he was—just not there.

She was down at the tent and bending to the guy-ropes before Rogan could move. She knew about tents. But the second rope was not off its peg before a firm hand grasped her shoulder and lifted her upright. For the draw of a breath Rogan had been sorry that she was not a boy; bending over the guy-ropes she had been in a particularly tempting attitude—but one could hardly

23

punt a lady through a tent wall; and the tent was not his, anyway.

She tried to jerk herself free, but Rogan had a man's grip on her. Her hat fell off. And forthwith, she twisted, lithe as a cat, and smacked him sharply on the angle of the jaw with a gauntleted left hand.

"Wow!" said Rogan, and smartly caught her wrist on the return.

"You brute!" she snapped unreasonably, and with the readiness of a boy grappled with him.

But she was in the arms of a man who had kept his feet in many a loose maul, and her back heel could not twitch that iron knee. He held her firmly in his arms and looked down into her blazing blue eyes; and with one ear he was listening for the horseman to come trundling down on them. He would just love that fellow to come down for a minute. But there was no sound from above.

III

Rogan Stuart with a fresh young girl in his arms—and she only rods and scorpions! Oh, but this was ridiculous! This led nowhere. What was he to do now? Hold her till she cooled? Hell! Suddenly he smiled into her eyes. "You poor kid!" he whispered, loosed his grip, swung her round and gently pushed her towards the tent. "Go on with it, then!"

He turned his back on her, strode up the slope, and slumped into the heather against his shady boulder. He looked up at the lazy horseman, who was grinning unashamed.

"You are no blasted use," said Rogan warmly, for that was how he was feeling.

But the horseman did not rise to the taunt. He

grinned amicably. He had a habit of grinning amicably. "Kicked you for a goal, son," he drawled.

"You for a referee!"

"No control—only her husband."

"You unfortunate—mutt!" said Rogan Stuart.

Below them the young woman stood for a moment looking down at the tent-pegs. Somehow, Rogan's words had checked the first hot flood of temper, but now the aftersurge carried her on. The guy-ropes flew, the pole swayed and leant over, and the collapsed canvas made a hump over the camp beds beneath it. She came round that lop-sided hump, bent, straight-legged from the hips, to pick up her hat, and faced the slope towards Rogan.

"You will have that tent out of here on my return," she ordered definitely.

"You—you great big bully!" Rogan mocked her softly.

She stopped in front of him, legs firmly apart; and he looked up at her smilingly. That deep red neckerchief suited her dusky cheeks, the sun had bestowed its tan approvingly, and her black hair had tossed itself nicely. But what in heaven's name could be the matter to whirl her into this tantrum? Surely her life must have gone all askew, and put her on the wrong road to get anything worth while out of it—if there was anything worth while in life.

On her part, she contemplated Rogan curiously. There was disapproval in her look, but there was speculation too. His eyes, deep-set under brow, were so steady, so cool—not caring about her or her temper. She had been in his arms and knew how futile had been her own vigour against their iron; and then he had carelessly loosed her, pitied her, ignored her. She was in that reaction that realises too keenly the disastrous display

25

of temper, and—and she usually did not give way to tempers. . . . But this man could not know that.

But this man knew. Well he knew the secret, gnawing anger that will sometimes explode on the first unlucky object. He could read the turn of her lips, the shadow across her eyes. And there he was on his feet and his hat off to her.

"I am sorry, dark lady," said he. "It was surely all my fault."

Her mouth quivered, but she turned away so quickly that he did not see. She strode to her pony, threw reins over lowered head, set hand on peak, and was in the saddle with one lithe twist; and next instant the pony was off in that peculiar fox-trotting walk-amble. Never had a man been ignored so completely as the young horseman who had proclaimed himself only her husband.

Rogan gazed up at him—so easily aslouch in his saddle, so serenely drifting smoke through his nostrils—and, for some unfathomable reason, a feeling of dislike arose within him.

But the horseman only grinned his grin, threw his leg over saddle-horn, and some touch of knee set the pony in motion. "Better get it out of there, fellah," he called back, gesturing a hand towards the tent.

"I don't like you," murmured Rogan, and kicked a foot in the heather. And then he realised that he had been fully alive for a matter of five minutes, knowing anger, scorn, the desire for war, as he had not known these things since life went into the abyss, as he had been certain he would not know them again; and all dealt him from the hands of a woman. "Blast it all!" swore Rogan Stuart, and turned his attention to the fallen tent.

"Silly fathead!" he chided himself. "You've gone and put two decent men into a nice hole." And what was to be done now? He rubbed the back of his head, he gazed over the green peace of the bay, he surveyed the bulging ribs of Slievemaol. For inspiration came a small temptation. Better go while the going was good! How easy it would be to set up that tent, take oneself away, and let any new tempest break where it liked!

CHAPTER III

BUT when Alistair MacIan and Paddy Joe Long rowed back round the point an hour later Rogan Stuart was sitting on the boss of stone as they had left him, and he was still peacefully smoking his short briar.

Paddy Joe was now rowing and Alistair lounged in the stern, his back against a loosely filled sack. Suddenly Alistair sat up.

"Snakes!" he exclaimed. "A cyclone must have hit hereabouts."

Paddy Joe turned his head, the oars trailed, and water rippled over the thin blades.

"That pole was sound as hickory," said Alistair, "and there's been no rain."

"I knew it—in my bones I knew it." Paddy Joe chuckled boy-like. "Alistair, *mo gaol*—my treasure— this life on a broken wing is done with: the hawk's pinion is again afloat."

Paddy Joe resumed his easy rowing, and the little coracle came smoothly to the mooring buoy. Alistair tied up unhurriedly, and the two clambered to the tent level and went round the collapsed canvas without seeming to notice it.

"Glad you stayed," said Alistair cheerfully.

Rogan Stuart, high-priest of ruin, looked at them out of a still face. "Had you gentlemen a permit to camp in this place?"

"We had and we have."

"I've gone and lost it for you," Rogan said quietly.

"Don't you believe it," said Alistair, and came to the ground limberly, joint by joint; he crossed his legs and felt for his pouch.

Paddy Joe stood over the two and looked lazily about him, at bay and brae and hill-top, and up into the blue dome of the sky, empty of even a bird's wing. "When I was a boy beyond in Kerry," he communed aloud, "a small twist of a whirlwind used sometimes come across the fields in still harvest weather, and twirl the hay twenty-forty feet into the air; it would snatch the caubeen off your head and play with it, and give yourself a lift and a whirl in the by-going; and every one knew that that whirlwind was the passing by of the good people— the fairy host—for you could hear the thin, mocking laughter of them as they scurried by. Could it be that the fairies came through this glen this morning?—God protect us all!"

"'This your camp?—This land is mine—have you a permit?'—like a lash. That kind of fairy!" said Rogan Stuart. He nodded towards the tent. "She did that all by herself. I tried to stop her, but she was too strong for me."

Alistair looked at the firm shoulders and deep chest. "Six feet high and as wide as a forge door——"

"Five feet seven in her long boots and scaling one hundred and fifteen," smiled Rogan. "I know, for I wrestled with her. And look! when she bent over the tent-pegs I was minded to punt her into the bay. Should I have?"

"You did the best you could," said Paddy Joe.

"I was asleep," Rogan started to explain, "up there in the shade of that rock; two American ponies came along the path and waked me. She was riding ahead, straight up and down—and behind her a lazy long fellow, dark and good-looking, in cowboy garb and speaking synthetic cowboy with a public-school accent."

29

Paddy Joe frowned. "Did he——?"

"No. An amiable hound! Rolled a cigarette and grinned, and offered me no help—she needed none; he did not exist as far as our little war was concerned. You know, she rode off and left him to follow like a tame dog—but had I not better tell you from the beginning?"

"It might be as well," agreed Paddy Joe.

Rogan pictured the whole brief drama succinctly. "So you see, gentlemen," he said at the end, "I have as good as lost you your permit."

"Not on your life," Alistair assured him firmly. "We have that permit in Sir Jerome's own handwriting."

"But she said, 'This land is mine—have that tent out of here when I return.'"

"Return she must," said Paddy Joe, pointing at the red house across the water. "That lady and her tame husband live in that place."

Alistair hopped nimbly to his feet and sprang down to the level. "She will find this tent tight as a drum, then," he cried.

"A bold bit of strategy," agreed Paddy Joe, and went to help. Rogan followed.

As they moved round the circumference of the tent Paddy Joe mused aloud.

"When I was a boy in Kerry——"

"Nothing else but, wherever you are," Alistair interposed.

"—From Knockanore to Moyvala I knew the people, two hundred and fifty to the square mile, in seed, breed and generation—and they knew me. We had to."

"What you mean is," said Alistair, "that, having staked a claim in this place for a matter of three weeks, you flatter yourself that you have got below the skin of the aborigines."

"Once a Kerryman, always the itching mind. Haven't

30

I a tongue in my head? Come now and let us rest ourselves, and I will put a few facts before you, so that ye
shall not be playing a part in the dark when the time
comes. The itch is on me to break my well-known
silence."

Alistair wagged a hand helplessly.

II

The three men moved up into the heather below the
track and squatted in a triangle; and Rogan Stuart felt
in himself an unusual comforting warmth that these two
should take him into fellowship as a matter right and
proper.

The sun poured on them; the warm air flowed over
them; in that wide-flung panorama of sea and mountain they were like three standing-stones amongst all the
grey stones lifting out of the heather. Into the great
stillness that enclosed them their voices went out and
died, for it was the heart of the day, when no bird sings,
no fish plays, when the crow of a distant cock is weighted
with a devastating loneliness, when life dulls down under
the dominance of the slow sun.

Paddy Joe's voice was a quiet lift and fall. "Sorry am
I to tell you that that big house over there beyond the
water was erected—erected is the word—by a country-
man of my own—out of the North."

"Oh well!" said Rogan excusingly.

"He got small good out of it. He was one of these
here famous business magnates who scrape their wealth
in the brutal places of the earth, in wheat and wine and
oil—and bloody sweat. And at the long last he came
home and built that house—and died; and maybe
God was more merciful to him than many a man would
be.

"He died, whatever, and his wealth flowed in other channels—or the same. This thing and that thing was disposed of in due process of law, but yon house stuck in the hands of the trustees; for, mind you, the English sportsmen and the French nuns and Hindoo princes, who would be buying, are austere people and know what a house should be. That house is built of red Belgian brick, and the corners and astragals and stepped gables are of yellow French brick—a bastard cross of Dutch and Scots Baronial styles. That's the sort of house that's in it. Still an' all, one man had such a liking for this glen and the people in it that he rented the house from year to year, and he's there yet, though the house is no longer his to rent: Sir Jerome Trant, Baronet. Wait, now!

"Sir Jerome Trant was what you might call a British proconsul in a small way—West Indies, East Malaya, the islands of the South Seas—and, his galley-service over, he drifted back here to his native soil, still a youngish man, not a day over fifty this minute—and a decent sort of man as well, and a sound drinker. Not wealthy—no proconsul is since the days of Warren Hastings—but he has his virtues, and I misdoubt if his son Ambrose is one of them. He lost his wife early on, and she left him Ambrose. You saw Ambrose this morning, Rogan Stuart, riding cowboy. What's this you called him—'an amiable hound'?"

"Did nothing but grin. He refrained——"

"You've hit the nail on the head. That's the lad. All his life—but once—he refrained—refrained from persisting. He tried planting in Penang, where good men survive and make money and a name; he tried pearling out of Cape York; and recruiting black labour in the Solomons; and smuggling vodka into Oregon; and he made his one big kill on a ranch in Arizona—one of these dude ranches run to give the Easterners a kick. Between the three of us he was as near a remittance man as be damned—but not quite, for he lacked the negative virtues. Howsumdiver the dude ranch must have suited his style, for he did there the one definite thing of his life: got himself a wife.

"Elspeth Conroy was her name. That is a Gaelic name, and it means daughter of kings, and, by all accounts, she was the daughter of a cattle king or an oil king—at any rate a money king. She fell for Ambrose—his good looks, his breeding, his amiability, how do we know? Anyway she married him, came over to the old country, and, according to precedent, set out to acquire house and estate. There they be, over yonder! She owns that house, she owns the fishing of the bay and the rivers that fall into it from away back by Loch Aonach; ben and glen and stream, she owns them all. The land is no longer ours, Rogan Stuart."

While these two looked at each other understandingly Alistair laughed. "And she smote him with a south paw," he said, and turned to Paddy Joe. "You certainly have been routing about in local history. And is Ambrose still . . .?"

"They call him Amby—every one," said Paddy Joe.

"That settles it."

"Don't know—just guessing. I never set eyes on him or her; they came back from a trip to North Africa yesterday—with a small house-party, I believe. But look you, this day is not done yet—but never mind. What I want to point out may give you a line on them. Listen! Though she was in the devil's own tantrum this morning and behaved unkindly to a stranger taking his ease, yet, from what I have heard, she cannot be adjudged either hard or bitter; and Tom Whelan, the harbour-master, says she is a darling girl and the heart o' corn." He looked at Rogan speculatively, smiling. "There's nothing about you would send a girl up in the air?"

"There must be," said Rogan gloomily. One thing he knew: he had no power with women.

Paddy Joe rose to his feet. "Now ye are as wise as myself, and your talking makes me thirsty. Stay where you are, Rogan Stuart. See to the vessels and utensils, youngster—I'll be back in a minute."

He went up the shore some fifty yards to a fold in the slope where a small trickle of water came slipping down between fox-tongue ferns and made a miniature fall over the beetle of a rock. There he lay on his breast just above the little trickle, pulled up a sleeve, and inserted a long arm behind the apron of falling water. One by one he brought forth three dark dripping bottles, and again groped in the cache.

"One—two—four, and the boy is honest for once; but if you couldn't trust him with nectaire honey how could you trust him with lager beer—and the weather that's in it?"

When he got back to the tent Alistair was ready with three glasses and a cap-lifter.

Paddy Joe, out of the tail of an eye, watched Rogan drink. The lad knew how. Men who are incontinent might be apt, on a thirsty day like this, to quaff two-thirds of the glass at the first pull; but the civilised and cultured man would take no more than a round sip to savour the liquor and attune the palate, and after that—well, all depended on the depth of the flagon and the capacity a man was blest with.

"Slainthe!" toasted Rogan. "You fellows are too kind—especially after the mess I've made. Here's hoping nothing will come of it."

"Fate had a trout in the frying-pan for you this morning," said Paddy Joe cryptically.

"Here is to what comes," toasted Alistair. He lifted his glass and paused to listen. "And it's coming now, old-timers."

III

A click of shod hooves on quartz gravel, and the two ponies came back round the buttress of the hill. The young woman led as before, straight-backed as ever, and, behind, her slim husband still slouched lazily in his big saddle.

Rogan Stuart never hesitated. He bent his knee to the slope and halted at the side of the track; Alistair and Paddy Joe glanced at each other and followed him. They stood side by side; three big men waiting for a slip of a girl, and not one of them at all confident. Their glasses, two-thirds full, were gripped in their right hands as in some ridiculous ritual; but they were men enough not to mind.

Level with them the leading pony came to its quick, sliding halt; the girl swayed forward from the hips, supple as a wand, her firm young breasts outlined against the thin silk.

Rogan spoke the moment her eyes reached his—and to him her eyes came first.

"I am sorry, madam, that I gave you a wrong impression. I was entirely to blame. This is not my camp. These gentlemen were kind to me—a stranger passing through."

"A stranger passing through"—on the road to nowhere. That is all he was. That is all he would ever be. His deep-set eyes smiled at her, and for a single moment a grey light of intuition hinted to her the trouble at this man's core.

She looked closely at him for a moment longer, and then her eyes moved on to Alistair.

35

"Madam," said he coldly, "we hold a permit to camp in this place from Sir Jerome Trant."

Perhaps it was the coldness of voice and eye that made her frown, but he gave her back frown for frown under level brow. "You and I are Americans," he told her. "It is a pity that we sometimes make ourselves ridiculous in foreign lands."

Elspeth Trant had her temper well in hand now; her frown grew no deeper; no retort came from her. Her eyes moved on to Paddy Joe, and Paddy Joe smiled his old, melancholic friendly smile.

"Don't be minding him, my lady." His voice took on a quaint gentleness. "The thing you did you were impelled to do. Don't I know! And it wasn't badly done. You are a Conroy, I'm told, and the Conroys were the same always. Where I came from they had houses and lands and once were kings—and now they have nothing but their spirit. Hold you that! Let not your spirit break, and life will not break either."

And to Paddy Joe she smiled, but it was a smile that, somehow, made the heart stound. Suddenly then her knee twitched inwards, and, at once, her pony started off in its quick walk-amble. Not a word had she spoken.

The three men stood looking after her and, like her, completely ignored her husband.

"By the jumping Moses!" cried Paddy Joe warmly, "the first time in history that a woman achieved distinction by silence. She up and licked the three of us."

IV

Ambrose Trant's laugh recalled his presence. "You— and a bear-cat on the side," he drawled. "Good thing you were heeled for dry work!" His eyes were on the glasses, lit amber in the sun.

36

He met their considering gaze unabashed. He was young, sleek, handsome, without a single mark of weakness or vice, except, it might be, that fish-bellied pallor about a mouth that was sensitive rather than sensual.

Suddenly Paddy Joe spoke up. "Care for a glass of beer, Mr Trant?"

"You've done saved my life," said Trant, and was out of the saddle as he spoke.

Alistair glanced at Paddy Joe speculatively, and, without a word, turned and strode off towards their cool cache. He came back with two bottles in each hand, and found Trant sitting with the others on the track edge, reins over elbow, and his pony, head alean, behind him.

As Alistair poured the beer slowly, so that a misty film clouded the outside of the crystal, Trant's mouth opened ever so little and a pink tip of tongue ran across his lips and back again; and his hand was out before the glass could be presented to him.

"Here's how, fellows!" And there was only a trace of white froth slipping down the inside of the glass.

Already Alistair was levering off a second cap. "Try another," he invited casually.

"Thanks! Don't mind if I do. That first did not get below my collar stud."

He was more continent with the second bottle, and, between sips that he seemed to strain over his palate, looked about him at the camp.

"What is your stunt?" he enquired. "Fishing?"

"Some. We have a permit for tidal waters."

"You should try Loch Aonach—up the glen, a morning's hike. Stocked with rainbow trout." He jerked his head to where his wife had disappeared round the point. "Might wangle a day for you."

"Thank you," said Alistair dryly.

"No trouble." Trant's eyes strayed to where the two

full bottles were lying in the heather, but Alistair ignored his look. The man was restless too, and his glance kept shifting to the path. After a pause he got slowly to his feet. "Thanks! Saved a life." He pivoted into the saddle and the pony started off in a smooth hand-gallop. "Owe you a day in harvest," he called back, waving his hand.

"Tame husband goes," said Alistair. "And a couple of bottles of good beer wasted."

"Hoots!" exclaimed Paddy Joe, coming out of his introspection. "We've found out that he does not matter a damn—and that's the hell of it. But do you know, I like that young woman, Elspeth Conroy—or Trant—but Trant is wrong. Did you observe the line of her mouth and her clear eye? She is as unhappy as a stray pup and plucky as a blue terrier."

"There goes the sensational novelist—the unspeakable imagination of P. J. Long——"

Paddy Joe paid no heed ; he mused aloud. "Oh, youth and the clean line, and unhappiness turning down the corners of the mouth! It is the most dreadful thing in the world for youth to be unhappy. It leaves its mark —that unhappiness. It darkens the sun, chills the grey dawn, draws out the length of the gloaming——"

"One gets used to it," said Rogan quietly.

"The devil bite the tongue of me!" Paddy Joe cursed himself warmly and turned to Rogan. "Where are you thinking of going from here?"

"Nowhere in particular—nowhere at all."

"There's no hurry on that road."

"Stick by us a bit," Alistair invited warmly. All the morning he could not get this man out of his mind. Now he warily approached the question of poaching salmon with a net, for he could not be sure how a law-abiding citizen would react to their project.

"Anything short of dynamite," Rogan took him up.

Alistair liked him better.

"A friend from Moray has failed to turn up for to-night—and there's a third camp-bed."

Rogan hesitated.

"Stay by the fun while it lasts," advised Paddy Joe. "Seems anyway as if luck has stacked a hand for us three."

"It's good of you," smiled Rogan, "only—Fate has no game I'll play."

"Fate will decide that, maybe," said Paddy Joe.

CHAPTER IV

I

THERE was no moon, but the still summer night was not dark. High up in the sky the stars were faint and few, and the northern glow outlined, stark and black, the great humped hog-back of Garabhmore mountain. Out at mid-bay the little coracle seemed to float on a pale nothingness out of which the oar-tips created a faint shimmer of phosphorescence; and when Alistair, pulling smoothly, opened the head of the inlet, small twinkles and gleams rayed away from them over the pale surface towards the lighted windows that were scattered and strung on all the wide curve of hillside.

"Quite a population up yonder," murmured Rogan Stuart, acrouch in the bow at Paddy Joe's feet.

"Good land all the way up Glounagrianaan," Paddy Joe murmured back. "Pull your left, son; the current is getting you."

"I feel it," grunted Alistair. "Watch out for the bridge."

He buckled down to steady pulling, not for the head of the bay but quartering across towards the north shore. Rogan, peering forward, made out the black bulk of trees closing in on either hand; and presently, the high, faintly outlined arch of a bridge loomed overhead.

"Nicely gauged," commended Paddy Joe's whisper.

This was the Dunmore River coming down from Loch Aonach. The water gleamed roily as it went by, and the coracle went bucking forward under the jerk and kick of the oars. Above the bridge the current was easier, and Alistair, now rowing noiselessly, brought the boat close in to the wooded bank on his right.

Paddy Joe whispered in Rogan's ear. "This is the enemy's territory, and you are now without the pale of the law. But our little lady owes us one salmon at least."

They slipped along outside low-growing water-willows and below trees that, here and there, trailed a branch in the current and made a low gurgle. In a few minutes they came to a squat building, the open-arched gable of which, jutting out into the water, showed it to be a boat-house.

Alistair swung the nose of the coracle to the shore on the downward side of the building, and Paddy Joe's fingers scraped along a wooden wall. There they lay and listened. No breath of air moved in the warm dark; everything was remotely hushed, still, watching; the great black bulk of the trees seemed to know that they were there and seemed not to be concerned; the very highest and faintest star seemed to be looking down at them detachedly, with a strange aloofness that, yet, had something inimical in it.

"Here's where you get off," whispered Paddy Joe. Rogan lifted to his feet carefully, and the other's hand steadied him while his voice went on whispering:

"Keep to the front of the house—this side. The keeper and the kennels are at the back. If danger threatens, give the plover's call—as I told you—and slip back here as soon as you can. If we are here first we'll give you the call. Ach! there's nothing to fear really—but one never knows. Watch your feet, son! Give us an hour if you can."

Rogan looked back and down from the bank, but the boat was already gone, and not even the creak of a thole-pin showed its direction. Feeling forward with his feet, guided by the wooden side of the boat-house, he worked round to the rear and found gravel acrunch under shoe-soles. This would be the path back into the grounds. He could not see a yard; down here below the trees the night was close about him and all the stars were hidden.

He paused there and listened in a stillness drawn out and fine as a wire, and waited until his tenseness relaxed and he became in tune with the mood of the dark. Alone there in the night, he yielded to it, became part of it, was no longer awed by its detached awareness. Slowly then he moved forward on the gravel, his progress a mere drifting on the stream of the dark. Now and then his left shoe grazed along the grass edging of the path. After a time the darkness seemed to retire, to thin out, and faint sheens and glimmers cut across and between the tree trunks; and, quite suddenly, he came out between two thick clumps of shrubbery and found himself looking across a wide reach of lawn at the lighted front of the big house.

*　　*　　*　　*　　*　　*

A full hour later the coracle came drifting down at mid-stream, Paddy Joe leaning on the oars and Alistair perched on the high-cocked prow.

"Our scout has given us good measure," whispered Alistair. "Hope he hasn't lost himself—listen—listen! Is that your signal?"

"And well whistled at that," said Paddy Joe, and dug in the oars.

Across the night, very part of the night, came the plaintive shaken call of the grey plover, beginning softly, lifting, pulsing, dying away—that call in a minor key that is of the true spirit of loneliness in the summer hills.

In less than two minutes the coracle scraped round the corner of the boat-house and Alistair's hand steadied her against the wooden wall. He looked up at the bank. From his position low down the angle and eaves-edge of the boat-house were clearly outlined against the sky, and a dark figure leant against the corner, bent-over and peering down towards them. The only thought in Alistair's mind was that this was Rogan Stuart; and his mouth was pursed to greet him, when a voice that was not Rogan's startled him.

"Who is down there? What boat is that?"

There was no mistaking that voice. It was Ambrose Trant's.

Alistair crouched back in the bow of the coracle, quiet as a mouse.

"I see you—I know you." Trant was lying boldly as he bent and peered. "Poaching too! Come right up here—come on!"

Alistair grinned in the dark. If Paddy Joe and himself obeyed that urgent order, Ambrose Trant might experience a few busy and unhappy minutes. But these two were old hands and would not move till the right time.

"Very well!" warned Trant. "Let her rip. I'll damn soon round you up."

His figure disappeared, his feet crunched on the gravel; and then came a short explosive epithet and the thud of a heavy fall, followed immediately by a scramble and a squeal and another thud on the ground.

"Ride him, cowboy!" whispered Alistair. "Hang on, Paddy Joe!" And he disappeared over the bank, leaving the coracle arock behind him.

"Blast it!" swore Paddy Joe.

II

Rogan Stuart, who had smothered in his time tough, international out-halves, did justice to Ambrose Trant.

43

He got him with a devastating low tackle, clumped him flat on his back, and locked him across the hips. But Trant was lithe as an eel and was by no means a physical weakling. Vindictively he kicked and squirmed, twisted to his knees, and got an arm round his opponent's neck. And thereupon Rogan broke all holds by cleanly somersaulting him over his head. This time he did not seek to bottle him; instead he crouched back out of distance and waited. Man-handling was no part of the job in hand, and he hoped that Ambrose, with the wind knocked out of him, would cry enough or even scurry away for help. All that Rogan wanted was a chance to make the boat.

But Ambrose Trant was now fighting drunk and entirely without the better part of valour. He bounded to his feet, exploded an ugly oath, and charged blindly in the dark.

Rogan instinctively ducked under a swinging right, and the two bodies came together and fell. They rolled, they heaved, they scrabbled on the gravel. Twice Trant squealed as vindictively as a weasel. The drink he had recently taken gave him, for a time, a really astonishing and explosive energy; but, for all that, after every roll and every tumble Rogan Stuart was invincibly on top.

And then the struggle ceased as suddenly as it had begun; as it will, when a drunk man is down to the dregs. Trant's clutching hands went loose, and he flattened out limply on his back. His breath hoasted broken-windedly and his diaphragm heaved below Rogan's smother.

Rogan rolled clear and to his feet at the same time. And a voice spoke softly in his ear, "Nice work, son! Let us be going." Alistair's hand slipped inside his arm.

"Will he be all right?"

"Fine! As soon as he gets his wind back—watch out for rain. Come on!"

Paddy Joe had the boat handily waiting for them, and they slipped in over the bow.

"H-s-s-sh!" warned Paddy Joe, and they stilled to listen. There came to them from the pathway beyond the boat-house the sound of running feet—feet running lightly and quickly—feet running lightly as a woman's. . . .

With silent hand Paddy Joe levered the coracle backwards along the wall, gave one final push, and let the current take them. Twenty yards down, he dipped oars, brought the boat bow on, pulled softly until the bridge loomed behind, and then drove forward with all his might.

"Not a word," he whispered over his shoulder. "Sound travels to-night."

Rogan was getting his wind back. He sat up in the bow and looked around him. It was better out here in the open where one could see across the summer night. The great hog-back of Garabhmore stood out against the sky, and, in the blackness below, was hidden the big ugly house where ugly things were happening. Let it stay hidden there. He, at any rate, was finished with it and its ugliness.

Out beyond mid-bay Paddy Joe slowed down to a leisurely gait and blew deep breaths through his lips. "And that's that, my children," he said in a low voice. "We are now circulating on our own affairs in a free country." He looked over his shoulder at them. "Where's your hat, Rogan Stuart?" he asked, and stopped rowing.

"Here in my pocket," said Rogan. "Put it there when I cleared for action."

"Sound man! That hell of a hat would hang us all."

"I'll get you into trouble yet. Didn't keep a very

45

good watch, did I? I never meant to tackle Trant, but he ran right on top of me."

Alistair, acrouch at Rogan's feet, chuckled happily.

"You earned your slice of the fun. I was hopping about outside the vortex and counted eleven flying-mares in as many seconds. Poor Amby will be gey sair the morn."

"Had you some fun yourselves?"

"Some, about fits it," said Alistair without enthusiasm.

"It does too," said Paddy Joe exultingly.

"What in thunder could a fellow do against that current?" Alistair wanted to know.

"You see," explained Paddy Joe with satisfaction, "the poor mutt anchored me on the shore with one end of the net and then tried to make the haul up into the throat of the pool——"

"Where the fish lie," pointed out Alistair.

"Anyway, the weight of the net and the current was too much for him, and he finished up with a figure of eight and landed below me. Such a snarl——"

"With a nice ten-pounder in the bottom loop." Alistair looked up at Rogan. "Did I see all the fun you had back there?"

"You did," said Rogan, a little grimly. "The rest was not funny." He looked across the water into the darkness where the house was hidden. "There are ugly things going on in there," he said in his deep voice.

"There is unhappiness in there, we know," said Paddy Joe.

"And worse. Here are two problems for you. Why should father and son hold a drinking bout, with hell for a wind-up? And what makes a woman *caoine*—lament— to herself in the dark?"

"Phew-w!" whistled Alistair. "You saw a whale of a lot in one hour."

"More than I should—and none of my business."

"Why should father and son——?" wondered Alistair.

"Leave it," admonished Paddy Joe. "Leave it now! Here we are at our own quiet place."

Above them the brown of the tent showed dimly on its flat, and behind it the great breast of Slievemaol, facing the northern glow, was a serene grey shimmer.

"And now," said Paddy Joe, shipping his oars, "we will rest ourselves and drink one drink to wash all ugliness away."

"We drank all the beer."

"And who would drink beer in the dead hours? What we will drink is what has been drunk in these hills under the cover of darkness for a thousand years."

CHAPTER V

I

Rogan Stuart and Paddy Joe Long sat on two convenient boulders, smoked a contemplative, after-breakfast pipe, and looked down at Alistair unmooring the coracle. He was taking back the harbour-master's unsnarled poaching net.

"I'll freight back a cargo of beer," he called up.

"Good boy! Don't be more than two hours," called back Paddy Joe. "That fellow likes beer any hour of the morning," he told Rogan. "'Twas I larned him."

But Alistair was not two hours away. In less than a quarter of that time he reappeared round the point, and he was coming at a fast pace.

"Hello!" exclaimed Paddy Joe. "The boy is in a hurry."

"Hope young Trant did not recognise me last night—" began Rogan quickly.

"What harm if he did?" said Paddy Joe lightly. "A month in jail never hurt any one—I was there myself."

Alistair buoyed the boat—with never a glance towards them—clambered up the boulder and skirted the tent. When they saw his face they knew he brought bad news. He was anxious-eyed and frowning and came directly to his subject.

"Bad news, boys!" he said evenly. "Ambrose Trant was killed last night—strangled."

Rogan sat as still as the stone under him; Paddy Joe came to his feet.

"God have mercy on him," he prayed. "Strangled?"

Alistair addressed Rogan. "He was found lying where we left him, and he had been choked to death. The finger-marks were on his throat."

"But my hands never——"

"I know that," said Alistair impatiently. "Your hands were never near his throat; nevertheless, some hands were. Remember those feet we heard running on the gravel—well?"

Paddy Joe nodded, his eyes on the ground. "Light feet, light feet!" he murmured. "Could it come to that?" He looked quickly at Alistair. "Who told you?"

"Tom Whelan."

"Did you happen—ah—happen to say——?"

"Where we were last night?" Alistair snorted. "Tom met me at the head of the ladder, bundled the net out of sight, shoved the cut of salmon under his vest, and then told me. I just listened, expressed regret—only saw the man once, and so on, and came away. I didn't start digging out till the first bluff hid the pier."

"Fine! Not that it would matter with Tom Whelan—but never give a friend a secret to keep unless there is great need."

"A secret?" said Rogan Stuart enquiringly.

Alistair strode back and fore in front of them and tapped palm with clenched fist. "Look here, fellows! We are in this, and we had better consider it from all angles—here and now."

"Here and now," agreed Paddy Joe. "Sit down, son! We are in conference."

The three sat in a triangle. It was again a grand June morning, and, in the sunny stillness, they were again like three standing-stones leaning to each other out of the heather, and set to lean there forever.

They were silent for a space, gathering their minds to the problem.

"Go on, Alistair," said Paddy Joe. "Tell us."

"Little to tell—what the harbour-master told me: Ambrose Trant's body was found by Sir Jerome, shortly before eight this morning, just at the back of the boat-house—strangled—with finger-marks on his throat, and every sign of a fierce struggle round about—there would be plenty of sign, of course."

"The police have it in hands?"

"Naturally."

"No action taken—no arrests?"

"Tom had heard of none. That is all he knew."

The three considered for a few seconds, and Alistair lifted an open hand and placed middle finger on thumb. "Here are the points," he said. "Ambrose Trant was killed; we did not do the killing; we do not know who did it; and, as far as we know, no one knows we were about the place last night——"

Rogan lifted a hand. "Pause there," said he steadily. "Young Mrs Trant knows I was in the grounds last night —I talked with her for half an hour."

"Then," said Paddy Joe, desperately calm, "we are in it up to our necks."

II

Alistair and Paddy Joe were silent—they had nothing to say. The cue was now with Rogan Stuart, and they waited for him to go on—if he wanted to go on. He was ready enough and frank enough. He shook his head sadly.

"I might have known I'd bring you bad luck. I am the bringer of it these many days. Now I've got you implicated in this killing, but, of course, I'll take anything that's coming. Look here, friends! I had better put everything before you." He paused for a moment and went on. "Last night, over there, I played eaves-dropper for half an hour, foolishly, driven by some sneaking impulse, and I saw and heard things that were not meant to be seen and heard; and later on I did not think it right to divulge anything."

"Correct!" said Alistair firmly. "Forget it."

"No. My obligation is to you. It is essential that you know all that I know. After all—well, I see only one thing that I can do."

"Very good!" said Paddy Joe. "I think you are right, Stuart. Carry on."

III

That previous night, when Rogan came in sight of the house across the wide lawn, he paused to examine his territory. Veiled in the night, with turrets and stepped gables outlined against the glow above the hills, the house looked imposing, even dignified. The upper floors were all in darkness, but, here and there, along the ground level, light glowed behind blinded windows, and the glass front of the big porch, bulging from the façade, showed a pinkish gleam of lanthorn alight in the front hall; and, on the far side of the porch, a French window was wide open, with a strong ray of light splaying out across the lawn, and turning the grass a bright metallic-looking green.

He stood there for perhaps a minute, looking and listening. Nothing moved, not a leaf rustled; and so he set out to make the traverse in front of the house. Scattered over the lawn were dark patches of flower-beds and shoulder-high clumps of rhododendron, and, keeping these clumps between him and the open window, he drifted slowly across until he got beyond the splay of light, and there started edging in towards the house.

He did not know why. That open, lighted French window attracted him curiously. Eavesdropping was not in his mind; he would just take one peep, and so, perhaps, learn if any of the household were abroad. Conveniently enough, the dark cone of a young cedar grew close to the wall at the side of the couple of steps leading to the window, and he slipped in amongst the branches and peered through them into the room. He could smell the fragrance of the fronds, and the points of them stung the backs of his hands.

It was a man's room that he looked into: part snuggery, part office, part library—shelves of leather-backed books and ledgers on the opposite wall, maps and plans on the end wall, and in the far corner a white door with an old-fashioned bronze handle. Big leather chairs were scattered about, and the soft glow of an electric bowl under the ceiling gleamed back from a silver tray, a decanter of amber liquor, a soda-water syphon, and some empty glasses standing on a flat-topped writing-table at mid-floor. That cool-shining soda syphon made Rogan feel thirsty, for it indicated the need of a man on a sultry night—and it was sultry, even out in the open. But for the job he had in hand he might have been tempted to walk in on the two men in the room and hold them up for a drink.

There were two men in the room. One was Ambrose Trant, sleek-haired and young, a high colour on his cheek-bones and that odd pallor about the mouth—abnormally good-looking in his white linen and black dinner-jacket. He lounged in a red chair at the far side of the table, and his long fingers were restless on the short stem of one of the empty glasses. The other man was striding back and forth close inside the window. He was striding slowly but with a remarkable soft litheness, and his wide shoulders swayed in time to his light feet. A

52

small man, but not insignificant in face and figure. His hair above the touch of grey at the temples had a dark leonine sweep, and his eyes a fine youthful sparkle. He held a cherry-wood pipe firmly in his teeth, and now and then his wide under-lip pouted out under the stem. He could be no other than Sir Jerome Trant.

Rogan was on the very point of slipping away into the night, when the clink of glass against the silver tray made the elder man turn his head.

"That the signal for another whiskey?" he enquired, and his voice lisped a little on the sibilants.

"Just a last one, Dad." There was a note of suppliance in Ambrose's voice, and, when he turned his head, Rogan saw the unfocussed eyes of the man who has had several drinks too many.

The father looked at the closed door in the far corner and his ear was bent as if listening. And then he strode quickly to the table, laid down his pipe, caught up the decanter, and poured a stiff drink into each glass—stiffer drinks Rogan never saw for that time of night; and the hiss and splash of the soda made him thirstier than ever.

"We'll drink fair, Amby," said the father.

"Whatever you say, Dad," agreed the son.

The dipsomaniac drinks in one of two ways: either gulping the stuff down or straining it over a titillated palate. Ambrose strained it; the other took one decent drink and laid his glass down. And again Rogan, to avoid further temptation, was on the point of slipping away when the father spoke, and what was said held him by sheer surprise. Sir Jerome was leaning forward on the table on strong square hands, and his voice was calmly matter-of-fact.

"I wonder, Amby, how long it will take me to drink you into hell?"

53

Calm as a post he said that, and Amby took it as light as thistledown.

"Not a chance, Dad! I thrive on this. Old Satan and yourself will grow sick of waiting."

"Never, my son! Any gods there be will think twice before damning me for ridding the world of you—you poor swine!"

The calmness of the tone and the searing words made Rogan's flesh creep. If these two were father and son, this house was already hell.

Rogan stayed on. In fact, he had no time to get away. As Sir Jerome lifted his glass the bronze handle of the white door turned, and he put the glass back hastily on the table-top. The door opened inwards, and the lady of tempers—young Mrs Trant—stood there in the opening. She looked at the two men, she looked at the tray, she said not a word, but her face, though it never altered a line, gathered, somehow, a still, hopeless look.

"Just having a last drink, Else," said the older man deprecatingly.

"So I see," she said, and there was no feeling in her tone. "It is very warm in the house—I'm going out for a breath of fresh air."

She left the door open behind her, came past her husband's chair, without looking at him, and across towards the open window. Her dark hair was bare, a silken scarf was careless about her white shoulders, and her arms, slim and long, reminded one of the shaft of a lily.

As she stepped down and out on the lawn the fringe of her scarf brushed the fronds of the cedar, and Rogan held his breath—and kept on holding it, for Jerome Trant came to the window and stood watching her as she moved out along the broadening band of light. He was swaying a little on his heels—and Rogan heard him whisper distinctly.

"It will be all right, Else, my girl.   It will be all right."

And in the room behind Ambrose Trant laughed, shrill as a woman—a queer laugh for him, for it was full of bitterness and mocking.

His father turned away slowly from the window.

Rogan Stuart looked across the room, and a shock went through him like a knife. He trembled a little, stilled, and again trembled. Over there in the doorway, framed in the dark, stood a third man: a tall, slim-waisted, supple-shouldered man, with a face of clean pallor, and close-set black curls over a white brow—calm, sure of himself, but with the very devil in leash behind his brilliant eyes. The open door shielding him, he was outside the vision of father and son.

Rogan Stuart knew that man. Too well he knew him. He was Captain Eudmon Butler, the Black Captain, "terror on two feet in love or war," as Paddy Joe had said. He stood there looking across at the open window, and a small smile came suddenly about his mouth—a smile that was greedy, sure, calculating, possessive. Then he stepped lightly back into the darkness, and his feet made no sound. Perhaps he remained there in the darkness listening, or perhaps he had slipped away to reach the grounds—and the woman—by another door.

Rogan stayed where he was behind the cedar. He could not move. There was a buzzing sound within his head, and an intermittent tremor still shook his whole body. What happened in the room after that he saw and heard as in a dream.

Ambrose was still laughing bitterly, and his father looked at him out of frowning eyes.

"It's all right, old fellow," said the son. "I was only laughing at this hell of a house."

"The house is all right."

"So might Hell be but for the damned."   For the first

time there was character in the voice—taunt and hate and despair. "A hell of a grand house! With a father trying to drink his son to death—and in love with his son's wife."

Jerome Trant moved as swiftly as a boy on those light feet of his, and was bending over Ambrose, his head forward in menace, and his voice rasping.

"What did you say?"

It was either the drink or the hate—or both—that gave the younger man force. He wrenched himself to his feet in his father's face. "It is true!" he almost screamed. "You know it is true. It is in your eyes. You love——"

The father thrust a big clenched fist into the son's breast and knocked him clump into the leather chair. "You foul-minded young fool!"

The force of that fist cowed the son and calmed him. He stared up at his father and wagged his head helplessly. And the father threatened him: "By God! if ever you speak of your wife and me in the same breath I'll kill you."

He stood glaring down at Ambrose, who could not meet those stern eyes.

After a time the father nodded his head and shook it, just as if he said "What's the use?" and came back round the table, his face saturnine. "We can do nothing, Ambrose," he said, dejectedly now, "just nothing at all! There is no hope for you. All the tests of manhood have been applied and failed. You are only a spineless, good-looking hound. Elspeth Conroy married the husk of a man, but she is loyal, she is kind. What can you do about it, Amby?"

"Nothing," said Amby the spineless.

"Yes, you can," said the other quickly.

"What?"

"Leave her."

"To you—or Eudmon Butler?"

"Damn you! I warned you. No, not to me. And if you bring dangerous company to this house, that is your folly—and her risk. Think how unhappy an active young woman tied to you must be. Clear out and let her live her own life. She is no cheap woman. I will go with you. Look! we could slip away quietly, saying nothing. There is a place in the Mautopas that I know —a white beach under palms—a kindly sun—drink— any damn thing you like! A complete careless drifting. Ambrose! I will stick by you till you peter out, or till I do. Will you come?"

Rogan began to admire Sir Jerome Trant. He was a man; but he might as well have spoken to the wind. Ambrose sat crouching forward in his chair, his head between his hands; and he was rubbing his sleek hair desperately.

"No, no!" he whispered. "I cannot."

"Why not?"

"I don't know. I can't leave her. She is the only thing I have left. I can't—I tell you I can't!"

Rogan understood him then. She was the only fine thing he had, and he must hold her. But the father laughed bitterly. "There is the final failure of all. That finishes you, Ambrose. Very well, then!" Suddenly, he shoved the tray aside and leant right across the table. "But listen, my son! I want to retain my own self-respect, and I want Elspeth to respect me too; and if you dare couple our names I will not be responsible for my actions. Do you hear?"

"I hear."

"Bah! Don't make a promise! You never kept one." And then, under some uncontrollable impulse, Sir Jerome brought his open hand in a savage smack over the other's ear.

The son crouched and cowered in his chair, and the father straightened and walked up towards the fireplace out of Rogan's line of vision. And, after a time, Ambrose lifted his head, smoothed his hair, and his hand reached forward towards the tray where his glass still held a half-inch of liquor.

And there Rogan left them. He did not want to hear any more. He had looked upon the raw stuff of tragedy.

If Rogan Stuart had, at that point, given the plover's call to his friends the night's venture might have ended harmlessly. But Rogan Stuart was no longer his calm self. The mere sight of Eudmon Butler had shivered to atoms all his hard-won calm, and now he knew that that calm had been only a rind over a volcano where the old torture and desire were ready to flame in the presence of the man who had wronged him. Behind all, he was dismayed at himself and for himself.

Out on the dark of the lawn he halted on braced feet and brought his hands up to his head. What was the use—what was the use! All that ugly past should be dead and damned. Nothing could restore what was lost, nothing could make life flow in him again; and why should this flame leap alive to drive him? Pull yourself together, man! He ground his teeth savagely. What are you here for? To protect the flank of two men that trusted you. Get on with it, buckle your mind down to it. Already there was one person in the grounds in front of him, and at any moment there might be another.

Resolutely he shook the tremors out of his body, and moved away into the dark, working steadily across the lawn from clump to clump. He was very careful now, very alert—but deep down he knew why. Elspeth Trant was somewhere in the grounds, he knew; and if Eudmon Butler ran true to form he would not be far away; and some inner devil in Rogan Stuart gloated at the prospect of coming against Eudmon Butler in the dark. No! he urged himself, get on with your scouting; but the inner devil grinned.

Somewhere behind the shrubberies he stumbled over the edge of a path. He hesitated, listened, and decided to prospect forward. He was pulled up in less than twenty yards by the looming bulk of some sort of rustic building —a thing with white walls, and with a conical roof outlined against a patch of sky. The black gape of the doorway some feet above the ground was facing him; and the thought came that the woman—with or without a companion—might be in there. Without hesitation he stepped sideways on to the grass, and edged his way right up to the building. His teeth were tight clamped, and he could hear his blood beating in his ears.

The conical-roofed summer-house was erected on a platform that jutted out all round to make a railed veranda, and three wooden steps led up to the doorway. He sidled his way to the steps, and peered and listened into the blackness within the house. Not a stir, not a sound, but his own blood beating in his ears. No one was in there.

He had been a long time on his feet now, and, somehow, his legs were strangely weak. Why not take a short rest here and consider his next move? He sat down on the top step and leant shoulder against the veranda post.

The scene in that ugly house back there was still in his mind. It was the raw stuff of drama—or melodrama. The eternal triangle with a vengeance: a live woman, a degenerate husband, and—oh, bah! it was none of his business. He was merely the passer through, catching one glimpse and passing on. And yet he found himself thinking of the woman with interest. For it was not the son or the father who would soon matter to her—only Eudmon Butler. And this very night he could save her from Eudmon Butler—with his bare hands. Was she worth saving? He smiled at himself that an excuse like that should come into his mind. Yet the interest remained.

As he sat there he found himself wanting a smoke, and wondered that this desire should obtrude on the turmoil of mind and body. It would be too risky, of course, yet his hand went instinctively towards pocket. It never got there; for in that instant he got his second surprise that evening, and goose-flesh ran all over him. A woeful sound stirred the air around him: the low keening lament of a woman wailing out of the night, sad with all sadness.

He turned and looked into the dark of the summer-house, and, at once, realised that the sound did not come from there, but from the veranda at the back. And, as he listened, he knew that the woman was not really keening but softly intoning an old Gaelic lament, sad as loneliness, but not plaintive; too strong and bitter to be plaintive, too wise in grief, too indomitable for despair, knowing the beauty of defeat and desolation:

> O Seas that roll over me !
> O salt Seas falling !
> Whence roll ye, where fall ye,
> O desolate Waters ?
> *Out of my dark into thy darkness.*

He knew every word of that song and the spirit behind it: but could this be Elspeth Trant intoning these deep notes? An American woman singing a Gaelic lament! But she was a Conroy—daughter of kings—and laments like that were her heritage. Sorrow! but she had cause to lament. Let her sing, then. And if she could sing later when the inevitable cup of sorrow flowed over, she would have the fibre that should be in a king's daughter.

He listened, and from somewhere there flowed over

him that final freedom of weariness and despair. And then he realised that the singer was coming nearer round the veranda.

The lament stopped short and a voice spoke quickly, but not in alarm. "Who is it?"

He remained still. He knew that the thing to do was to maintain in her and in himself the mood of the song—its fatalism, its fearlessness; and he knew, by the spirit that dwelt at the heart of that song, that he could do it. He lifted up his head towards her, and softly, deeply, intoned the second verse of the lament:

> O Wind that cries over me !
> O cold Wind piercing !
> What cry you, where pierce you,
> O desolate North Wind ?
> *Cold of my grief into thy grieving.*

"Who is it?" she whispered.

"One passing through—on the road to nowhere." His voice was deep and slow.

The rustle of her dress, the sound of her light feet on the wood came nearer. "Who are you? Do I know you?" She was not in the least startled.

He did not move.

"This morning," said he, "you stood me on my ear when the referee was not looking—and I deserved it."

"Oh!" And after that exclamation she was silent and still for so long that his confidence grew, for it is only when woman acts on impulse that she makes the welkin ring and upsets beehives.

She was close above him and bending down boldly to look right into his face. There was the darkness of her eyes, the blackness of her hair, and a faint pleasant little waft of perfume.

"It is you, then!" She was upright now. "What are you doing here?"

"I—don't—know. Paying a visit to Hell out of season."

He could hear the intake of her breath before she spoke again. "But you *are* trespassing this time."

"I am sorry for that. This is a place I would not trespass in if I could help it."

The memory of her lapse that morning, or the spirit of the song, held her; to-night she was patient—even gentle. "Why are you here, then?"

"Trying to waste half an hour of your time—drifting with the stream of the dark to feel its dominance—the final dominance, you know."

"I know that."

That quiet agreement surprised him.

"You are too young to know," he told her sadly. "It is the evil of all knowledge. Forget it, and remember the advice that Paddy Joe Long gave you."

"Paddy Joe Long?"

"The long man who advised you not to let your spirit break and life would not break either. But I assure you that both will."

"Oh! that was the wise man of you—but I suppose you are all that—you three wise men?"

Though she said that a little derisively, already he had got hold of her mind. She had seen him for the first time that morning, and, yet, he seemed to put finger on the secret canker of her soul. She was trying to think that out. It puzzled her, aroused her curiosity, and once that was aroused, she forgot the strangeness of this meeting in the dark. And she was not afraid, not physi-cally or mentally afraid.

"Don't think about it," he said; and then suddenly, "Will you not sit down? half an hour is a long time," and he slapped the top step clear of dust with his hat.

"Sitting down seems your favourite occupation," she said coolly. "Why this half-hour?"

"If I told you that you'd be as wise as myself."

"Wise—wise—wise—how wise are you?" Her deep voice mocked all wisdom.

"Not very, but I knew that lament you were keening. It should explain us to one another."

And there she was, sitting within a yard of him, her shoulder against the other veranda post. Once the spirit was aroused in her she forgot all ordinary conventions. He smiled to himself in the dark. He had intrigued this young wife. He would keep on doing so. Suddenly, then, he remembered that smoke he was craving, and felt in his jacket pocket.

"Care for a cigarette?" He held the battered silver case across to her.

After a pause he felt her fingers fumble softly. "Thank you," she murmured.

He scraped a match and cupped it in one hand for her, and as she leant forward the line of her face was outlined in the wavering glow. In that light she looked so young and fragile—her forehead so delicately white below the black hair, the shadows so deep below long lashes, the round of her chin so full of youth and tenderness—that a wave of pity flowed over him. Paddy Joe Long was right. There was nothing more desolate than for youth to be unhappy. And she might be loyal, too, to a spineless husband—but for how long would she remain loyal, tempted as she must be? Not for long— and after that a slow hardening, a creeping degradation, tragedy inevitable.

He leant back and lit his cigarette, and she, in turn, saw his face: the crag of brow above the deep-set eyes, the high bones of the cheek with the leanness below them, the line of the mouth so firm—and so grim! A strong face, but a face that had to husband its strength desperately.

63

They sat there silent in the dark, and Rogan Stuart had no desire to break that quietness. They were, indeed, only two scraps of flotsam, drifting and touching and fated to drift apart and never touch again. And yet this quiet sitting in the dark was rather pleasant. Less than twelve hours ago they had been inimical, but now, under the dimness of the stars, in the tie of an old Gaelic song, there was all about them a new atmosphere in which their minds seemed to move along parallel lines.

She spoke first. "I fear I was rather on my dignity— and out of it this morning," she said. "I am not always like that."

"What of it?" he murmured. "I merely came between the two poles and got the whole discharge. You've got a handy left hand."

"Would you please answer my first question? Who are you?"

"Rogan Stuart is my name," he told her, and waited for that name to rouse a memory. He had never hidden his name. What was the need? For, though the name of Rogan Stuart was very well known not so long ago, very few now remembered it. Man was a lonely, self-centred beast after all.

It roused no memory. All she said was, "That's a Scottish name?"

"Yes, but my mother was Irish."

"My father was," she told him. "He taught me that old song and many more."

"You sang it well," said he. "You sang it too well You are too young to know how to sing that song."

"I don't feel young," she whispered.

"Only the young feel that way," he murmured back.

They were silent again, the cigarette tips glowing and dulling lazily and dimly outlining chin and nose. Rogan felt very sure of himself now. He had got firm hold of this young woman's mind and could sway it as he willed. But, though she felt his influence, her mind was thinking along lines of its own.

She was unhappy. She had taken a fatal step in marrying a man without morale. What could she do? There was some spirit of race in her, some spirit of self-penance that kept her loyal—loyal and no more. And, recently, fear had entered her life, for she had met a man, a tall, dare-devil Irish soldier, who had attracted her strangely and disturbingly. . . . And now, here in the quiet night with her, was this strange impersonal man, sure of himself—sure of her too, and knowing her trouble. That morning his arms had held her against all her strength, and then he had smiled and looked at her out of deep-set eyes, and let her go. "You poor kid," he had called her, and she had felt no resentment. He knew, and was sorry for her in an impersonal way. Impersonal! That was it. An uncanny impersonality, secure in its own citadel. Could not she too seek after that impersonality? Could she? She contemplated what it meant, and there, in that mood that rayed from him to her, she had a brief blinding knowledge of what that impersonality meant. It was unhuman, it was awesome, it was the surcease of pain and despair, the final refuge of a soul too strong to wrest itself from the trammels of the body. She shivered and spoke to him just above a whisper:

"You were sorry for me to-day, but to-night I am sorry for you."

"You need not be," he told her sternly.

"It is not good—to be alive yet dead."

"The only good there is."

"I don't care—I will be sorry for you if I like."

And that was that. Whatever else they might have said was cut off short; for across the lawn came the high voice of her husband. "Hello, Else! Where are you?"

Rogan ground the cigarette under heel and came to his feet; and she whispered: "Your half-hour—is it up?"

"Just about."

"Tell your friends they may have a salmon in daylight if they want one."

"Thank you, wise lady," said he, "and good-night! Go on living! That yonder is not death; Death only walks at his shoulder." Surely the spirit of prophecy was in him then.

He turned to go, paused, turned and leant close over her. "I am sorry for you too," he said. "There are three men about you, and one only is a man. Beware of one other. Keep your own soul, daughter of kings!"

He left her there on the step and slipped across to the shrubberies, and, as he got there, heard Trant call once more. She never answered back, and Ambrose did not call again. He paused behind a clump to take his bearings. There was the house; then, over there to the left, would be the path to the boat-house. He kept trending that way; and, with folk moving about on the lawn, he thought it better to give the signal; so he tapped cheek with finger-tip and whistled the plover's call. As he went he wondered what had become of Eudmon Butler.

Rogan was not aware that Trant was at the boat-house before him until he heard the sudden challenge in the dark immediately after the coracle bumped the wooden wall. The night was dark down there, and he was within ten yards when Ambrose turned and ran straight into him before he could slip out of the way. The rest followed as night the day.

The substance of the foregoing Rogan Stuart narrated
to Alistair and Paddy Joe. He did not, of course, dwell
on his own reactions to the presence of Eudmon Butler,
but he intimated that he was aware of that man's reputa-
tion in love affairs. The two listened quietly and closely
to this narrative, and a considering silence held when he
had finished. Then Alistair spoke wonderingly:

"Strange! the little things that kept moulding events
all night."

"What else are little things for, dammit?" said Paddy
Joe, and turned to Rogan. "Thank you, son! You've
put the thing before us."

"I suppose," said Rogan, but a shade doubtfully,
"the proper thing to do is to make a clean breast of it
to the police——?"

"Do you think so?" queried Alistair smoothly.

"I don't know—hate getting you fellows implicated.
If only you had kicked me out yesterday!"

"Don't be minding us," expostulated Paddy Joe.
"Men should be adventuring things to the risk of life
and limb once in a while, and not be always tied to a
woman's apron-strings—but what am I saying?"

"What you'll be blame sorry for when your wife
hears it," Alistair told him.

"Wait you! Here we are, the three of us, and at the
moment we are calm and cool, and we have a little time
in hands—not much, but enough maybe. I read somewhere that the time to come to an unalterable decision
is before the issue is joined—and now is the time. Just
as a lead, let us narrow the issue to my own view. Look!
As far as I know and deduce, one of five people might
have killed Ambrose Trant."

"Five?"

"You two and——"

"This is serious, Paddy Joe," Alistair stopped him.

"I am merely clearing things up for myself as I go. I saw nothing with head under my oxter, and all that I know was that there was the devil's own dog-and-cat fight above, and at the end of it you two come tumbling into the canoe. Well?"

"I didn't kill him," Alistair humoured him, "nor did Rogan Stuart. Trant was getting his wind back as we left."

"Very well!" He held up five fingers and turned down two. "Accepting your plea, who then are left?"

"The father, and the wife, and—" began Alistair.

Rogan's voice, smooth with emphasis, stopped him.

"Eudmon Butler does not usually need to kill to get his own way—with women."

"The worse for him at the bitter end," said Paddy Joe. "Leave him for the present and take father and wife."

"Looks pretty black against the father," said Alistair, "taking a line by what we know. But consider this: if Jerome Trant killed his son, the reasonable thing to assume is that the wife knew nothing about it; and the reasonable conclusion that she would arrive at was that Rogan Stuart and ourselves had a hand in it. She guessed we were poaching."

"And the natural thing she would do," pointed out Paddy Joe, "would be to report to the police where Rogan Stuart was last night, and where he was yesterday, and where——"

"Hell and the lid off!" cried Alistair, and turned to stare at the point of land that hid the harbour.

"Exactly," said Paddy Joe. "I have been waiting

an hour or more for a policeman to come round that point. None has come. Well?"

"She has not told," said Alistair in an awed whisper.

"And that would imply that she knows that we did not do the killing."

"Just a moment," put in Rogan. "If the woman did the killing—or if there was collusion in the killing between father and wife, might she not seek to implicate me?"

"If she did, the police would be here," said Alistair.

"Exactly," agreed Paddy Joe. "Why postulate in her sheer criminal wickedness? One thing we do know: she is not wicked."

"I don't know," said Rogan heavily. He knew the surprising and tragic things a woman was capable of.

"I do," said Paddy Joe firmly. "Listen, now! Let us put ourselves in her place. We know she is under a strain, and we know she is subject to sudden tempers. Very well. She was in the grounds, she heard her husband squeal, and she came running; she did not answer his previous calling, but that fighting squeal she would answer, knowing that Rogan was in the grounds. Remember the light feet we heard running?"

"Let us be fair," said Rogan. "Many men are light-footed too."

"Wait, now. She comes up, she finds her husband on the ground getting his wind back, as you say. She would naturally help him to his feet. He was drunk, he was fighting mad, he had already called to her twice and she had not answered, and then he had been set upon by a strange man. Who was that strange man? What would Ambrose think, what would he do in his drunken state? She was holding him there where he had been man-handled a minute before; why, he might even strike at her, he would certainly use the unforgivable word. And what would she do?"

"Choke it in his throat, by heavens!" said Alistair fiercely.

"And there you are. Mind you, it would take very little then to finish Ambrose Trant. The drink had probably rotted the life sources—you saw his pale mouth; he was after a real man-handling, and a finger pressed on each side—there—and he would go out like that." Paddy Joe flicked thumb and finger. "Why, she would not even know that he was gone! He would yield under her hands and she would throw him from her, and away—straight to her room. . . . It is more than likely that they have separate rooms. She would not know that he was dead till this morning. That's my reconstruction for you."

"And she has said nothing?"

"Evidently she has said nothing, but how long will she stay silent? I wish I knew."

"But what should we do?" demanded Alistair.

"The move is with her, is it not?" He jerked a thumb towards Rogan and smiled. "But I'm afraid there is one amongst us with one of those tender, Presbyterian Scots consciences."

Rogan looked up. "I? Oh, I don't care a damn what happens—to myself. No doubt the proper thing is to report all I know to the Civic Guard, but how am I to keep you out of it? What do you suggest?"

"We are not worrying," said Alistair.

"Alistair, son," said Paddy Joe, "do you want to be hanged or to hang anybody?"

"Not at present, Paddy Joe."

"And you couldn't put your hand on the slayer?"

"I wouldn't, you mean."

"You have a helluva tough conscience, boy."

"Raw-hide."

"Like my own. You have us now, Rogan Stuart. Suppose you put this thing entirely in our hands?"

"Certainly," agreed Rogan readily. "I will do exactly what you tell me—and nothing more or less."

"I thought you would."

"You'll do to take along." Alistair gave the supreme words of Western praise.

"Events will wait on us," said Paddy Joe, "so we'll sit tight for the present. If the police appear we will know why, and tell them what they should know—and that is about everything——"

"And if they do not show up?"

"There's our bit of lunch—fried salmon——"

"Damn that salmon!"

"And a vegetarian entrée, and a cup of coffee—'cause we have no beer. And in the afternoon—listen, now! In the afternoon we will pull up to the pier and dare all Dounbeg, walking about, having a drink or so, talking to this one and that one; and when we see a policeman we'll nobly swallow our hearts, for the bold road is the best road, and whatever is guiding us will direct us to the next bend."

CHAPTER VI

1

THEY rowed round the point, and the green long glen of Grianaan opened out before them—sunny green slopes, house-dotted, and the rounded hill-tops brown in heather. A rocky mound behind the pier hid the village of Dounbeg, but, above and beyond the grassy crown of this mound, the chimneys of the Harty Arms Hotel smoked thinly. The clean deep tide of the bay lapped and shimmered between the square green-slimed piles of the pier, and sea-urchins pulsed in the clear, translucent green of the water.

A squat wooden building stood at mid-pier, and, as the coracle appeared round the point, a shirt-sleeved, massive, rugged-faced old man came out from the doorway and strolled heavy-footed down the resounding platform. He was at the head of the iron ladder as Paddy Joe tied up at the foot of it, and his voice rolled and rumbled like thunder.

"More line, lubber—the tide's making."

"Interfering sort of people in this place!" mused Paddy Joe aloud.

The three mounted the ladder and Alistair introduced Rogan. "Rogan Stuart—Captain Tom Whelan, late mercantile marine, now king-pin of the busy harbour of Dounbeg, where you behold as many as two Galway hookers unloading peat."

"Late pirate," added Paddy Joe, "or what's his mug for?"

"You're in good company—maybe, Mr Stuart,"

72

rumbled the harbour-master, his Colleoni-like face not changing a line. "You'll be from Scotland, then?"

"He is not," said Paddy Joe.

"And don't be speirin', Thomas!" warned Alistair. "We did not kill Ambrose Trant, if you want to know."

"God rest him!" ejaculated the harbour-master. "That was bad work at the big house!"

"It was queer work, too. What's your latest?"

"Nothing—nothing at all. Sergeant MacGrath is keeping his mind to himself, which, maybe, means that he has nothing in it to keep. Myself, I'm thinking it was strange poachers done it—from down Corullish way. A bad breed, them fellows! would throttle their own father if he came between them and as much as a dog-fish. But whoever did it didn't mean to kill."

"How do you know?"

"Who would, man? He was a friendly lad, Amby Trant, with the laughing word—and him ready to take and stand his drink with Tom, Dick and Harry——"

"And Shawn, Mick and Larry?" put in Paddy Joe.

"'Tis so—he stood it well," agreed Tom Whelan.

"Has the father been up from the house?" enquired Paddy Joe.

"Sir Jerome? Up at the Garda station twice, I hear. They say he looks broken."

"And young Mrs Trant?"

"The poor girsha! My little heart o' corn!" his voice rumbled softly. "She'll be feeling it. No—she hasn't been up. But, sure, she's young and maybe——" He stopped.

"Maybe what?"

"I dunno, Paddy Joe. She's young, thank God."

He stalked up the pier and the three of them went with him. "Thanks for the tail of the salmon," he said in a growling murmur at his office door.

"Try it?" enquired Paddy Joe.

"I would if Friday wasn't in it—that's the one day I don't like fish. I have it here yet."

"Take it home to the missus—if you like," said Paddy Joe smoothly.

"I'll be thinking about it," Tom rumbled, and left them.

They walked on up the pier, Rogan in the middle.

"A queer thing!" mused Paddy Joe aloud. "Old Tom is sorry for Ambrose Trant, but, at the back of his mind, he has the thought that, for the girl, her husband's death might not be such a bad thing. And what is more, a good many in Dounbeg will be thinking the same thing. They knew Amby, liked him even—but they have a strange warmth and understanding for Elspeth Trant. You will note that. And note another thing: no one seems to know of any strained relations between father and son. Queer?"

"Has the harbour-master any doubts about us," enquired Rogan.

"He might, but the doubts will stay in his own mind. Don't worry about old Tom Whelan, even if he does know where we killed that salmon last night."

They skirted the rocky mound, and the long straggling street of Dounbeg opened before them. The flat-fronted houses were lime-washed in staring and badly matched colours—yellow, light green, livid blue, pink, red ochre—and the puce-slated roofs were at all levels. Left of where they stood a big modern hotel towered above a green lawn whereon was slung a dilapidated tennis-net—but the lines of the court were not yet marked.

"Here's the Harty Arms," suggested Alistair.

"I'm dry too," said Paddy Joe.

The hotel bar was empty, but the bang of the door brought the proprietor himself, a red-haired man famous

74

for his droll, and often salacious, stories. To-day only one subject obsessed him.

"Bad work last night, gentlemen," he said, his hands busy at the beer levers. "God rest the poor fellow!"

"Amen!" responded Paddy Joe.

"A bad thing for the town—and the season nearly on us—and no blame to the town either. There isn't a man in this place would put a hurting hand on poor Amby. The devil blast them Corullish poachers——!"

"He was well liked?"

"A friendly man! devil the friendlier ever stood on two feet. I've seen him, myself, in this bar stand a drink to a tinker off the road."

"And take one?"

"Ay, begobs! He had a head like a rock."

Alistair thought he would test Paddy Joe's theory.

"They will feel it at the big house?" he half queried.

"Surely, then! I saw Sir Jerome passing in the car, and he looked a broken man."

"And Mrs Trant?"

"Wishan! the poor darlin'. The poor young widow! —God be good to her! But she's young—she's young; an' after all—sure, if you insist, Mr Long, I'll try a small taste."

II

They left the bar and walked up the straggling street as far as the Central Hotel, a long two-storied building fronting the road with a glass-roofed veranda along the length of the ground floor.

"We'll rest ourselves in the sun here," suggested Paddy Joe, turning into the veranda.

Alistair stretched his legs from a sagging wicker-chair and felt for his pipe.

"You have set us in the public eye, if you so intended," he said.

A flaxen-haired waitress put her head round a glass door.

"'Tis all right, Mary Josephine," called Paddy Joe. "We might want you in a small while—or we mightn't."

Rogan Stuart relaxed and looked about him. The seaside season had not yet opened and very few people were in the street, but every now and then heads appeared in doorways and surveyed the scene; the citizens were keeping tab on events. Opposite the hotel veranda was the post-office, with its green letter-box taking up half the window, and twenty yards farther on a square house showed the square plaque of the police-station. Alistair pointed to a barred window.

"The lock-up," he said. "We may be in there before night."

Presently, a tall man in the dark-blue uniform of the Civic Guard strolled carelessly into the street and stood looking about him.

"There's Sergeant MacGrath," said Alistair. "No flies on him either!"

The sergeant saw the three lounging on the veranda and waved an easy salute. Paddy Joe lazed to his feet.

"I'll have a look at his eye," he said. "Hang on!"

He slouched across the street, and Alistair and Rogan saw the guard grin at something that was said.

"We have been here a bare three weeks," said Alistair, "and Paddy Joe has the place in his breast-pocket. The sergeant spent an evening with us last week, and I lost half a dollar to him at a card-game called forty-ones. He bent the lid of the bacon-box every time he took a trick."

They smoked leisurely and watched the two men in talk. It seemed to be a wholly friendly dialogue, and

76

Paddy Joe kept emphasising points with finger on palm.

As a matter of fact, Paddy Joe was trying to get a line on the policeman's thoughts and succeeding just as far as the policeman would let him.

"You're taking it damn easy, Dan," said Paddy Joe in the course of the exchanges, "and it your first big case."

Sergeant MacGrath looked him over with a derisive brown eye. "Maybe I am, Paddy Joe, but many a man hanged himself by getting a longish bit of rope—and can't I lay my hand on you any time I have a mind?"

"You'll have to throw a wide loop, Dannie. How many have you to cover at the big house?"

"Only a couple that count." He held Paddy Joe's eye. "My work would be much easier if another man had been killt last night instead of poor Amby."

"Meaning?"

"I'd be saying a word to the lad sitting beyond with your friend."

"Oh!" Paddy Joe swallowed his surprise. "You know him?"

"Rogan Stuart—and a good man in his day. I played football against him when I was at the O'Connell Schools and he at the Mountjoy, and, dammit, he would think nothing of gouging your eye out in a loose scrum. Was he with you all yesterday?"

"And all last night!"

"Don't tell me where. The lamp was not lit in your tent till past midnight, but that's nothing new."

"Watching us?"

"What else? But I'm leaving you out of this—for a piece anyway. Ye'll tell me the truth if I want it."

"Don't overlook any one."

"That's the policeman's rule."

"Even the father and the wife——"

"The girl was a mother to poor Amby."

"Yet it would appear that she never missed him through the night."

The sergeant shook his head in mock pity. "Easily known you come from a backward place like Ballybwingan. In our society we no longer share bed—and board, only sometimes."

"You astound me. What about the father, then?"

"Sir Jerome? When a father like that drags a son up to man's estate—a lad like Amby without much harm in him—what would he kill him for?"

"What?" Paddy Joe wanted to know.

"You've the bad Kerry mind," chided the other, "but we'll consider your suggestion."

"Go to hell! you Bandon Orangeman," said Paddy Joe politely, turned on his heel and strolled back towards the veranda.

"'Tis the wrong man was killed, all the same," called the sergeant, and, with a glance up and down the street, that shrewd man disappeared into the station.

"What we suffer from in this country," said Paddy Joe grouchily, throwing a leg over a corner of the glass-topped table, "is an intelligent police force."

"Was he too slick for you?" enquired Alistair.

"He was bright all right, but he is stumped this time, I do believe. Mind you, he guesses we were out on one of our stunts last night, but that is all he does know."

"If he guesses——"

"'Tisn't his guesses we need trouble about," said Paddy Joe. "Hullo! Who is coming now?"

The throb of a motor came up the street from the direction of the harbour; and a big car came sliding to a stop in front of the post-office.

"From the big house," Paddy Joe told them in a low voice.

The far door opened, and a slender woman, dressed in black, got out and entered the post-office.

"Herself—God help her!" said Paddy Joe.

"Has she seen us?" speculated Alistair.

"You couldn't be knowing. Women see more than we give them credit for—and sometimes it does them no good. Wait, now!"

Rogan Stuart waited two minutes and then drew himself slowly to his feet.

"I'll have a look at her eye," he said in Paddy Joe's very drawl, and stepped down from the veranda.

"Let him alone," murmured Paddy Joe. "He has a hard streak. I couldn't do it myself."

The meeting was perfectly timed. They came together at the post-office door, and their eyes met. The colour had receded under the smooth tan of her cheeks, and there were dark shades below her eyes, but her gaze met his steadily. Yet she had started ever so slightly, and her tones tremored in spite of her.

"How can you stay here?" There was pain in her voice. "You must not stay here."

He inclined his head, and his voice was equally low but steady as a rock. "Go you too, while you are still free."

And that was all. She entered the car, which slid away almost soundlessly, and Rogan disappeared into the post-office. In a brief while he was back on the veranda.

"I bought some stamps," he said, "but I don't use any." He sat down as before, and the two friends waited. "We did not bandy words," he told them. "She merely told me to go away from here."

Paddy Joe considered that for a long time. "It was good advice," he said at last. "I was afraid that time would not be given us to move in any way. For your own sake and ours it would be a good thing if you could disappear—like a needle in a bundle of hay."

"What chance has a fellow of losing himself in this blanket-spread of island?" Alistair enquired sceptically.

"That's our problem."

Rogan smiled grimly. "There are many ways of losing oneself."

"None that you have in mind will do, Highlandman," said Paddy Joe evenly. "The sleep that knows no waking is not in our cosmos."

"I do not know what sleep is," said Rogan Stuart sombrely.

"God ha' mercy on us!" exclaimed Paddy Joe, and brought both feet to the ground. "Come, boys! let us back to camp and work this problem out."

III

As they paced thoughtfully down the middle of the road the creak of an axle from behind made them edge on to the pavement. Paddy Joe looked over his shoulder and stopped.

"Here comes a friend of mine who has solved the problem of living," he said. "Jamesy Coffey, King of the Road. Wait till we see who he has in his tail."

An old white horse plodded by them, drawing a caravan painted strongly in green, white and orange, with high-set windows red-curtained, and a black stove-pipe protruding from the arched top. A keen, swarthy, tousle-haired lad of some twelve summers held the reins on the driving-bench, and softly tapped the rump of the old horse with a hazel-switch. By his side sat a woman of late middle years—a remarkable woman; upright she would stand close on six feet, and she carried no extra flesh ; black-haired, black-eyed, aquiline, dusky, with heavy jet ear-rings almost touching her shoulders, she sat placidly smoking a short clay pipe. Her big, dark eyes stared away into the distance at something evolved out of her own mind.

And then, suddenly, she turned and looked piercingly at Rogan Stuart—and at Rogan only; just one piercing glance, and again she turned away into her own abstraction.

"That's Maag Carty—and Daheen Coffey her stepson," Paddy Joe told them. "She's cross-bred out of a gypsy and a MacCarthy More, and has the second-sight. Look at this one now!"

Close behind the van a small, hardy, sleek jennet, walking daintily on narrow hooves, drew an ancient tiltcart covered with patched canvas. A young woman sat on a box under the front arch of the tilt and held the reins loosely.

"Glory be!" said Paddy Joe. "The strangeness of her hits me every time I look at her. That's Julie Brien, daughter to Maag Carty by another husband. That hair is redder than your Margaret's, Alistair?"

"Red like that is broken-down black," Alistair remarked, "but she is a flaming good-looker."

She was young and vital. Her tight-fitting cloth jacket outlined her virgin bust, and, though all her days must have been spent in the sun, there was not so much as a freckle even on the bridge of her nose. Her complexion was of that peculiar texture that is smooth yet matt, and was of one even tint, darker than cream, lighter than lemon; and her lips were red and grave. Her dark-brown eyes looked at them and smiled at Paddy Joe, who waved a hand at her, placed it over his heart, and shook his head. She showed her white teeth then.

"She's a darling," said Paddy Joe. "But I wonder

where Shamus Og is. Shamus Og is Jamesy Coffey's grown-up son and a devil on two feet. By what I hear, he shouldn't be far away from that red hair."

Under the axle of the tilt-cart trotted a wise-looking, brindled lurcher dog, with its nose within an inch of the jennet's sprightly heels.

And on the tail of the tilt sat Jamesy Coffey himself, his black-gaitered legs and brown boots swinging loosely. He was a squat, wide-shouldered, oldish man, with a black bowler hat on the back of his head and a blue stubble on his round chin. He was gloomily smoking an impossibly short stub of briar, and gloomily contemplating the legs of a colt that walked soberly behind the tilt— a tall, nicely-coupled colt with a reddish chestnut hide above black points, and with just the smallest trace of a limp in the off foreleg.

Paddy Joe lifted up his voice above the rattle of the axle: "Hullo, Jamesy Coffey, you old robber!"

Jamesy looked up and stared at Paddy Joe out of a choleric blue eye, and then nodded shortly and sourly.

"Where's Shamus Og?"

The old fellow gestured a hand widely over the breadth of Ireland and resumed his gloomy contemplation of the limping colt.

"Where'd you steal him?" called Paddy Joe. "A splint, a spavin, and a ringbone if I looked for it!"

"Go to hell, Paddy Joe Long!" His voice was a high ringing tenor.

"That's Jamesy Coffey for you," said Paddy Joe, grinning, "and I number him amongst the best half-dozen men I know. A great and kindly heart——"

"He doesn't sound like it," said Alistair.

"Och, that's only his way! The best man on the road, and if the tinkers of Ireland had a king, that king would be Jamesy indisputably. But mind you, Jamesy

82

is not a tinker as we know tinkers. I'm worried about Shamus Og. I'll have to look into this."

"Are you the grand vizier of tinkers?"

"A title worth while, too," said Paddy Joe. "Come on."

When they got down to the pier they found that the man of the roads had drawn his van and tilt on to the green common that fringed the road beyond the rocky buttress.

"Good!" exclaimed Paddy Joe. "I thought he might be making for Corullish without a stop." He walked on a few paces, hesitated and stopped. His eyes were quite vacant for half a minute. "God is good!" he said then, and looked up at Alistair. "Let you and Rogan go across in the canoe, and, later on, I will climb over the point. Have a pot of tea ready in an hour—and don't forget to call in at the Harty Arms for the beer we ordered."

"Yes, father," agreed Alistair mildly.

CHAPTER VII

I

Two hours elapsed before Paddy Joe appeared on the
path round by the bluff, his tweed hat on the back of
his head, hands in pockets, a gay whistling in his mouth—
with never a problem in the world to trouble him. The
westering sun, low down, shone on his face up the length
of the bay, and there was a rich orange glow on the rocks
and heather amidst which he strolled.

He stopped his whistling. "Good men and all!" he
shouted. "Is my tay ready?"

"Biled!" called back Alistair. "What did Jamesy
Coffey spiel to you?"

"Cute fellow! What did I spiel to Jamesy Coffey?"

"A jugful, I'll bet a hat!" chuckled Alistair. He sat
cross-legged on top of the bacon-box, and poured a brown
stream of strong tea into an earthenware mug, flipped in
some sugar from a blue paper bag, and squeezed half a
lemon on top.

Paddy Joe hopped to a seat on the bacon-box at
Rogan's side, looked at that man round the rim of the
mug, imbibed deeply, and sighed with satisfaction.
"Jamesy Coffey is a sound man," said he, "and a friend
of mine. He would be king of the tinkers if the tinkers
needed a king. They don't. He's a cut above the real
tinker. His da had ambitions outside his class and gave
him some schooling, and Jamesy ran away to the States
and came back with money in his pocket and took to
the road, an aristocrat of travelling men and an un-
crowned king——"

"You said that before."

"I want to impress on you the sort of man he is. He is of the son of the real tradesman tinker—and there are few left, for, barring one or two, there isn't a so-called tinker could use a soldering iron to bottom a tin pan. And Jamesy himself, though he still carries his father's budget—that's what the tool-kit is called—does not work at the trade."

"How does he live, then, caravan and all?" Alistair enquired.

"He is not poor, wherever you set the standard. He has worked himself out of the slough of tinkerdom to be plutocrat of the road. Added to his money during the war dealing in scrap-iron, jobbing in horses, mules, asses—anything on four feet. He could retire into a house any time he likes, but he knows where his happiness lies and enjoys himself rambling about the South and West, doing an odd horse deal, buying scrap in bulk, dickering for a gun or fishing-rod—and helping out a friend in his own cross-grained way."

"A sort of busman's holiday?"

"That's it. I know him since I was so-high; and in those days he used to have a tail of twenty or more— Coffeys, Cartys, O'Briens, Sheridans, *tre-na-ceile*, mixum-gatherum, a robbing, roaring, fighting crew, with their own code and their own morals, roystering it from Bantry Bay to the source of the Suir. Did I ever tell you about the time Jamesy married Maag Carty, his present wife?"

"You will," said Alistair resignedly.

"Why wouldn't I? Maag Carty is not his first wife— nor his second, maybe. The tinker's life was a hard life on women and children, and, even now, the tinker's clan is a dwindling one. They died early and they died strange, and they were buried in their own secret way. Not one man in ten thousand has ever seen a tinker's funeral. I saw one and couldn't get it out of my head for days——"

"Hooch?"

"Some. And the *caoining*—lamenting of the women: the same old laments that were lifted shrill and weird over O'Sullivan Bere and Hugh Roe and Brian—over Niall and Con, and Eochy of the Firbolgs—timeless laments to tear the heart out of you, and drink to make the tears soften the pain. But about Maag. The Cartys boast the blood of MacCarthy More, Prince of South Desmond, mixed with the older blood of a gypsy king. The Carty women were ladies in their own right. As a matter of fact, some authorities hold that the tinkers are descended withershin from the bards and romancers of royal houses—and true it is that there never yet was a tinker who couldn't sing a ballad to stir the blood, or tell a lie finer than any truth——"

"We will get to Jamesy Coffey in our own time," murmured Alistair.

"Why not?—Another boast of the Cartys was that they were always married by a priest before the altar rails ; and that is not usual amongst tinkers. Jamesy's way and the tinker's way is by that unique ceremony called 'jumping the budget,' a ceremony as old as fire-worship and sprung out of it——"

"Snub it!" Alistair urged him. "Put a hitch on it, fellow!"

"Anyhow, it was over at Ballybwingan in the summer season—four or five years ago—and the Coffeys and the Cartys were there, running a show and telling fortunes for the visitors and stealing on the side. Jamesy had buried two or, maybe, three wives, and Maag Carty had buried one or two men. I rather think they had always been attracted to each other and antagonistic at the same time—as two strong characters will be; and now, with the fires cooling, they could be easy companions on the road. And I think, too, that Jamesy saw that Maag was lonely and poor, with a growing daughter too precious for ignoble selling. 'Jamesy,' says Maag, 'you poor darling chicken-stealer, isn't it time some woman buried you?' 'Try it yourself, you long rip,' invited Jamesy politely. And that completed the courting.

"I knew Jamesy well and he knew me, and in matters relating to the outside and alien world he treated me as a sort of consultant. So up he comes to our bungalow, sees Norrey my wife, and takes a good long look at her. 'Poor Paddy Joe Long!' he says, shaking his head, ' little the sense was at him one bad day. Is he inside?' 'What do you want?' Norrey questions him, 'and if it is an old coat, he is wearing it.' 'He would be,' says Jamesy, 'and you in silk.' I came out then to save Jamesy. 'Long Maag of the Cartys,' he tells me without any beating about the bush, 'is marrying me like a Christian—how does a priest do it?' 'Like you might bottom a can,' I told him. 'Sticks for all time and leaks in many places.' 'Solder will mend a leak,' he comes back, 'and the butt of an ash-plant cure a wife. Did you ever try it?' And he jerked a thumb at Norrey. He has a tongue like a rasp and a heart of corn.

"Next day I took Maag and himself to the Presbytery to interview Canon Mulney, as decent a shepherd as ever cursed a flock, even if he was a bit fond of the dollars. 'Are you in a hurry, Jamesy?' the Canon wanted to know. 'I am not,' says Jamesy, 'but this one is, for she knows damn well I might change my mind any minute.' 'In that case,' says the priest, 'the special licence and my little fee will cost you five pounds.' 'That's enough,' shouted Jamesy. 'That ends it. I never gave a pound to a priest, to say nothing of five.' 'Never mind the poor darling, reverend father,' says

Maag. 'Five pounds it will be, and more if you want it.' 'Will it, begobs!' says Jamesy. 'Very well so.'

"And the next morning Norrey and I led them up to the altar rails, the whole tinker clan watching us through the door; they were afraid to come in lest the roof fall on them and the holy-water blister where it touched. The Canon is there in his white surplice, and looks knowingly at Jamesy, and Jamesy slips across a crumpled note. The priest, being a gentleman and in his vestments, does not examine the note, but slips it out of sight somewhere, and there and then binds the two in wedlock bonds. In the sacristy after the ceremony, where we were signing the register, Maag lays a five-pound note face up on the table. 'Father,' says she, 'say a Mass for Timmy Brien I buried last, and when the time comes say one for Jamesy Coffey.' 'Dear—dear!' says the gratified Canon. 'This is too much, my dear Mrs Coffey.' 'You will find it little enough, father,' says she.

"Such a wedding! Thunder and lightning and heavy showers! A tinker's wedding bothers description. Wait till I tell you—no, I won't, then! Some time next day, I was in amongst the breakers on the long strand to cure my head, when the good Canon himself pops his head out of a roller by my side. 'Paddy Joe Long,' he wants to know laughingly, 'was it you taught Jamesy Coffey the way to trick me?' 'I would if I knew how, Canon,' I told him. And then he tells me how he came to slip hand in pocket and had found Jamesy's note, and instead of a five-pounder, it was only a crumpled oblong of butter paper; you know the sort that has the feel and crinkle of a bank-note—that was it. The Canon and I had a good laugh.

"But, coming up the village street afterwards, whom did we meet but Jamesy himself, and he as bold as brass.

'Ha, you scoundrel!' cries the Canon. 'You can't trick me like that!' 'Can't I, then?' says Jamesy back at him. 'To trick a man at his own trade is a fair game.' 'And a dangerous one too, my gambler,' says the priest, 'for I always keep a trick up my sleeve. Do you think your marriage is valid?' 'What's that?' Jamesy cries suspiciously. 'A bargain broken breaks all bargains,' the Canon gave him jokingly. 'The words I said over ye are no more binding than the wind, and ye'll have to come to me again—or live in sin.' 'Powders o' war!' cried Jamesy. 'Them's the grandest words I heard in a year of Sundays. Sure, I'm sick tired of the ould devil already—and there I leave you.' 'Come back—come back!' shouted the Canon in dismay. 'You are validly married—I was only joking.' 'Joke or earnest, you can't be changing your mind that way, Canon,' shouted back Jamesy, and in with him to Carroll's bar. Ay, faith!''

"You know the ways of the tinker clan," half-mused Rogan, appreciating what Paddy Joe was leading up to.

II

Paddy Joe shook his head slowly. "I know only the edges. But if I had my way—if Norrey would let me, and she will not—I would go and live a year or two years with Jamesy Coffey, and write one book worth while. But even if I got the chance I don't suppose I could stick the life for a year. I am getting past my toughness, and, to be a man of the road, a travelling man, an enemy of all settled life and settled men, calls on the best qualities of a man—and sometimes the worst. A great and cleansing life—for good or ill."

Rogan smiled understandingly. He had to lose himself from this place, not only because of the killing, but because of a man who still remained alive; and Paddy Joe was indicating a way.

"What are the qualifications of a passable tinker?" he enquired mildly.

Paddy Joe felt for pipe and pouch. "I'll tell ye," said he, grimly cheerful, "if it takes a year. The rain shall wet him, and the sun dry him, and he not heeding the wetting or the drying. The winds shall blow over him, the frost nip his edges, the sun pour its hot lead on the back of his neck—and these shall be but as the sounds of lyres and scorpions. Yes, sirs! A man impervious to all the scorpions and gentlings of nature that in the end shall kill him without his knowing of the onslaught. And, not caring about the weather, he shall have an instinct for it like a black-backed gull. He shall know a bird by the flutter of its pinions, and stalk the grey-lag and the curlew on their own flats. Two fields off he must be able to say 'That's not a tussock of grass but a hare in its form,' and his hound-dog shall round that hare into his poacher's pocket, and he shall sell it to the owner or make soup for his clan. A pheasant twenty feet above the ground, on a branch of a tree at the gable end of the game-keeper's house, shall not be safe from him in the dark of a November's night. A wise salmon in a pool below a hazel bush shall rue the day when his eyes peer into the deep of the water. He shall hear a hen cackle and know whether the cackle is over an egg or over a worm—and the egg shall be for his tea. He shall know an unsound leg on a horse, and sell a donkey as a Spanish jennet——"

"You remind me," said Alistair, "of Mr Polly at the Potwell Inn. When your tinker finds nothing more to do, how does he amuse himself?"

"He shall be happy with the lean belly and the belly that is too full—and when his shirt needs washing he shall wash it. He shall take a woman or leave a woman just as it pleases him, sing a ballad at a fair, lie splendidly to common men and to gentlemen, and when he passes his word he shall keep his word. He shall be friendly to any man worth friendship and be tied to no man, and his enemy he shall fight at the drop of a hat. Amongst his own clan he shall fight his way to his own level and fight harder than ever to keep that level, but in the alien world outside he shall not fight at all, except at a last and desperate extremity—and then he shall be deadly. . . . Wait, now, till I get my breath, for I am not much past the beginning."

"Could I become that sort of tinker, Paddy Joe?" enquired Rogan simply.

"You could," said Paddy Joe, looking at him with level eyes, "because you must."

Rogan nodded in an abstracted way.

"You must go for your own sake—and ours. Remember how this afternoon we were stumped by the problem of getting you away, and Jamesy Coffey came along. He was sent."

"It is a sound proposition," said Alistair musingly. "The only way to lose oneself in this island is to lose one's identity."

"And no sleuth will ever find him under the skin of a tinker's curate—if the skin fits," said Paddy Joe, and turned to Rogan. "What was your mother's name?"

"Mackay-Rogan."

"A good name. We will adopt and adapt that name. You are no longer Rogan Stuart. You are Rogue McCoy, travelling man—outcast from heaven and from hell—going the twisty roads of Ireland in Jamesy Coffey's tail, and abiding by Jamesy Coffey's code. If you are the man we think you are, you won't shame us, and you'll have experiences that may—you'll have experiences, anyway. And look! Will you give me one year of your life?''

"It is yours—for what it is worth."

"It may be worth nothing indeed, but I'll keep a string to it. Jamesy Coffey has a circuit that he keeps to, more or less: the great fair of Puck, the big horse fair at Cahiramee, the sale of colts and young hunters at Castleinch—these in the fall; then into the hunting country and game preserves, Mallow, Cappawhite, Thurles, Templemore, and across Loch Derg into Galway; and the summer season here or Kilkee or Ballybwingan. I live at Ballybwingan all the summer, and about this time next year you will report to me at that place, and the yoke will be taken off you by the goodness of God."

"When do I begin—to-morrow?"

"To-night. Every hour is urgent after the darkness falls, for there's a woman in the game. I talked two hours to Jamesy, told him as little as I could, and got him to move his camp down to Sand Cove below the Narrows. We'll pull down there in the dark."

"Thunder!" exclaimed Alistair. "You'll take the oars yourself, then. The tide will be meeting us full pelt."

"Rogue McCoy will take an oar—we'll make it. Mind you," he warned, "our pull may be fruitless, for Jamesy, the old hedgehog, will not give a final assent until he and Maag Carty have put Rogue through what he calls his catechism—and it is no easy one. That will be enough now. The tea is cold, but beer is cooler, and talk is a grand thirsty thing, glory be!"

III

"Are we making it?" Alistair panted, rowing forty to the minute.

"Fine," whispered Paddy Joe encouragingly. "Two full inches every tug. Hold it, ye devils, another minute, and I'll give you time to draw a breath."

"Easy for you, scrimshanker!" grunted Alistair.

Alistair and Rogan at the oars had bucked the coracle more than half-way against the smooth rush of the tide in the Narrows. Out of the dark, big black rocks towered close over them on one hand, and, on the other, not a hundred yards away, the face of the mountain blotted out the stars. Little pale flecks of foam on the face of the tide rushed past them and gave the illusion that they were progressing at a mighty pace, but, as Paddy Joe had said, the coracle was making bare inches at each bending kick of the oars.

Presently Paddy Joe leant forward. "Keep pulling, Rogue—ship oar, Alistair!"

The coracle slewed in towards a steep boulder, and Paddy Joe, leaning out from his perch in the bow, fended off and got a good hand-grip. "Easy all!" Alistair added his grip and the little boat hung close to the rock.

"Some spell!" panted Alistair.

"Get your wind, and then we'll work her by hand to the next bend."

Thus they came to where the Narrows began to open to the outer bay.

"There's a throw-off in the current here," said Alistair. "I can feel it. We'll make it this time. Are you ready, Rogan—Rogue, I mean?"

They made it this time and came to reasonably slack water.

"We'll pull across now," directed Paddy Joe. "Sand Cove is round the point."

They skirted a rocky jut and found themselves in still and shoal water; in the half-light of the calm summer night the sea had a fine green tint over a pebbly bottom, and the curving shore of the little cove showed a gleam of bright sand backed by dark clumps of furze and black-thorn. The round curve of the coracle grated in the shallows ten feet out, and Paddy Joe, splashing carelessly into six inches of water, lifted the bow to the edge of the sand.

A voice spoke at his shoulder. "Blast ye for all that noise! Come away into the bushes, quick, and be damned to ye!"

Paddy Joe looked over his shoulder at the squat figure bulking out of the night. "I'd know you by the kind word anywhere, Jamesy Coffey. Hurry up, boys—this way!"

At the thorny edge of a tangle of blackthorn they bunched into a group round the old roadman, who was about as prickly as the bush behind him.

"A damn fool I am!" he grumbled unamiably. "An' mind you, Paddy Joe Long, I'm under no obligation to you!"

"You are, Jamesy," said Paddy Joe equably. "Didn't I marry you to Maag Carty?"

"The devil melt you for that! Listen to me, now! Had ye robbers anything to do with the throttlin' up at Dounbeg House? Ye didn't kill young Trant, did ye?"

"Not quite," said Alistair.

"I wouldn't put it past ye. That long black bastard of a peeler put me through me catechism this evening—where was I yesterday—what place I robbed last night—where was Shamus Og——?"

"Where is Shamus Og?" Paddy Joe queried.

"Didn't I tell you? Bla'guardin' up east with a dirty tribe of Wards from the County Wicklow." He jerked a thumb over shoulder. "Julie Brien, that carroty-haired rip behind, wouldn't jump the budget with him because

94

of his goin's-on—so he up and off with Rody Ward. Is this the lad?"

"It is," said Paddy Joe. "Vet him."

The squat, wide figure breasted close to Rogan, and the blue-jowled face came within six inches.

"Say, four pints of Guinness at a rough guess!" murmured Rogan.

"Go to hell! I saw you up at Dounbeg and didn't like your looks."

"A sound judge," agreed Rogan.

"A face that would hang a dog. I hear you're Scotch —what name?"

"Rogue McCoy."

"Whoever baptized you had second-sight. Up in Down once, we ran across two hangmen out of Scotland— a Williamson and a MacFee—and Shamus Og bate the two of them——"

"If Rogue McCoy was there three men might be beaten," said Rogue cryptically.

"And Shamus Og one of them," suggested Alistair.

"You're a liar. There was never a Scotchman pupped that Shamus Og couldn't belt."

"Some vetting!" remarked Alistair, a little nettled. "Any time I run up against the great Shamus I'll be tempted to take a whirl at him for the honour of old Scotland—if he's anything like his dad."

Jamesy Coffey ignored the bite; all his attention was concentrated on Rogan. "Tell me, now, Rogue McCoy, is there blood on your hands?"

"No." And after a pause he went on firmly. "But I will tell you the full truth that you want. There is one man I am afraid to meet lest I kill him."

"He did you hurt?"

"He quenched the sun for me," said Rogan deeply.

"We will kill the hound in our own time," said Jamesy

95

calmly, and turned to Paddy Joe. "He'll do. The honest drop is hidden in him somewhere. I don't know why you ask me, and I don't know what the hidin' is for—and I don't want to know—but if Maag Carty finds nothin' agin' him I'll take an' make a dacent man of him. Come on with me now!"

The short grass was grey-green between the clumps of furze and juniper, and they wound their way in and out until they came to the open where the camp was pitched. The old white horse was already hitched to the van, the jennet to the tilt-cart, and the colt tethered at the rear. The lad of twelve, Daheen Coffey, his fingers slack on the reins, leant in a corner of the jut-over of the van and was sound asleep. The lurcher growled softly under the axle and Jamesy Coffey cursed him silent.

"Good!" exclaimed Paddy Joe in a low voice; "ye are for the road already?"

"What else, you *bosthoon*? We'll put twenty long miles between us and that peeler before cockcrow—a fellow that would hang his own mother!" He turned away and by some trick of tongue and teeth emitted the peculiar night-call of the jack-snipe. "They are up by the road on the look-out," he explained.

And in a little while they—the two women—appeared out of the night, their light, accustomed feet making scarcely a rustle.

Jamesy's hand found Rogan's arm, and, somehow, his grasp was queerly gentle. He led him to the tall old woman. "There he is for you," he said in a petulant grumble, "and you can say whatever you damn well like, Maag Carty—he's coming."

"Be easy, childeen!" Her deep voice had a lovely, smooth, bell-like quality that caressed one remotely. She did not look at Rogan, but went and crouched down on

96

her heels against the wheel of the van. Then her bell-voice caressed him.

"Stoop down here, my darling, and let me know you!"

Rogan, smiling grimly to himself and at himself, went unhesitatingly and crouched on his heels before her. He placed one hand on her knee to steady himself, and leant close. He could make out the dusky leanness of her face, the black pools of her eyes, the long jet earrings trembling and faintly glinting. "I am here, dark mother," he whispered.

She would know him! She would never know him. No woman breathing air would ever know him again.

Her long arm came out and over his shoulder, and he felt long smooth fingers gentling down the hair to the back of his neck, and so under his ear and along the angle of his jaw. So, those fine fingers came round his chin and there held him, and though their grasp was gentle he felt a force greater than his strength.

"My poor love! My sad love!" she murmured. "You need not tell me. One woman you trusted too much."

Perhaps it was those fingers and the wisdom and force behind them that put their spell on him. A sudden cold anger surged in him. He felt cold as ice, and a desire to hurt poured through him.

"I trust no woman. Solder will mend any leak, and the butt of an ash-plant cure any woman." His voice was iron. He had heard those words that evening used jestingly, but he was not jesting now.

"Powders o' war!" cried Jamesy Coffey. "He'll do!"

The long fingers loosed his chin and Rogan shivered. He rose to his feet and with difficulty kept himself from swaying. It was long since he had been so shaken.

Maag Carty was on her feet too, and now there was an ancient sadness in her voice, like a deep bell rubbed softly in the dark.

"Some leaks no solder will mend."

The girl, who had been standing quietly at her mother's side, laughed shortly.

"What are you opening your mouth at, tin-can?" Jamesy Coffey wanted to know.

"At myself, kind man—and at men too." Her voice had a soft huskiness.

"One of them'll make you laugh at th' other side of your mouth, maybe," Jamesy reprimanded her.

The old woman came close to Paddy Joe. "'Tis hard you are to please, Paddy Joe Long, my dear one," she said, "and a hard task you have put on Jamesy Coffey and me, but we will do what we can—we will do our best. Your friend is in our keeping."

"Where I would have him, mother mine."

"That'll be all, now," cried Jamesy, his voice high with irritation. "That will be dam' all. Young fellow, you'll get under the tilt, and you'll stay there under a sack for twenty miles—smother or sweat. Off ye go, Paddy Joe! Bad company ye are for that telegraph-pole of a lad with you—and he is bad company any road."

"Well I know it, Jamesy."

"And 'tis you is the lucky devil always in the choices you make."

"That's the finest compliment for you, Alistair," said Paddy Joe.

"To hell with ye!" cried Jamesy, and squattered to the front of the van. He poked the sleeping lad in the ribs. "Wake up, Daheen, you lazy little brat, and watch the gap in the ditch, or I'll belt the hide off you." He hurried to the back of the tilt-cart and scrambled and kicked into the tail seat. "I'm ready now, an' if I have to come down off me perch, I'll—I'll——"

And then his voice changed and softened. "Next summer at Ballybwingan, Paddy Joe Long, I'll be tellin' you where we buried Rogue McCoy. God bless ye—God blasht ye!"

PART II:
ROGUE McCOY, TINKER'S CURATE

***

CHAPTER I

I

IT was the late autumn of a fine year, and the harvest season was about done. All across the great curving sweep of upland on the Cork-Kerry border the purple of the heather was washed with brown; the pastures were sage green, but the after-grass of the meadows was still vivid, patches of swede blue-tinted, and mangold fields a polished green; the potato shaws were sere and withered, and where the yellow corn had been was now brown stubble, though, here and there, the stooks had not yet been gathered into the rickyard; and over stubble and field the rooks went on lazy wing and the blue rock-pigeons flitted nervously.

A whitish-brown road came winding over the eastern horizon and down into the immense shallow bowl that was the barony of Castleinch. Half-way down the slope it crossed a little rushing clear stream by a high-cocked bridge, and curved round a patch of green common, scattered with clumps of furze and briar. From that green common the eye commanded that whole grand sweep of country, softly filmed in the tenuous autumn haze.

Down the slope, a mile away, was the purple-blue, straggling roof-line of Castleinch, with faint smoke-wreaths drifting and fading in the still air; and, beyond the scattered town, the small whitethorn-hedged fields sloped upwards mile on mile, dotted with white-walled farm-houses and their backing of cone-pointed corn-stacks and clumps of fruit trees. Above the farm lands the brown curves of moor swept their splendid lines to the horizon, and over that far horizon, as if out of another dimension, the sharp strong peaks of the Kerry mountains lifted heads into the void. High up in the pale-blue, fragile-looking sky a few copper-tinted clouds floated sluggishly and far apart, and out of the immense dome, over the wide and placid landscape, poured the golden, haze-warmed richness of the sun.

The roadman's camp was established on the green common on the downward side of the high-cocked bridge: a van, painted brightly in green, white and orange, a cart with a canvas tilt of many patches. An old white horse, forelegs hobbled, grazed industriously at the edge of the road; a brown jennet nibbled daintily amongst the bushes ; a lean lurcher dog was fast asleep in the shadow of the van.

Across near the curve of the hurrying stream a small fire of peat and bog pine was cradled in a cunningly built hearth of rough stones, and, over it, a bellied three-legged pot bubbled ruminatively and gave out an odour that might be hare or partridge or barn-door fowl. Watching the pot, a lean, brown-faced, eagle-nosed woman sat acrouch on her heels; jet ear-rings dangled to her shoulders, and a short black pipe drifted smoke from the firm line of her mouth. Behind her, at the brink of the rivulet, a slim, red-haired young woman knelt on a flat stone and industriously washed a rough grey shirt; the soapy water made a blue spreading film on the limpid surface of the stream. The brown cloth of her sleeves was turned up above the elbow, and her shapely arms were exactly the same tint as her face, lighter than lemon, deeper than cream; the ardent sun of that long summer had not flecked as much as freckle even on the bridge of her nose.

Between the fire and the van an oldish, squat, blue-jowled man, wearing a highly respectable bowler hat on the back of his head, sat on an upturned soap-box and smoked an unbelievably short briar pipe; his choleric blue eyes were fixed on the forelegs of a tall, rangy, chestnut colt, that was being groomed by a strongly-built—but not tall—man. A tousle-haired, swarthy lad of twelve held the halter, whistled a soft tune to himself, and, occasionally and lovingly, patted the soft muzzle of the colt.

The groom was a veritable man of the roads. His dark-brown hair needed cutting, but it had a fine healthy lustre, waved rather becomingly over his ears, and curled drake-tails on his smooth red-brown neck; his strong-boned lean face was one shade of tan under the kiss of much sun, a vigorous, short bristle had sprouted on his upper lip, and a two-day film of light brown stubble covered chin and cheek. A red silk kerchief was in a hard knot about his neck; his blarney-tweed jacket was patched at the elbows, but not a button was missing; his cord breeches were patched on both knees; his leggings of tan cloth were frayed at the ends; and his brown-hide boots were innocent of polish. A man of the roads, indeed.

The squat man on the soap-box removed his pipe and swore a preliminary oath. "Rogue McCoy, if you put as much as a brush above his elbow I'll take my hands to you."

Rogue McCoy looked out of a serious face at the lad holding the halter, and winked his off eye.

"Daheen," said he, and his voice was a rich round blend of Highland and Irish. "Daheen, your da, Jamesy Coffey, hasn't a stem of sense."

"The world knows that," agreed Daheen.

"Daheen, you brat," cried his father, "I'll belt you for that as soon as I get your pants off."

"'Tis the truth, whatever," protested his son.

"Mark that, Daheen," said Rogue McCoy. "It is for the truth that a fellow gets belted."

"I never got no beltin'."

"The conclusion is obvious. Hold by it. And moreover, whom did Jamesy Coffey ever belt—I'd like to know?"

The tall woman crouching at the fire spoke over her shoulder. "Darling, the last man he killed was home before himself."

"Shut your gypsy mouth, Maag Carty!" urged her husband. "Myself that's melted by the two of ye, and not a dam' day's luck since I met aither of ye."

"If you said anything else, heart's treasure, it would be time to say prayers for your soul."

"Damn my soul, then!"

Maag Carty crossed herself devoutly.

"I am wondering, Daheen," spoke up Rogue McCoy, "why we are not allowed to groom our *Copaleen Rua* above the elbow?"

"Any fool 'ud know that," said Jamesy Coffey derisively. "The buyers to-morrow will take him for a fresh colt out of the hills, and that's what they do be looking for at Castleinch Fair."

Rogue McCoy had acquired the strange habit of interrogating his chief through a third and, sometimes, imaginary person.

"Tell me, Daheen, do the Irish horse-buyers never look at a horse's mouth?"

"They do," said Daheen. "I saw them myself often."

"I'm tired teachin' ye," said Jamesy. "He's only risin' four at the outside, and 'tisn't the jobbers will be looking him over, but some foolish horsy woman from Kildare or Meath, or Dublin, maybe."

Rogue McCoy straightened up and stepped back from

the chestnut colt till he was close beside Jamesy Coffey on his soap-box. Quite naturally he placed a hand on the old man's wide shoulder and leant his weight on it easily; and the old man took no notice.

"His legs will pass, Daheen," criticised Rogue. "That touch of firing on the off fore did him no harm, and might be mistaken for the brush-aside of a kick. It isn't his legs that I'm afraid for." He stepped forward and felt the colt's shoulder with gentle, searching fingers. "There's where the wrench was. See, he doesn't wince now. Another week's rest would mend him; and there, Daheen, is where Jamesy Coffey fell down on us—with his tearin' and rampagin' across the country."

"He did, then," agreed Daheen.

"Blood-an'-turf!" screeched the baited Jamesy. "Didn't I crawl like a snail for the last fortnight, an' you walkin' *Copaleen Rua* on the soft edges of the road?"

"And that's all we could do, Daheen. But, if we were camped in this place for that fortnight, you and I would have that shoulder right as rain—right enough to sell, anyhow. As it is, if we are asked to give him two runs to-morrow he'll be left on our hands same as at Rathkeale and Puck."

"Don't give him two runs, then, you——"

"Not for man or devil. Take him away, Daheen boy, and give him your çapful of water and six hands of oats; and I will let you ride him down to the fair if you have your lessons and can spell Nebuchadnezzar the king of the Jews."

"Mother o' God!" protested Daheen. "Amn't I on my holidays to-day and to-morrow?"

"Your holidays are past and gone a full month, small man."

"But, Rogue McCoy——?"

"That's right, Daheen," encouraged his father. "Tell

him and his lessons to go to hell. What do you want with book-larnin'?"

"I'll have them, then," cried Daheen, "and I'll spell rhocherinos as well."

"That's the boy, Daheen," commended Rogue. "'Tis a bold man would come between us."

He turned and walked down to the brink of the stream and picked up Julie Brien's slab of soap.

"Th' other side of me—or you'll dirty my washing," she ordered in her pleasantly husky voice.

He stepped round her, bent at her side, and began scrubbing his hands briskly.

"Wait, Julie," he offered, "till I get this embrocation off and I'll wring out the washing for you."

"You will not. You'd twist it into rags."

"I would," he agreed, playfully fierce. "I would twist it into pieces as easy as I'd twist yourself."

She sat back on her heels and laughed at him, her teeth showing and a friendly gleam in her eyes of dark amber. She was a taking slip of young womanhood as she leant there, the shadow of her chin on the slender shaft of her neck.

"Would you?" she taunted him. "Wait till I finish this shirt, and I'll try you a fall, fair collar-and-elbow."

"If you put a hand on him, you *sthreel*," threatened Jamesy Coffey, "I'll tell Shamus Og as soon as I see him, and that's the boy'll tear his lights out and yours with them."

At the name of Shamus Og a sullen light displaced the twinkle in Julie Brien's eye, and she again leant forward to her washing.

"You will not tell Shamus Og anything, darling man," came the bell-voice of Maag Carty. "And what is more, no son of yours will ever lay hand on a daughter of mine, for that is against the laws of God and man."

"Jamesy Coffey—and his people before him—made their own laws."

"One day, little love—the day I married you—you obeyed another law, and I have Paddy Joe Long of Ballybwingan to prove it——"

"To hell with Paddy Joe Long! That black thief would swear to any lie and you putting him up to it."

II

The clack and squeak of many ungreased axles came from the road, and over the crown of the high-cocked bridge poured a ragged regiment of tinkers. There were half a dozen ass-drawn carts, piled with women, children, crooked poles, old sacking, osier-work baskets, gleaming tins; a dust-covered scamp sat in the front of each cart, feet dangling at each side of the donkey's croup, and, at regular intervals, as a matter of mere routine, a dangling foot kicked the animal in the belly—and the animal took no notice. Bringing up the rear was a whole drove of donkeys—all colours, all shapes, all ages, but scarcely a decently-bred one among the lot. They were herded by a scatter of ragged urchins and three or four mongrel dogs.

Jamesy Coffey's lurcher tumbled from under the van, charged forward a dozen yards, stopped short, and set up a bold and threatening clamour. A wise dog. For, as soon as the mongrels saw him, they came tearing like one dog across the green. Whereupon Jamesy Coffey emitted a wild yell, leaped to his feet, and rushed to the stream-side for ammunition. The yell halted the mongrels; the first missile made them fall back over themselves; a second, shrewdly aimed, brought a yelp of pain and a scamper for safety; and the whole wild band of tinkers set up an extraordinary shrill cheer of encouragement. Then a great voice bellowed forth:

"Well hit, Jamesy! I'll peg you for that to-morrow when Maag's not there to save you."

They were a gay and ribald clan, and the greetings they shouted across were more than Rabelaisian: "Maag, you ould b——, when 'll you give us the wake? What's the Buckie-Highlander lookin' for? Shamus Og was in Abbeyfeale yesterday threatenin' to (unprintable). Is Julie Brien (wholly unspeakable) . . .?"

The band moved on towards Castleinch, and Jamesy came back, to find his soap-box occupied by Rogue McCoy. He glared at him explosively. "Shove west, you grabber—there's room for two."

They sat amicably shoulder to shoulder, and Rogue, setting an ancient briar between his teeth, began leisurely slicing a plug of villainous-looking tobacco.

"Them's the maggy-men Flynns," said Jamesy witheringly. "I wouldn't take no notice of them."

"Big Plucky himself was there," said Julie with satisfaction, "and he didn't open his mouth."

"He knew better," remarked Rogue grimly.

"All dam' fine!" derided Jamesy, "but Big Plucky went as near as two pins to lickin' you that day at Lisdoonvarna—and he would if he hadn't a pint too many."

"The poor ladeen will be able to spit through his teeth the rest of his days," said Maag Carty.

"Another will be able to do likewise when I meet him," said Rogue quietly, grinding the tobacco in strong palms. "I took a good look at the lad who insulted Julie——"

"Leave them be!" advised Jamesy. "They're only low maggy-men." (Maggy-men are Aunt Sally men.)

"Damn the hair I care," said Rogue. "Any man that insults Maag Carty or Julie Brien—or Daheen Coffey——"

"And what about Jamesy Coffey, you devil's pup?"

"Let that fellow look after himself—and how could one insult Jamesy Coffey?"

"Herrins alive, you caffler!" protested Jamesy. "We'll have a fight on our hands every fair and market, and spend the time between in Stranleigh Jail." But there was a warm light in his eye that belied the protest. "An' what's more, me haro, if Shamus Og turns up—and the same lad can be as insultin' as a kickin' mule——"

"If he's Jamesy Coffey's son he'll surely have a wicked, abusive, scorching, vitriolic, mustard-plaster of a tongue, but—oh bah! Go and insult your grandmother!"

"I ask God to witness," cried Jamesy hotly, "that I haven't an hour's comfort with you. I'm afraid to open my mouth for fear I would insult any one—and Rogue McCoy drive me teeth down my gullet. Wait till I tell Shamus Og—an' if I was only five years younger——"

The rattle and roar of a motor came down the hill, and an old Ford tractor swung round the curve and over the culvert. It was trailing two large vans, one covered, and the other loaded high with poles, canvas, rolls of oilcloth, swing-boats, and yellow-painted boards showing gaudy red-and-gold lettering.

Jamesy had one look. "Speak of the devil!" he exclaimed. "That's a Ward outfit, all the way from Wicklow; robbers, dog-stealers, horse-copers, the Wards would steal a glugger from under a hatchin' hen. They'll be buyin' up all the old crocks to-morrow, and sellin' them as trained hunters to the Templogue Hunt."

"They might buy our *Copaleen Rua*."

"Hell to you! I wouldn't sell that little colt to them an' I starvin'." There came an interested gleam in Jamesy's eyes, and the mouth above the blue chin softened strangely. "I wonder would Shamus Og be with them? If he is—an' 'tisn't often I do it—you'll hear me give someone the rough side of me tongue. You will so."

Julie Brien, still on her knees, half-turned and looked intently at the vans as they rattled by. The tractor did not slow down, but, opposite the camp, a tall man swung out of the rear door of the leading van and dropped to the roadside with superb ease of balance.

"'Tis himself," said Jamesy in a voice unusually mild.

Julie Brien turned to the stream and resumed her washing. Rogue McCoy looked at her and smiled gloomily. The shirt she was washing was his, and once already she had scrubbed it thoroughly. It had been thin enough in places, and this added scrubbing would not improve its durability. She seemed quite composed over her work; there was no suffusion of colour in her smooth cheeks, and he could not see the sullenness of her eyes ; but, as she turned her head, he saw the round of her neck, and in it a pulse beat furiously. He turned to watch Shamus Og coming across the green between the furze bushes.

He was worth looking at. A tall young fellow, lithe and strong, with the round, blue-shaven chin of his father, a bare head of thick black curls, and eyes blazing black with devilry and temper. A thoroughbred, whatever his ancestry. He was wearing a sound suit of heather-mixture and a soft collar with a flowing blue-bird's-eye tie.

He strode into their midst and halted, feet apart. He looked down at his father, he looked across the fire at his step-mother, his eyes did not once rest on Rogue McCoy. No one said a word. Then he walked slowly to the brink of the stream and looked down at the girl so busily scrubbing.

"Well, Julie Brien! How goes it?" he saluted her in a loud voice.

"Fine, thank you. Hope you're well yourself, Shamus

Og?" Her voice was low and cool and husky—and she kept piling lather on lather.

"Never better. Isn't it busy you are? And whose shirt are you washin'?"

"A decent boy's shirt."

"You never washed a shirt for me?"

"You chose your own shirt-washer."

"Did I? By Christ, then! I never asked a woman to wash a shirt of mine and she not willin'."

"You need not ask me, Shamus Og."

He stood there looking down at her, his black eyes blazing; his broad shoulders restless, his jaw muscles ridging and rippling; rage, torment, desire struggling in him. But he did not speak to her again. He turned grindingly on his heel and spoke to his father, and only his eyes betrayed the inner turmoil.

"Well, old solderin'-iron! I hear you are no longer boss in your own camp?"

"'Tisn't what any one hears bothers me," said his father mildly. The rough side of Jamesy Coffey's tongue seemed to have been mislaid for the moment.

Shamus Og looked full at Rogue McCoy for the first time, but Rogue McCoy was not looking at him. He had lit his pipe and was calmly smoking, his strong-boned, bronzed face a little stern, his eyes on the distant moors and serene as the hills. Shamus Og searched in his mind for something to say, found nothing adequate, and turned to the woman at the fire.

"Maag Carty," said he, "haven't you a word for me?"

"I have, dark love, and it a word of welcome, and your dinner here in the skillet for you."

"Thank you for that; but I'll not take bite or sup where a grudge is."

"In your own heart the grudge is, tall son."

"Ho-ho! is it my fortune you'd be tellin'?"

"And a luckier fortune than you or any man deserves— and I might hold your luck from you if I could."

"Luck!" he exclaimed bitterly, and swore terribly. "Little the luck a man has going the lonely road to death."

At these bitter words Rogue McCoy looked at him, and their eyes locked for a moment. Somehow, in a single flash, the two men came to a subtle understanding. Shamus Og turned away to where Daheen was watching the chestnut colt lip its oats out of a tin pan. He walked across slowly.

"Hello, nipper!" he greeted his half-brother pleasantly, and caught playfully at his tousled head. "Japers! but you're growing a tarnation big fellow. In no time at all you'll be givin' our da one of his own famous beltin's."

Daheen grinned, and there was admiration and affection in his face.

Shamus Og looked over the colt, felt forelegs with knowing fingers, prodded here and there about the shoulder, and nodded to himself.

"Still got the crowbait on your hands, Jamesy," he called. "I'll give you a fiver for him."

"Where'd you steal it?"

"That's askin'." He jerked his head down the road, where the vans were jolting towards the village. "All them's mine—bought 'em off old Rody Ward."

"Maybe the fortune with his daughter?"

"No, by hell! There is no woman tied to them or on them—or ever will be." He slipped something into his brother's hand. "Watch it!" he advised. "When I was your age devil the copper I could call my own with the ould fella."

"Oh, Shamus Og!" whispered Daheen urgently.

"Why wouldn't you be staying? The times you and me and Rogue McCoy would be having! Man, you should see him snig a salmon out of six foot of water."

"'Tisn't a salmon out of a pool him or me is after," said Shamus Og, and strode away towards the road without another word or glance.

Rogue McCoy came to his feet and stretched himself lazily. "I think," said he, "I'll be going a piece down the road."

Jamesy looked up at him quickly and doubtfully. "What for?"

"To see could I find the rough side of Jamesy Coffey's tongue."

"Take it to hell with you when you find it."

"And he with a string to it all the time," said Rogue reproachfully, moving away.

"Darling, your dinner—and it ready this minute," lamented Maag Carty.

"Nice and cold for supper, mother," he called back.

Jamesy swore furiously. "Isn't it time me own dinner was ready? Am I nothin' at all?"

Down by the stream Julie got to her feet, all the resiliency gone from her young limbs, and sighed deeply. She held up Rogue's shirt and stared at it in dismay. "Oh goodness!" she cried ruefully. "I have washed three holes in it."

"'Tis the dumb suffer always," said Maag Carty.

III

Shamus Og heard the feet on the road behind him, and turned head over shoulder. He did not halt, but gradually slowed his gait until Rogue ranged alongside, and then the two marched straight ahead without a glance at each other. So they went for a space, two yards apart, Rogue smoking unconcernedly, Shamus Og's brows down over dare-devil eyes.

The latter was the first to break the silence, his voice surly. "You're this Rogue McCoy I'm hearing about?"

"I am."

"I heard about you up in Tipp—at Templemore."

"And came down to look me over?"

"I might do more than that at the heel of the hunt."

"You might," agreed Rogue equably.

"I hear you gave Big Plucky Flynn the father and mother of a weltin' at Lisdoonvarna." He glanced aside quickly and away. "Why?"

"Because you were not there to do it."

"I see. Maybe you'd be ready to take my place other ways as well?"

"Are you sure you have a place I could take?"

Shamus Og laughed his wild and bitter laugh. "I don't care a damn, but I'll be a dog in that manger." He halted and faced Rogue impulsively. "And let me tell you, fightin' man, I'll say what I like about Julie Brien."

And Rogue faced him, eyes stern, face grim. "Say it."

The other glared at him, his teeth clenched, his mind searching for the word to say. Then, and suddenly, he shook his black curls. "No—it can't be done that way," he said regretfully. "I can't say it."

"I know you can't," said Rogue shortly. "I'm glad you're honest."

Like men at drill the two turned and strode onwards, not quite two yards apart now; and the tension between them had slackened.

"Your father and Daheen—and others as well—were hoping you would join up," said Rogue easily. "But now that you are on the road yourself——"

"I will keep to it—by myself," said the other briefly.

"Yes! I can see you going that road, and I can see the finish of it too, Shamus Og Coffey."

"Has Maag Carty been givin' you the second-sight?"

"And you will not keep that road by yourself either. You will take some strange woman and kill her; and you will take a second, and she may kill you. Drinking, roystering, fighting, in jail and out of it; and, in the end, dying in a ditch."

"Make it ten years and welcome the finish."

Rogue laughed. "Maybe you're right. There may be no better way with life."

"Not your way, anyhow! Bossing old Jamesy Coffey, jumping the budget with Julie Brien, finishing your days with the old age pension."

"Let me be honest too, Shamus Og. If you want my sentiments about women they are easily given. To hell with them!"

"Amen to that."

"You do not mean it."

"As God made me——"

"You are only talking to hide the hurt."

"And you too," retorted the other. "Could it be that Julie Brien has twisted the heart in you as well?"

Shamus Og looked aside at Rogue out of a suspicious and threatening eye, and Rogue was silent. He knew the desire in Shamus Og's heart, he had seen the pulse beat in Julie Brien's neck. He made up his mind resolutely, though his secret soul flinched.

"Look here, Shamus Og! The heart was twisted in me and out of me long before I met Julie Brien." He threw his hand out, clenched it tensely, and flung it away open. "Squeezed and wrung and thrown away—like that."

"Is she on the road?"

"Dead, and better dead—and my child dead—and the

114

man that was I dead too. I am only Rogue McCoy, travelling man, on the road to nowhere. Let it be."

"I knew you were not always on the roads the minute you opened your mouth."

"My mouth is again shut," said Rogue McCoy.

"I know, I know!" said Shamus Og. "Man, but I had hard thoughts against you, and wanted only the wind of a word to be at your throat; and to that it may come yet—I don't know and I don't care; but if it does it will be for no small trumped-up reason. Begobs! Castleinch is for a big day to-morrow—look at the crowd."

It was the eve of the great horse fair, and Castleinch was full and busy; and from the long lines of stables at the rear of the houses came the rattle of block-chains, the stamp of hooves, the champ and aroma of horses. Every third house in the town was a public-house, and every one of them doing a roaring trade; and the long street was scattered with groups of men, mostly of the small-breeder type, but amongst them could be distinguished the universal horsy man: the hard rider from Kildare, the tall English hunting man from the Shires, natty French officers in mufti, flat-polled Germans in spurred boots, high-breasted Italians with tight waists. Castleinch was in the heart of that limestone country that builds bone in the finest half-bred in the world, and its famous fairs horsed some of the crack cavalry regiments of Europe.

Castleinch was comprised in one unusually wide street a full mile in length. Half-way in that length it bulged out to a width of a hundred yards, and in the middle of that space stood the two-storied market-and-court house. On the sunny side opposite was the principal hostelry, the Desmond Arms. It was fronted by a big balustraded porch, four steps off the street, and at each side of this, along the ground-floor windows, a temporary railed wooden platform had been erected to enable the patrons to look over the parade of horses. Needless to say, the professional buyers never used this platform in judging a horse, for these knew how close to the ground one must be to estimate the qualities of a "lepper."

Rogue McCoy and Shamus Og moved slowly down the uneven flagged pavement, their eyes observant. They knew where they were going. In every Irish town there is the showman's pub—the house of call for travelling men. It is not necessarily the lowest pub, and certainly not one selling inferior or doctored liquor; the roadman can tell by taste the seven whiskies of Ireland in age and degree, and a pint of stale stout is as often as not poured over the barman's head. All that the roadman asks is a good drink, a sawdust floor to spit on, plenty of shoulder room, and a quiet place at the back to clinch a bargain or settle a difference. Moreover, when the roadmen are in town, the showman's pub is the popular resort for many respectable members of society; for in it are recounted all the new stories of the winding roads of Ireland, mad, wild, strange stories of love, war, and roguery. Many of the richest, raciest, most salacious stories originate in the showman's pub, and well-conducted men have been known to collect these stories for re-telling in well-conducted clubs.

"It might be a good fair, too," remarked Shamus Og. "The foreigners are in full strength."

"We'll sell the chestnut," said Rogue hopefully.

"If you can bribe some vet not to know a lame shoulder."

"That shoulder is coming right—and it will pass to-morrow if we are not asked to show his paces too often."

"Stick to the lady buyers, then."

They were passing the Desmond Arms, and a loud, ringing tenor voice hailed them from the balustraded porch.

"Hullo, Shamus Og! Have you a horse to sell?"

IV

Shamus Og halted and looked up, and Rogue McCoy halted with him, but Rogue McCoy did not look up. He knew that ringing tenor voice—he knew it too well. He knew it in his dreams; it had waked him to many despairing dawns. Now it made his heart leap and sent a cold thrill through him. A blinding spark leaped across his vision and made him dizzy for an instant, and then his heart began to beat, a heavy, slow, thick beat that was almost sickening. He dare not look up, for surely his eyes could never hide their knowledge. "O God! has it come again?" his mind besought.

Shamus Og was speaking. "No, captain. Are you on the look-out for one?"

"Could do with a young lepper."

"Rogue McCoy here has a chestnut gelding risin' five——"

"Rogue McCoy! A name like that needs watching, Shamus Og, and I'll watch him. Can your gelding jump, Rogue?"

Rogue had to lift his head now, and he did so with a quiet slowness that was strangely menacing. He looked the man leaning down from the balustrade in the face. It was he, Eudmon Butler. A splendidly tall man in horseman kit. Riding-breeches outlined the shapely long legs, a waisted coat emphasised the great spread of shoulder. The man might be blood kin to Shamus Og Coffey; he had the same handsome pallor, the same blue-shaven slit chin, the mass of black curls; and an infinitely worse devil leaped in his brilliant black eyes.

But there was no mutual recognition. This tall man, after his kind, had a careless memory for the men—or women—he had injured. All he saw was an unkempt-haired, horse-coping tinker, with a craggy, unshaven, unsmiling face, a short bristle of moustache, and deep-set eyes that looked like grey limestone.

"Can the chestnut jump, Rogue McCoy?"

"With leading-strings only." His voice was deep and steady.

"Sir, to you," ordered the other sharply.

"Captain Butler," said Rogue.

"Oh, you know me?" He laughed ringingly. "You tinkers do. Bring him along to-morrow and I'll vet him—and if he's crocked I'll give you what I gave Shamus Og at Cahirciveen last year. Eh, Shamus? Been fighting lately?"

"Done my share, Captain," said Shamus Og without rancour, and laughed. "Some time, I wouldn't mind havin' another go at you. I was reduced last time."

"Right! Do a deal across me, and you'll get your bellyful."

And there Rogue McCoy got his second shock within a minute, a shock that was, somehow, more disturbing. Two people came through the door behind the soldier, and a pleasant low-pitched voice spoke:

"Starting in to deal already, Captain Butler?"

Butler turned with abrupt readiness and bowed over the lady with that pleasant voice, and his own voice had a welcoming caress.

"My dear Mrs Trant. No, I was just saying a needed word to a horse-coper."

Yes, this was Elspeth Trant, whose husband had been killed less than four months ago. She was still wearing black, and none of her good looks were lost in that colour. And the man behind her was Sir Jerome Trant, her father-in-law, sturdy on his short legs, his hair a little whiter, his aquiline face a little ruddier, and his eyes frowning as he looked at Captain Butler bending over the woman.

She had not taken the advice that had been given her that day at Dounbeg. Alas! poor little moth fluttering about the flame. The inevitable must happen, and the whole sordid affair go forward stage by stage. And what stage had been reached now?

She came to the balustrade and looked down at Rogue McCoy, and her eyes widened and grew intent; her fine strong hands grasped the railing and firmed there. Her woman's eyes were never deceived by the tinker's garb and the tinker's stubble. Rogue met her look fairly and squarely, his firm crag of a face giving no sign. Indeed, at that moment, he did not care one small curse what was going to happen next.

Captain Butler spoke peremptorily. "That will be all right, McCoy. Bring the colt along, and remember what I said."

Rogue did not reply. He turned at Shamus Og's side, and the two went on down the street.

"That's Captain Eudmon Butler," Shamus Og remarked. "You know him?"

"I know him."

"The Black Captain—black in and out! The greatest devil on two feet in all Ireland! A bloody terror! Women an' horses—love or blood—any damn thing at all!"

"I know."

"You heard him? An' I may as well tell you that he is the only man I ever tackled who gave me my bellyful and a bit over—and I wasn't reduced either. A ragin' terror in a rough-and-tumble—hit and trip and the devil take the lavin's! Well, here is Mickeen's. Have one with me?"

"I'll be glad of it," said Rogue McCoy.

V

Mickeen's Bar was on the corner of a small side lane of stables. The front door opened on the usual tea and grocery store; the licensed premises were behind, with a couple of convenient doors giving on the laneway. The bar itself was a big low room with a high, zinc-covered counter making an L down and across; here and there, along this counter, wooden partitions made private alcoves. Behind the counter, amidst all the glittering paraphernalia, three stalwart barmen were ready for all the work required—serve, conciliate, or chuck-out. They were not yet busy, for the evening was young, and the alcoves were occupied by only a few farmers, some jobbers, half a dozen showmen, an odd tinker.

"What'll it be—a pint?" invited Shamus.

"Whiskey—a large one, if you don't mind."

"To be sure." Shamus **Og** glanced at him. "Wirra! have you seen a ghost?"

"The devil out of hell."

Rogue McCoy's face was livid below the tan; all the blood in him had gone to his heart. The bones seemed to stretch the skin tightly over the cheek-bones, and a cold glaze made his eyes like polished stone. His hand trembled as he reached for the glass of strong spirits.

"The Black Captain?" half-queried Shamus Og.

Rogue nodded, and took his whiskey in one deep gulp without water. "We'll have another," said he, and crooked his finger at the barman.

"If that's your way," remarked Shamus Og dryly,

"I know who'll be first in the ditch—and in no ten years aither."

"I needed that; we'll go easier with this one." Rogue added water to his glass, and drew in his breath deeply. "Damn fool to get a shock like that!"

The colour was returning to his face, and the beating of his heart was easier. The first fine kick of the alcohol was moving the maggots of salubrity and wisdom in his brain.

"The Black Captain didn't know you, did he?" said Shamus Og, full of curiosity.

"Not now," Rogue told him.

"You didn't happen to try him out any time?"

"No—" Rogue hesitated and went on. "Once I would have killed him."

"He did you dirt?"

Again Rogue used that gesture of the hand that clenched and flung away empty.

Shamus Og nodded. "That's his way. Leave it be."

But Shamus Og himself could not leave it be just yet. Half-way through his second pint he returned to the subject.

"Let me be giving you one word of advice, Rogue McCoy."

"I could be giving you a couple myself."

"I hear you—I heard you—an' thanks. You may be a good man of your hands—and any one that pegged Big Plucky Flynn can't be bad. And you might best me too, though I don't think so. But mark my words, with Captain Eudmon Butler you won't have a dog's chance. I'm tellin' you. The Black Captain is the toughest man within the walls of Ireland at a rough-and-tumble, and you haven't the weight or reach for him."

The whiskey had restored Rogue his own mature philosophy. He gestured aside with a hand.

"That is all right, Shamus Og; such folly is gone with the past. It was only the suddenness that got me. Let Butler go his own road—I never want to see him again. Leave it be, as you said."

"Very good!" agreed Shamus Og shortly. He had given good advice, but he had the regret of a fighting man that a great fight should not be fought. Perhaps he felt a little contemptuous too.

More clients were now coming into the bar, and, amongst them, three of the Flynn clan—the maggy-men. The three went into a partitioned alcove close by where Rogue and Shamus Og leant on the counter, and one of them, a loose, lank fellow with red hair, caught Rogue's eye and dodged out of sight like a fox into its earth. Rogue smiled grimly and finished off his drink.

"Just a minute, Shamus Og," he said. "There's a lad behind here I want a word with."

He stepped back and round to the rear of the alcove, and the three men in it looked at him. One was a big, heavy-fleshed man, who grinned, not unamiably, through a gap in his front teeth.

"Is that yourself, Rogue?" he greeted. "How are you, you devil?"

"Fine, Plucky, fine! How goes it?"

"Great, thank God! Come in and have one?"

"Do me a small favour first, Plucky."

"To be sure."

"Introduce me to that handsome red-haired fellow with the shy look."

Plucky grinned again. "Him's me cousin, Liam Rua —Red William.'

"Go to hell, Rogue McCoy!" exploded Liam Rua unhappily. "I want nothing to do with you."

"You'll be in the same way of thinking in about five minutes," said Rogue softly. "Will you be good enough to come outside for a word or two?"

"I want none of your words aither."

"The words will not be many." The voice sterned. "Come on out now or I'll——"

"Now then—now then!" roared the big barman, rapping the counter with a pewter pot. "No fightin' in here—you'll have your bellyful before to-morrow night. Any bloody man that wants to fight in here will have to go out in the lane—or I'll split his skull with the edge of this."

"There you are, Liam Rua," urged Rogue. "I won't keep you a minute."

"Sure it was only fun—but look, Rogue McCoy! Give me time to swallow two pints for courage, an' by the holy wars! I'll take a fall out of you."

"I wouldn't doubt you, Liam!" encouraged Big Plucky.

"It is afterwards he will be needing the pints, Plucky. I'll pay for them myself."

"That's dam' fair," agreed Plucky.

"Oh! Mother o' God!" cried Liam desperately.

"Pity you did not think of Her before you used the dirty word to a decent girl like Julie Brien."

Shamus Og, who had been grinning at the exchanges, stiffened and swore. "Hell's blazes! who spoke the dirty word to Julie Brien? Let me have a look at him."

He strode to Rogue, placed hand on shoulder, and pushed him aside. And Liam Rua, like a fox, chose that opportune moment to make his get-away.

The back-door opposite the alcove had opened to admit a jobber, and before it might be closed, Liam went for the opening, head down, under the man's oxter. He half-collided with the new-comer, and his flight was checked for just an instant. And in that instant Rogue McCoy's football training came to the fore. The toe of his strong brown boot reached its mark, and Liam Rua turned a somersault into the lane, landed on his shoulder, and rolled neatly to his feet.

"Oh hell! you bastards!" he roared, and continued his flight, accelerating every ten yards.

There was a gale of laughter over the bar, but Rogue did not join in.

"Dammit, Shamus Og!" he said, nettled. "It will be all to do over again."

"It will keep," said Shamus Og, his white teeth showing.

"Begobs! you won't catch Liam Rua this side o' Dingle," said Big Plucky cheerfully, "and the same lad won't sit aisy for a piece. What'll ye have, boys? Sure, there's no ill-will between us for what's past and gone; an' if it comes to that, I'll fight aither of ye when I'm in the mind."

VI

After the setting of the sun, when the desolate after-light of the gloaming began to possess the world, Rogue McCoy went campwards from Castleinch. Away in the west over the crown of the moors, a long band of glowing red lay above the horizon, and, below it, a rim of sky held the very soul and essence of green—a green lit intensely from within. Below that living green the hills cowered black and strange, mysterious dark places, strange to humanity and life as man knows it. Eastward, the grey upland fields sloped to the brown moors that were now of one even shade and strangely lacking in perspective. And, though a murmur rose from Castleinch, a great silence weighed down from the very sky and made that murmur fainter than a sigh. The rooks had done their cawing, no pigeon crooned, no thrush sang, no linnet was on the wing, all life was hushed, subdued, put aside for a little time in that pallid light of the gloaming.

But Rogue McCoy was alive and thinking wisely as he moved up the moorland road, all by himself, on feet that were a little wayward. He was not drunk, but, as they say, he had drink taken, and the wan glow of the twilight, that seems unrelated to sun or star, had taken possession of him and dowered him with its own aloof wisdom.

He stood without himself and looked himself over with a sort of detached pity, and, though he recognised himself as a self-centred fool, he had to acknowledge a sort of sneaking admiration for the man he was. Surely he did not matter a cent in this whirling atom of a world slowly running down to oblivion, but he had to go on acting as if life was centred in him. At the word of a wise man, whom he had known only for a day, he had placed himself under yoke for a year, and the yoke was pleasant. He could talk like a tinker, drink like a tinker, think inside a tinker's skin, and, by glory! he could fight like a tinker too. . . . And he pulled his weight in the camp. That is what pleased him most.

Sometimes, now, he found himself with an object in life. He felt that the little clan was under his oxter and he doing the honest thing by it, not because of any high sense of duty, but because he just liked to. Jamesy Coffey, growing old, relied on him and hid that reliance under a rasping tongue; Maag Carty, trusting him, could sit still and contemplate the working out of the destinies that she had some strange inkling of; Daheen Coffey— well! Daheen loved him, and was not yet subject to the risk of the degradation that destroyed most of his breed; Daheen was a lad of parts, of heart and head, and might be led to an appreciation of things that would serve him later. And Julie Brien?

Julie Brien, that slim red-haired one of mixed blood! What could he do for her? Nothing? What did he know of woman and her needs? Once he thought he knew one woman, but Captain Eudmon Butler taught him otherwise. Better not think about that. . . . Think about Julie Brien. Julie would go her own road, making men and breaking men, and was he one of the men she would not make or break? Give her credit—she did not want to. She was deep—or was she deep? She had stores of passion, she was afraid of herself, she was afraid of Shamus Og—the pulse in her neck beat at the very mention of his name. And with himself she was friendly and easy—and washed his shirt all to hell. A nice girl and nice in her ways! But what could he know? All the same, he would keep on giving her a sense of respect for herself, and after that let her go on as Fate—the God of woman—willed.

And himself would go on too. He would not look forward any more, though looking forward might no longer fill him with despair. And he might learn to sleep some time. God! if he could only sleep and not dream! Ah well! he could carry on. And he would not look back either, for looking back wrenched his heart for the little one that had so terribly died. . . . And yet, to-day proved that he had another nerve in him that could still be wrenched, as it had been wrenched at Dounbeg. For ten seconds in front of the hotel he had been insane, actually insane. But that was the suddenness—a mere reflex action out of the past. He was all right now. He could face Eudmon Butler this minute and dispassionately consider the hound that he was. . . . Strange, running against Elspeth Trant again! Wonder if she had recognised him? Her eyes had taken on a sudden startle.

If she had, he was the needle found in Paddy Joe's bundle of hay, and his tinker's curacy was of no avail. He must drop Paddy Joe a line this very night. No! he was too drunk to-night. In the morning before the fair. What would she do? What had she done? Four months had elapsed, and the killing seemed forgotten by the police—and by her. Perhaps she was too much taken up by Eudmon Butler to bother about dead things—and dead men. He could visualise the Black Captain's leaning possessive attitude, hear his caressing tone—too well he remembered these in other circumstances. Watch out, girl! You are playing with fire. Four months ago you were merely unhappy, and death broke the toils for you. And now, was Fate weaving round you uglier toils? That was Fate's way. Fate would never let a victim go. . . . And he was a victim too. . . .

A damn pity! There was something in her sib with himself—something in her breed and blood. There was that night at Dounbeg when the singing of an old Gaelic lament helped them to know each other for a minute. For a minute then they had been apart together, isolated and intimate, a mental and physical warmth gathering about them. He had power over her. She was a harp he could touch to his own tune—to his own tune. . . .

He swayed on planted feet at mid road, and, with the clarity that drink gives, he contemplated himself exerting that power once again; drawing her away from Eudmon Butler, using her for his own fitting vengeance. . . . What a superb, hellish joke! He threw up his head and laughed—laughed at himself and at her, and at Eudmon Butler—at all life. For in the very act of his contemplation, a strange warmth came about him, and his heart stirred. . . .

To hell with them! It was none of his business. A tinker's life was a cleaner life, where passion was brutal but not complex, where life set stark but simple problems. A tinker! That's what he was. A tinker rolling home to camp, with small worries for to-day and lively gay thoughts for to-morrow. And why wouldn't he be singing a tinker's song to help his wayward feet? He threw his head back, and his sound baritone broke the hushed stillness:

> Sure I haven't got a shillin',
> But be japers! if I had,
> 'Tisn't here you'd find me walkin',
> With a pub where I might sing.
> For to spend it I'd be willing,
> And to drink it I'd be glad.
> But what's the use of talkin'
> When I haven't got a wing?

Ah! Here was some one coming down the road towards him. A woman at that! Maybe Julie Brien, half-hoping, half-fearing that Shamus Og would be with him. But Shamus Og was back in his own van at the other end of Castleinch, and Shamus Og was not exactly sober. Good stuff in Shamus Og, properly used! No, this was not Julie Brien, though she was just as light-footed and lissome. This lady was in black, with a black close hat, and a scrap of black veil down to her nose. Yes, this lady was Elspeth Trant, walking the road by her lonesome—and a good way to be walking, if only she knew.

He swerved aside to let her pass, but she swerved too and stopped in front of him. He pulled himself up, planted his feet firmly, and brought his hand up in salute. He was quite sober—oh, quite sober—but he had a small inclination to sway backwards. She looked at him frowningly and intent; and though his face gave no sign, his eyes were watchful. She had not been deceived, then. She was graceful and slim as ever, and, in the half-light, her face below the film of veil looked fine and delicate and fragile.

She came directly to the point.

"You are Rogan Stuart?" She did not think of mistering him; and he knew that that frankness was not superiority.

He again brought his hand up in salute. "No, dark lady. I am Rogue McCoy, travelling man—on the road to nowhere."

"But you were Rogan Stuart?"

She would persist, then! He smiled at her, and, if he only knew, that tolerant wise smile gave him away completely to this woman.

"I am the needle found in the bundle of hay," said he. "Rogue McCoy, tinker's curate. What are you going to do about it?"

She shook her head a little impatiently. "Is that your camp up by the bridge?"

"That's a leading question, my lady."

"With the pretty red-haired girl sitting at the roadside?"

"Red-haired girls are as plentiful as blackberries in this place, thank God," he said perversely.

"I knew you at once, of course." She was patiently confident of that. "I've been on all the roads out of town, looking for you—I wanted to talk to you."

"Should have tried Mickeen's Bar."

"I should have. Might I ask you a question or two, Rogan Stuart?"

He swayed a step, replanted his feet, and "What's the use of talking, Elspeth Trant? Let the past be."

"I wish I could. It will not leave me alone." She leant head and shoulders to him impulsively. "Will you please answer one question?"

He saw that she was agitated—had been agitated from the beginning; her voice, her restless hands showed that. He would change his tone with her.

"Well?" he spoke quietly.

"Did you kill my husband?" There, indeed, was the direct question.

"I did not kill your husband," he answered firmly, and went on. "But, to tell you the full truth, I was compelled to use him roughly. Another pair of hands finished the job."

"Your—your friends?"

"No," he said fiercely, angrily. "Never my friends. My friends and I decided that the hands might be yours."

"Mine?"

"Yours."

"But why?—why should I——?"

"Because you were unhappy—because he was spineless—because he was drunk and might have accused you of the love of another man. You are hot-tempered, you know."

She swayed.

"You think these hands did it?" She threw her hands out for him to look at, small, strong, ungloved hands.

"Some hands were at his throat. Mine were not."

"You think mine were?"

He was sullenly dumb, though a chord in him cried aloud.

"I—I was afraid," she said, "but something—something said in drink—I don't know!" She hesitated, stopped, and then: "I am glad your hands are clean—that is all I wanted to know. Good night, Mr Stuart."

He stepped aside to let her pass, then turned and walked with her. "There are other rough men on the road to-night," he said. "I will see you to the edge of the town."

She made no objection. She was afraid to be alone at that moment. She was holding herself in all she could, but her agitation made her feet unsteady—more unsteady than his because so much weaker—and though she tried to hurry she could not.

"My lady," he proffered gently, "will you take my arm for a little while?"

She grasped his rough sleeve, and he steadied her with his firm shoulder. And he smiled to himself grimly in the half-light. Ah well! Surely, if he had any object in life, it was the helping of lame dogs—tinkers, tramps, rogues, a woman—if a woman could be helped. This woman was sorely in need of help now, and the bold way was better than the shrinking way.

"You are glad my hands are clean?" he put to her.

"Yes."

"You have only my word for it."

"And you would not take mine?"

"Does that matter?"

"I thought—I hoped that it might. Once—under the night—we understood each other."

She had not forgotten that night, then! It still moved her, swayed her. It moved himself too.

"Yes," he agreed. "Once, under the stars, a man and a woman understood each other in passing, and, because they did, nothing that has happened since should matter."

He felt her hand stir on his arm, but she did not speak. She understood.

They walked on side by side, and he knew that her resilient spirit was surely recovering its poise. She had no class consciousness—due no doubt to her Western upbringing amongst men who stood foursquare on their own firm feet. Now she held the arm of a half-drunk tinker and thought her own thoughts. And what might these be? If her hands were clean and she believed his were, was she wondering who killed Ambrose Trant? Eudmon Butler or Jerome Trant? And was she doomed to be the mistress—or even the wife—of her husband's killer? That was just the sort of trick Fate would play. By the Lord! he would make Fate's game a little harder.

"If I wasn't half drunk," he said, "I would not dare say what I am going to say to you now."

"Well?"

"Give up playing with fire."

"Am I playing with fire?"

"Or fire with you. Woman always loses that play. Let me give you the advice a wise man gave me. Break with your present life—absolutely."

"As you did."

"As I did."

"Why did you?" But before he could answer—if he could answer—she cried out, "Oh, please forgive me! I know. I learned of the tragedy of Rogan Stuart. I am sorry."

"Forget about it," he said shortly. "We are discussing you. In your case I would go back to my own country."

"But I have no one there any more. I am alone. This is my country."

"Very well! Ignore the past and start afresh. You are young, and life has not marked you deeply. Believe me, no life is so closely knit to you as a skin. You can change it. Go abroad for a little while and think things out——"

"You became what you call a tinker?" she said suggestively.

"I became a tinker only to hide away—and failed. No need for you to do anything as drastic as that. You are too frail a bud to stand the winds of that life."

"Think so?" she said with spirit. "I have wrangled and ridden my own horse from Wyoming to the Staked Plain, cooked grub—and sometimes shot it—for two, dad and myself, washed my own clothes—and his——"

"Could you wash a tinker's shirt?"

"Depends on the tinker." She shook his arm. "Oh!

I wish I could go back to those clean days in the wind and the sun. They were finer and rougher than any tinker's life."

"A hard life the tinker's—and a full one."

"With duties and obligations?"

"You make your own."

"To a pretty girl with red hair?"

"No," he said harshly. "Nor to a prettier girl with black hair."

And she was silent.

Rogan stopped. "You can see the first lamp from here," he said. "Think of what I said."

She loosed his arm and faced him.

"I did not mean to be rude," she murmured. "I am very grateful. Good night."

She put out her hand and met his in a firm clasp; then turned and walked away quickly and lightly.

Rogan stood and looked after her musingly. There she went—the other scrap of flotsam; and was all that he had said no more than the sighing of wind over the current that drove her? Was his advice to go by her like that wind? Was she too deep in the current that swept her to be thrown—where? *Faire-go-deo!* Pity for her! She was too much alive, too beautiful—and if once Eudmon Butler's net closed over her—God have mercy on her!

She had listened to him quietly, yet he had moved her. He knew that because of their sibness. And then he remembered that lament he had heard her sing under the night at Dounbeg. It was fitting. He lifted his voice and intoned the words:

> O Seas that roll over me !
> O salt Seas falling !
> Whence roll ye, where fall ye,
> O desolate Waters ?
> *Out of my dark into thy darkness.*

And her soft contralto came back to him like an echo:

> O Wind that cries over me !
> O cold Wind piercing !
> What cry you, where pierce you,
> O desolate North Wind ?
> *Cold of my grief into thy grieving.*

"And that goes for the two of us," said Rogan Stuart, and went his way.

VII

It was the dark of night when he got back to the camp. A calm mild night with the stars softly clouded, and no touch of autumn shrewdness in the air.

Julie Brien, a slim rod of shadow, met him at the roadside. A new mood was on him then.

"Tell me," he enquired, "did you see a nice slip of a dark colleen walking the road as if she owned it?"

"I did. A lovely lady. She smiled and gave me good-evening."

"Queer thing! She never said she saw you. It was a lovely red-haired girl she saw."

"Go on! You weren't speaking to her?"

"That's telling. Why are you out of your bed— telling your beads or waiting for that wrestle you challenged me to. Come on."

He half-circled her, crouchingly aleap from foot to foot, full of supple, explosive vigour.

"Silly! You've drink taken—you're drunk?"

"I'm not drunk, but I wish to God I was drunk."

She caught his arm and looked close into his face.

"You'll find no black eye," he told her.

"There was no trouble between you and Shamus Og?"

"Not yet."

"I wouldn't like you and Shamus Og to be fighting,"

134

she said soberly. "There would be no cause for that, Rogue?"

"If I was half a man there would be, Julie Brien."

"Don't say that, Rogue?" Her appeal was very serious.

"All right, then, I won't."

"Was he drunk?"

"That fellow? Like a rock. I was up at his stand—a good show he has—and ran the swings for a bit. Ten bob——"

"Did he give you your tea?"

"And it boiled."

"Hasn't he a good cook?"

"He has not." Rogue grinned into the dark, knowing what was in her mind. "That place needs a woman. Three men and a boy he has—a *gorsoon*—and the *gorsoon* made the tea. By glory! but I'll get Daheen to belt him day-after-to-morrow."

She dragged at his sleeve. "Come on and get your supper."

Side by side they wound among the whins to the covered van, where the fire was out within the stone hearth. Jamesy Coffey was moving about the tilt-cart and came at them truculently.

"By crums! Nice hours to be keeping, and the hard day before us to-morrow. Phew! you—! I can smell the drink from here. Did Shamus Og belt you?"

"No, but you should see him make Liam Rua Flynn jump."

"Did he, Rogue?" asked Julie eagerly.

"Like a kangaroo. He's running yet—down about Castlemaine, I'll bet a hat."

He went across to the steps leading up to the rear door of the van. The door was open, and he put his head over the threshold.

"You are back, darling," came the resonant murmur from the dark inside.

"Daheen asleep, dark mother?" he whispered.

"Maybe he would be, the little one."

He clicked his tongue regretfully. "Wo! wo! Them lessons do be a great trouble to us."

He climbed the steps and sat down on the out-jut, his shoulder against the jamb.

"You'll be killed with the hunger, boyeen," murmured the soft voice.

"Never thought of it, mother."

"There, then. Put it on your knee and make use of your fingers. 'Tis only the wing and the *preempeen*."

His hand felt for the plate. "God increase your store, woman-of-the-house!—I am hungry."

"'Tis the drink gives you the false appetite," growled Jamesy Coffey from below. "May the wish-bone cross in your thrapple—I saw her keepin' the best of it for you!"

Julie Brien came up the steps and sat in the corner over against Rogue. It was a quiet and peaceful little camp under the shawl of the gentle night, and Julie sighed softly and clasped her hands in her lap. Rogue felt in his pocket and reached across a rustling paper packet.

"That's a *thosheen* o' sweets I had for Daheen," he said. "But we won't be waking the cratureen. Hand them in to your ma and have a couple yourself, and leave the round hard boolies for him to suck in the morning."

There was a rustle of bed-coverings in the bunk nearest the door.

"Mind you," went on Rogue, "I am sorry in a way that he is asleep, for, though it is too late for lessons, it is not too late to continue the chronicles of the King o' Munster and relate how he employed the Black Thief of Sloe to steal the steed o' bells from the King o' Connaught."

A deep sigh came from the small bunk.

"Sh-h-h! Dinna wauken him," warned Rogue.

"Stop it, Rogue McCoy!" came the voice of Daheen. "Fine you knew I was only schamin'."

"How could I see in the dark?"

"You could so, then; you saw my eyes peepin'. The spellin's was hard, an' maybe I didn't do right by them —an'—an' Julie Brien wouldn't hear me at them."

"And who was chasin' rabbits with Tomboy till it was dark—and caught nothing?" Julie wanted to know.

"He took the scuts off two, anyway," explained Daheen. "You can try me if you want to, Rogue."

Rogue looked up at the softly-clouded September sky. "Could you spell the Precession of the Equinoxes?"

"That's a tough one. That's not in the book at all. Give me one I heard tell of."

"No, I will not, for you are half-honest—the half that's not Coffey. Instead, I will now tell, recapitulate, and relate the only true, verified, authentic narrative that has been handed down to us by the chroniclers, sean-nachies and bards, of the remarkable events, happenings and occurrences that astounded the populace, denizens and aborigines——"

"Japus!" said Daheen in admiration.

"Will there be no bed for any of us to-night?" Jamesy Coffey appealed to the far-off sky. "Oh! don't mind me—don't mind me at all—I'm off."

He stamped noisily into the dark towards the tilt-cart. But in less than a minute he came back very quietly, sat on the bottom step below them, and turned up a listening ear. After a time he rubbed a silent match on his tightened pants, and smoked peacefully. No one took any notice of him.

The packet of sweets rustled as it went from hand to hand; Rogue's plate clinked as he laid it down; his easy Irish-Highland drawl went on and on; and the night came close about them to listen. . . .

". . . and she was up on the battlements of the palace tower looking across the plain of Cashel, and when she heard the ringing of the bells on the steed and him prancing, she cried out: 'Bel! this is my unlucky hour. I come.' And over with her, two hundred feet into the ditch—and that was the end of her and my story."

"And a fittin' end," proclaimed Jamesy, on his feet. "A fittin' end for her and for most women ever I met."

"And for once I will not gainsay you," said Rogue, sliding down the steps. "Good night, people all," he whispered back, "and no dreams to ye. Come to bed, King o' Munster." He shoved the old man before him to the tail of the tilt, and the old man went without a grumble.

Rogue lifted his hands above his head and drew in and exhaled a deep breath that was almost a sigh. The drink was dying in him. "And that's another day over us," he murmured resignedly.

"It is, thank God," said Jamesy quietly. Alone in the night with Rogue McCoy, Jamesy Coffey was unusually gentle and soft-spoken. "Were you up at Shamus Og's camp?" he enquired.

"I was. He offered me ten bob a day to run the swings."

"Who has he with him?"

"He has no woman, Jamesy—if that is what you are asking. There's only one woman for him—and he has found that out."

"An' the wild devil took the wrong way o' findin' out. How'd you get on with him? Did you like him?"

"I did. He is the second best man of the Coffeys in

Ireland. He would settle down if he got what he wanted, and he has come down here to show us that."

"The ould black devil beyant in the van——"

"'Tis the young red devil he is looking to, Jamesy."

"And another fella might have a word to say to that," suggested Jamesy slyly.

"He might," agreed Rogue derisively.

"Out of my way!" Jamesy gave him a little push of shoulder and scrambled up under the tilt.

Rogan followed. "Maybe we'll sleep to-night," he said.

"An' have a head in the mornin'—an' you searchin' for a hair of the dog I've hidden on you."

"I'll not have far to seek," said Rogan confidently.

And so the camp settled down to rest. And through the quietness came little sounds of the night. There was not a breath of air adrift, and the streamlet seemed to lift its babble to some mystic, eternal, oft-repeated ritual; the hobble of the white horse clicked over there; something rustled among the furze, the bay colt snorted, the brindled lurcher, tied beneath the tilt, growled softly; and then, again, the full silence with the voice of the stream lifting untiringly and uncaringly.

Rogan Stuart—not now Rogue McCoy—heard these small sounds over and over again. Rogue McCoy, in the light of day, was afraid of nothing, but Rogan Stuart under the cover of dark was afraid of sleep; Rogue McCoy had an iron guard on himself, but, in sleep, Rogan Stuart's iron guard was down, and the dreams that came to him tore his heart and made his waking desolate.

The old man, like all old men, was a light sleeper. Two or three times in the night he wakened, stirred, and reached a hand to pull the old rag quilt over Rogan's bare chest; and his head was lifted to listen if Rogue

McCoy, his charge, was asleep. And Rogan breathed deeply for him and heard him whisper: "My poor lad— my poor lad!" and the thought in Rogan's mind was: "God! are there not grand men in the world!"

And thereafter he slept, and let no man pursue his dreams.

CHAPTER II

I

TEN o'clock in the morning and the heart of the big horse fair of Castleinch. Horses everywhere, clean-boned young horses, and the sound of horses and men going up to the sun-full September sky; men, honest men all their lives, this one day forgetting truth, decency, morals in a whole-hearted endeavour to sell a horse for a pound more than it was worth ; horsy men, hunting men, cavalry officers striding and halting, moving round a likely animal, rubbing down a doubtful leg, measuring hands-high with chin-tip on withers; veterinary surgeons examining teeth and going minutely into points and blemishes; shy colts protesting at a pinching grip on the jaw, vixenish mares letting out peevishly ; men swearing, protesting, coaxing, agreeing reluctantly; horses being led away, more horses coming ; lean country men clattering on lively legs down by the court-house and urging led horses to show off paces; a long line of sober farm horses with sunken heads waiting patiently for a purchaser ; and, from a field behind the street, the shouts of tinkers selling donkeys—not donkeys but Spanish stallions, wild asses of Tartary, noble beasts with crosses on their backs, fit to have palm leaves spread beneath their hooves. The shows and round-abouts in the market-place were not yet running; no ballad-singer yet raised a voice or hitched a pants; every man was concentrated on one of the oldest and most dishonest pastimes on earth — the selling of a horse.

Came now a small, swarthy, tousle-haired lad, leading a nicely-coupled chestnut colt with dainty-walking slim legs and ungroomed coat, and behind the colt strode a middle-sized, well-built man with calm, deep-set grey eyes looking out of a lean, strong-boned face. The colt reached out a dark muzzle and blew a soft breath on the lad's cheek, and the lad touched his head sideways against the black muzzle.

"Woh, boy!" and the chestnut came to a halt before the long front of the hotel. The small boy patted the black muzzle and spoke as an equal to his charge. "My poor *Copaleen Rua*—my little red horse—they'll sell you to-day, I'm feart. They'll be sellin' you on me to-day in spite o' God." The colt nibbled softly at his fingers.

The lean-faced man, after a quieting word, smoothed down the fine, long, sloping shoulder. "We'll sell him if we must, Daheen boy."

"You will if you can, Rogue McCoy."

A squat, oldish, blue-jowled man came hurrying, brown boots below black gaiters, a black bowler hat on the back of his head—Jamesy Coffey himself. He saw the chestnut, and halted in a surprise that had in it patent admiration. Then he walked round the colt, looking closely and separately at each leg, and ignored Rogue McCoy and Daheen Coffey.

"Are you selling him?" he asked at last, in a carrying tenor voice pitched unnecessarily high, his eyes never leaving the animal's legs.

"Are you buying?"

"Maybe—if you didn't steal him."

"Not in Kerry."

The old fellow made another circle and sniffed once.

"What are you asking for him?" He lifted his voice another note.

"Sixty pounds."

"Go to God!"

"Not selling a horse."

The old fellow became more particular in his examination. He bent down and looked closely at a foreleg. "Is that a firing?"

"Feel it!"

He did so. "No-o! A bit of a kick maybe—it might be worse." He straightened up and again lifted his voice. "I'll give you forty."

"Don't be wasting your time."

The old fellow walked away furiously for a dozen strides, swung suddenly and paced slowly back, his eyes all the time intent on the colt.

"Young fellow!" He addressed the lean-faced man as if he were a hundred yards away. "Have a bit of sense, blast you! I like him, though he is a bit on the light side—but I have a lady customer that he might suit. Look, now! I'll take a bloody risk and give you the top offer o' the fair. Give me your hand! Forty-five punds!"

"Sixty pounds," said Rogue McCoy stolidly; and then, "Go to God yourself out o' the way—here comes a lady who has an eye for a horse."

Three people came down from the hotel porch: Elspeth Trant, iron-grey Jerome Trant, and Captain Eudmon Butler, splendidly tall and gallant, towering over the woman possessively, his black eyes dancing.

Elspeth Trant nodded and smiled frankly at Rogue McCoy.

"Selling?"

"I am, my lady."

She looked over the colt, her eyes pausing on salient points; she knew about horses. "Steady, boy!" She spoke soothingly before running a hand down from withers to point, and the chestnut hide twitched under

143

her hand. She stepped back then and her eyes went up and down the fine legs.

"Would you mind letting me see his action?"

"Surely, my lady."

Rogue took the leading reins from Daheen, brought the colt's head up, clicked his tongue, and away they went. The man's action was as admirable as that of the horse; he was long in the thigh and ran lightly and easily on his toes. The animal walked, trotted, cantered, whirled fifty yards away and came back smooth as a bird soaring, pranced, halted, tossed his gallant head.

Captain Butler, hand on hips, feet wide-set, had watched the performance intently.

"I'll go over him," he said briefly, masterfully, and bent to the forelegs. "Call that anything but a neat bit of firing?" he enquired sneeringly. "Yes, the bone is right enough now." He straightened up, caught the colt's muzzle and forced his mouth open. "Rising five—and not yet sold. What is wrong with you, my lad?" He prodded the weak shoulder here and there. "Thought he was going a bit gingerly on that side. Eh? Give us another run, my fine tinker! Go on!"

"Does the lady wish?" enquired Roy McCoy quietly.

"I am speaking to you. Go on, damn you!"

"You or the lady buying?" enquired Rogue equably.

Butler strode at him where he stood at the horse's head, towered over him menacingly.

"Do what you are told, you dog! Go on!"

Rogue McCoy—no! Rogan Stuart faced him eye to eye. He realised in this crisis that this man was insane—that anger drove him over a narrow boundary into madness. A flare was alight behind the black eyes.

"If the lady wishes it," said Rogue steadily.

The Black Captain did not give the lady time to wish anything. And if he had only looked closer he would have seen that the man before him was a dangerous man, and a madman too at this moment; but with a cold madness that made the skin like drawn parchment over the cheek-bones, that made his eyes like cold bosses of glazed stone.

"I'll teach you, you dog!" said Butler, and thrust the flat of his fist into Rogan's face; not a hard blow, more an admonitory push than a blow. A little spot of red showed on Rogan's tight lips.

"I will kill you now, Eudmon Butler," said Rogan Stuart, cold as the wind. "You are better dead."

Something in voice and eye was a revelation to the soldier.

"Oh, it's you, Stuart?—you cuckold!"

"For your sins," said Rogan Stuart.

II

Some years have elapsed since that fair at Castleinch, but the men who saw the great fight between Eudmon Butler—the Black Captain—and Rogue McCoy, the tinker, will not let their friends forget it. Many of them still go to the fair of Castleinch and, from the hotel steps, point out to less lucky acquaintances the place in the street, and go out there and measure off the ground and wave explanatory arms. For the affair was about the most elemental and savage encounter ever seen in a county where fights are not infrequent, and, often enough, savage.

There was a rush of men and feet—surely there was a rush. And, before the ring could close, tall Shamus Og Coffey came from nowhere, threw a long arm round Elspeth Trant, and swung her clean on to the hotel porch. "See it from there, lady," he cried, and plunged into the crowd.

Jamesy Coffey, oldish and squat, was in the forefront, and remained there through it all. His great shoulders and long arms were pressed back against the force behind. "Give them room, ye bodachs!" he roared. "He's light, but tough; give him room to use his feet."

Came a tall sergeant of the Civic Guard, who ought to have known better, and burst into the ring. He caught Rogue, the fighting tinker, and dragged him backwards; and Butler struck Rogue savagely above the deep-set eyes. Whereupon, Shamus Og Coffey tore the sergeant loose, struck him terribly behind the neck, and threw him to be engulfed in the crowd. Came another tall guard, more wise, and shoulder-gripped two men at the edge of the crowd. "Hold there," he threatened them, "and put your back against me, or, by the powers! I'll arrest ye for killing Sergeant O'Dowd."

Horses plunged, horses kicked, horses bolted; but men shouted and forgot horse-dealing in the great game of the race. *Copaleen Rua*, the chestnut colt, no one to hold him, reared amidst the crowd and pawed with his fore-feet; men by a miracle dodged clear, and a nervy lad leaped in and caught forelock and nose in a steadying grip. Then came small Daheen Coffey, twisting and wriggling indestructibly amongst shifting and stamping feet, climbed somehow up a foreleg, got a handful of mane, and twisted on to the heaving withers. The colt, under that familiar weight, hearing that loved voice, quieted in the press of men and remained quiet though tremorous.

From his perch up there Daheen saw the fight, every phase of it. He was as white as a linen sheet; his nose, his mouth, his cheeks twisted and grimaced and quivered; and the tears of excitement, anger, fear, dismay kept running from his wide-open wild black eyes. And never once did he stop shouting, protesting, encouraging, warning, lamenting—though in after days he would indignantly and honestly protest that he had remained dumb as a fish. Strangely enough, the only thing Rogan Stuart heard amidst the storm and stress was the high voice of that lad who worshipped him; and it heartened him finer than any bugle.

"Bloody wars, Rogue McCoy! Up the men of the Coffeys, up the Carty men! Hit him again! O God, Rogue darling! Oh, my poor Rogueen! Don't let him kill you, boy avic! Twist him—twist him, you devil! On top of him now, and bite his ear. Take his black heart out and we'll roast it for Tomboy! O Mother o' God, what'll we do at all—what'll we do if he's beat on us. O mother, mother, his eye is smithereens in his head. Wirra, wirra, wirra! What'll we do—what'll we do goin' the road and us beat. Up again, then, and paste him down. He's grinning now. . . . We've the long day for it now—and a peg every minute. Who's the good man now . . .?"

And after a long time came the high clear cry of a woman, and thereafter came a great quiet.

CHAPTER III

I

THE court-house of Castleinch was crowded next morning. Men of the road, showmen, tinkers and their shawled
women-folk were there in full strength; a few farmers
and horse-dealers too, who had stayed overnight in town;
all the others were citizens keenly interested in the conclusion of the drama. Uniformed civic guards kept the
doors, lounged here and there in the aisle, stood to attention below and behind the prisoners' dock. Up on the
raised Bench the District Justice sat in his black robes,
white bands and scrap of grey wig: a youngish man
with a resolute jut of chin and a humorous mouth.
Directly below him sat his clerk in front of the low
oblong witness-table; and at either side of this table the
legal profession lolled carelessly on leather-backed forms.
Outside the railings of the sacred precincts the public
were packed in a slope that went up and back to the
oaken ceiling.

Behind the railing of the square prisoners' dock stood
Shamus Og Coffey and Rogue McCoy. Shamus Og was
his own tall self, handsome and dare-devil as ever. But
Rogue McCoy? A sorry spectacle! A veritable beaten-
up tinker! His neck was bare, for the red kerchief had
been torn from it; one sleeve of his blarney jacket had
been ripped from the shoulder; one eye was half-closed
above a dark-blue bruise; there was a patch of sticking-
plaster on craggy brow and another above a cheek-bone;
his mouth was swollen, his nose was swollen, his chin
showed a red blaze below the stubble; his right hand

rested gingerly upon the railing of the dock, and was swathed in bandages across knuckles and round thumb. A beaten-up wreck of a man? But no! For the half-shut eye and the other clear grey one were serene, steady, full of peace; and the face, though haggard and weary, was indomitably calm. No madness there any more.

The State, as prosecutor, had finished its side of the case. Its last witness had not been very satisfactory. That witness was Mrs Elspeth Trant. She had admitted that Captain Eudmon Butler was a friend of hers, but denied that he had been commissioned to buy a horse for her; Sir Jerome Trant, as sworn, might have requested his assistance as a well-known judge of horse-flesh, but in the examination of the colt in question she was the only interested party, and Captain Butler had interfered entirely on his own initiative, and had forced—she used that word—a quarrel on the seller without consulting her wishes and against her wishes. The prosecuting lawyer, swearing under his breath, did not press her, and the defending lawyer was wise enough not to seek to heighten the impression she had made.

Elspeth Trant now sat in a reserved seat inside the railings, her face pale, but collected, below a dark veil, and her eyes downcast. She had glanced once at Rogue McCoy, but Rogue McCoy had looked at no one.

The first and only witness for the defence was up. And he was Jamesy Coffey, squat, blue-jowled, grim. He had taken the oath, and now stood four-square on the witness-table, staring saturninely at the Justice.

"Sit down!" ordered the clerk, and Jamesy slumped into the windsor chair and carefully placed his bowler hat below the seat.

A plump lawyer, lounging amongst his brothers, yawned and came lazily to his feet: the solicitor for the defence—and no fool. He knew his witness, and he knew exactly how to take him.

"You are Jamesy Coffey?"

"I am."

"Travelling tinsmith?"

"And that's polite for tinker."

"Silence!" roared the usher.

"You know Rogue McCoy, the accused?"

"I do, then."

"Is he a friend of yours?"

"A friend? That fellow—only last week—told me I didn't know the differ between a get of San Toy's an' a spavined mule. A friend, says you!"

"Silence!" roared the usher.

"You saw the whole affair from beginning to end?"

"I did so—every peg and belt, cross and counter, hit-me-high, hit-me-low, tumble and pitch, and the devil help the man underneath."

"Silence!" roared the usher.

"Tell his honour what you saw."

The solicitor sat down and lounged, his work finished.

"I will," said Jamesy Coffey grimly, turned to the bench, leant forward, grasped knees firmly with both hands and cleared his throat.

The Justice pushed the grey wig back on his forehead, leant over the narrow desk, smiled at Jamesy, and nodded familiarly. "Go on, Jamesy!" He knew Jamesy, had known him all his life, had bargained with him for fishing-rods, fowling-pieces, lustre ware, such things; and he knew that if Jamesy got his own time justice would not be ill-served.

Justice and tinker looked at each other; as far as they were concerned the court-room might be empty; and Jamesy took his own way to it.

"It was a good tough fight, your honour—a goodenough fight; since me own young days I dunno that there has been e'er a better. You didn't happen to be there, your honour? No! A great pity! There was one or two things worth seein'. An' who knows? I might have won a hatful off you, an' you bettin' on the wrong man. Any one would, the first half of the road, and it a long road. This is how it was, your honour:

"This Rogue McCoy was sellin' a horse to the lady— and a nice lady, as ladies go. Dam' all he knows about a horse, but the colt was a good one, an' the lady nibblin', when up comes the Black Captain—Eudmon Butler. Mind you, the colt had shown his paces nate as a trottin' pony, without stumble or knock, splay hoof or cross, when here comes the Captain with his head high as that ceilin' and shoulders fillin' the street. 'Tinker man,' says he, 'give that colt another run!' What right had he to interfere in another man's sale, an' the man doin' his best? God be with the days when, if any man did that across me, 'tisn't as quiet as Rogue McCoy I'd take it; for all he says is: 'Does the lady wish it?' 'I wish it,' says the Black Captain and swore a mighty oath. 'If the lady wishes it,' says Rogue again, quiet, like I'm sayin' it now. An' without another word, without lave or licence, the big man smashes his fist into the lad's face, and meself saw the blood follow the blow—down his jaw there. 'Tis the Black Captain's way; the whole world knows it—you know it yourself, your honour. He done it before an' often before, an' maybe—but I doubt it—he will do it again; but by the 'tarnal! he will not do it to Rogue McCoy.

"I ask any one in this court—I ask yourself, your honour, what would you do, an' you after bein' hit across the gob without rhyme or raison? Answer me that, now?"

"I would not care to say, Jamesy," said the Justice, a sudden gleam in his eye.

"I know what you'd do—fine I know! An' the thing you would do is what Rogue McCoy did. Look at him there, now; he is not big, an' maybe he goes hungry many a day—an' maybe he should too—but, small or hungry, he rose to the insult; and they were at each other like a blue tarrier and a mastiff dog.

"Listen to this, now, your honour. At the first grapple, in tears a big . . .—I beg your honour's pardon— a big peeler, and if he is not from the County Cavan I'll eat my caubeen. In he comes roarin', an' grips Rogue by the throat, an' 'twas then the Black Captain gave him that cut over the eye—a dirty blow. An' all that Shamus Og did was to catch hold of that peeler an' give him a small push behind—an' if he fell down in the crowd an' had three ribs broken 'twasn't any one's fault but his own.

"Men in this chair to-day, your honour, have swore that it was a rough fight an' a dirty fight; an' I ask any one here to-day what chance would any man have against the Black Captain with parlour tricks? No, your honour, 'twas two hardy men full of hot blood, face to face and nothin' barred. Up and down, in and out, on the ground and off the ground, over the guard and under the guard, collar and elbow, the inside lock and the back heel, the point of the elbow, the pan of the knee—they were all there an' more besides—an' need for them.

"An' did the small man have the worst of it? Maybe he had—at the beginning—an' maybe he hadn't. He was light surely, an' the big man flung him about. But if you saw him land on his feet like a cat an' spring like a tiger, you would know that it was he was callin' the tune an' payin' the piper. An' when they fell, was he under, an' if he was under did he twist in the air an' come on top before they touched the ground? He did so. An' when he struck, his blow was the dunt of a sledge; an' the blows lit off him like a light hammer off an anvil.

"The Black Captain did all he could—an' it the dirtiest—an' he was worn down an' worn down, an' he knowin' it. An' the grin on his face! To a thread he was worn, an' Rogue McCoy shook him like a tarrier shakes a rat, an' bate him like a carpet. And then, your honour, a lady up in the hotel porch let a screech out of her. "Enough—oh!—not any more!" she cried. And at that Rogue dropped him on his face, and backed away like a lamb—an' his face the face of a man below the blood.

"Yes, your honour! An' they took the Black Captain —what was left of him—to the hospital above on the back of a door. An' Rogue McCoy stood like a rock on his two feet, with two of the guards at his side an' no hand touchin' him. He was as quiet as that when it was all over. Pity you didn't see it, your honour."

"It was not so bad at second hand," murmured the Justice, and he bent over his papers to hide his twitching nostrils, the fighting devil in his eye. He turned over some documents, picked out one, and looked down at the witness.

"Thank you, Jamesy." He glanced across at the defending lawyer, who came to his feet.

"That is our defence, your honour."

The State prosecutor hesitated, decided not to cross-examine, and spoke hurriedly. "The case rests."

Jamesy Coffey sat stolidly in his chair, and, strangely enough, it was to Jamesy the Justice addressed himself.

"I accept your evidence, Jamesy Coffey—most of it. It is reasonably corroborated by the last witness. My mind had been almost made up to return the prisoners to the County Court, considering the present state of Captain Butler ; but in the circumstances I have decided to give a verdict—and if the defence wishes to appeal I will consider any views put forth."

"We will not appeal, your honour," said the defending solicitor promptly.

"As you please! It is clear that the injured man, Captain Eudmon Butler, was much to blame in the whole bad business, and I am taking that into account. You have heard the doctor's evidence, and his opinion that Captain Butler is in no danger unless unforeseen complications ensue from the terrific body punishment he received. I will accept that opinion as fact. But Captain Butler received such a savage beating that I cannot accept such a beating as necessary or unavoidable, allowing for all extenuating circumstances. In my opinion this was no ordinary fair-day brawl; it was deadly to the point of extreme malice. Apart from minor injuries, not unusual in a bout with bare knuckles, Captain Butler's nose and three ribs are broken, and a muscle very nearly wrenched from his thigh. In the circumstances I sentence Rogue McCoy to one calendar month in Stranleigh Jail, with hard labour. I am sorry, Jamesy, but my Court cannot overlook a street fight of this description."

"An' what about the man that started it, your honour?" Jamesy Coffey wanted to know.

"Do you not think his punishment already severe enough?"

"Begorrah, your honour! it would not go well with me to gainsay you."

"As for the second prisoner, Shamus Og Coffey," went on the Justice, "the evidence is conclusive that he assaulted Sergeant O'Dowd while the sergeant was doing his duty. I will not accept the accusation that he broke three of the sergeant's ribs, nor will I accept the plea that he only administered a small push behind. It is too apparent that the sergeant will not be able to hold his head up for some time. This is not the accused's first offence, and I am compelled to sentence him to three months with hard labour. The Court stands adjourned."

"That will cool the pair of them," said Jamesy Coffey philosophically.

II

Shamus Og Coffey and Rogue McCoy sat side by side on the plank seat in the temporary lock-up at the Garda barracks, where they were being detained pending the departure of the afternoon train for Stranleigh Jail. Shamus Og's right wrist and Rogue's left were hand-cuffed together, for the *gardai* were taking no chances with two such fighting men. They were talking quietly and in a friendly fashion.

"A whale of a Jonah I am!" remarked Rogue. "I carry trouble about with me. You know, at the very start of this sojourn, I very nearly ran two kindly men in for—manslaughter at least."

"I'm not surprised," said Shamus Og, "after the things you done yesterday."

"Never mind that! I am thinking of the trouble I've run you into."

"An' never mind that, you! 'Twas worth it—an' I was in quod before—twice."

"A tough experience, isn't it?"

"You'll find it tough enough, after bein' used to the open and three good meals a day. Man, you'll be hungry as a pike the whole month, an' only gettin' used to it at the very end. They starve the first-timers good an' hard. I'm an old hand with a friend in camp, and an odd fag on the quiet. An' think of all the money I'll save in three months?"

"What about your show?"

"Young Terry Ward is all right. The season is over

anyway, an' we were going up to Limerick for the winter. That's a good stand."

"Could I run up there and look it over—I'll be out long ahead of you?"

"No-o! Next summer I'll be glad of you; but Terry is all right, an' might think you were spyin' on him. Moreover, he won't cheat me more than is proper."

The key clicked in the lock, and hob-nailed brown boots clattered on the stone flags.

"There's our pair o' fightin' men—God forgive me for lyin'," came the high tenor of Jamesy Coffey.

Tall Maag Carty came behind him, and the door closed slowly. Shamus Og looked at that closing door; perhaps he hoped for a third visitor.

Each of the old people carried a stout parcel. Maag Carty, before she spoke, opened hers at the end of the plank. She was ever the provider; her parcel contained two bottles of soup wrapped in woollen socks to keep in the warmth, two quarts of brown stout with the corks half drawn, and a great pile of sandwiches.

"I knew my darling men would be hungry, and they going where hunger is. There now! Take it in your hands, white loves. Sad day to see you handcuffed together! But I saw it in a dream two days ago, and it was not a bad sign."

"One month an' three months in jail was a dam' fine thing to see," said Jamesy Coffey dryly.

"No, quiet man! Only these two men with a friendly tie."

"It is tight enough, whatever."

She ministered to the two, and they thanked her with words and with sound appetite.

"Sore all over you'll be, *mo gaol*—my light," she said to Rogue.

"Not my jaws, dark mother, as you see. I'm right

156

enough, and needing the month's rest from the slave-driving of Jamesy Coffey."

"An' fine you'll look pickin' oakum with a busted thumb," came back Jamesy. "That was one piece of awkward work, me boyo. Maybe you had the best of it, but look at the time it took you; an' me bold Shamus Og that had not sense enough not to hit a peeler till his back was turned."

"True for you, da," agreed Shamus Og.

"Go to blazes!" said Jamesy.

"How's Daheen?" enquired Rogue.

"The poor darlin'—" began Maag.

"Roarin' his head off," Jamesy interrupted, "an' me after beltin' him twice to cure him. He would shame us in the town if we brought him in—an' Julie Brien bawlin' with him."

"And who is Julie Brien bawlin' for?" enquired Shamus Og darkly.

"For company, what else—an' because she hadn't a clean shirt to send down to Rogue, havin' washed three holes in his spare one—the *ownshuch*!"

Shamus Og went on eating sandwiches gloomily.

"Anyway," went on Jamesy, "I'll have peace for a month, an', come high, come low, I'll be boss in me own camp. Was it Lyon's fifth reader you was talkin' about for Daheen—Julie Brien told me to ask?"

Rogue smiled secretly. "Yes. But it will cost you half a dollar."

"He'll do without it, then."

"Put your hand in my pocket—the handcuff side—an' you'll get a handful of silver," Shamus Og invited.

"To hell with your silver!" Jamesy threw his parcel on the plank. "There's a hand-me-down coat an' vest in there, an' a red neckcloth Maag Carty had. I'm off." He turned from the door. "When you come out, maybe you won't be so keen on the winter roads, Rogue McCoy; an' you'll be off your own hook—or lookin' for that ten bob a day Shamus Og promised you, *moryah*!"

"He will be welcome," said Shamus Og.

"Maybe I will, Jamesy," said Rogue cryptically. "Where will you be?"

"I dunno where—but it'll not be Stranleigh. That place in October would make a duck squawk for dry weather."

Maag Carty stood before Rogue and ran gentle long fingers over brow and cheek and chin; and he felt a queer, soothing, sleepy balm flow where before had been a dull, hot ache.

"Don't be troubling now at all, childeen," said the crooning bell of her voice. "Don't be troubling one bit. Sorrow for me that the power is not in me to help you and you dreaming, *mo lanaveen oge*—my young little child!"

She looked at Shamus Og and shook her head. "I have no word to say to you, Shamus Og, son of your father. Don't hold it against me."

"No, Maag Carty, I will not. The right thing you always did."

"And you too strong for me." She went to the door. "God be with ye!" she blessed them, and followed her husband.

III

An hour later they had another visitor. A lady. Not Julie Brien, though Shamus Og looked up eagerly. This was a dark lady in a dark veil; and she was Elspeth Trant. Her face was still white below the dark film of veil, and her eyes were big and very tired. She was agitated, but hid that fact very well.

Rogue McCoy rose to his feet and Shamus Og rose

with him; and her shoulders drew together when she saw the manacled hands.

"I am sorry to see you like this," she said quickly.

Rogue was so slow in finding his tongue that Shamus Og had to answer for the two.

"You needn't be sorry, ma'am," he said politely. "'Tisn't your fault we're here."

For the time she seemed to ignore Rogue; she came across to Shamus Og and stretched out her hand, and he shook it awkwardly with his left.

"I want to thank you for getting me out of harm's way yesterday."

"Nothing at all, ma'am."

"I am sorry you got into trouble—you didn't deserve to."

"All in the day's work," said Shamus Og, grinning.

She glanced at Rogue. "Sit down, please," she urged, and made to push them to the bench. "I want a word or two with you, Mr—Rogue McCoy."

They sat down, and she too took a seat on the plank next Rogue; and Shamus Og, his handcuffed hand behind his hip, turned his shoulder away from them and looked up at the narrow barred window.

"This is bad work, Rogue McCoy," she said.

"Which? A month in jail?" He smiled equably, and she looked away.

"Yes—that only. The—the other thing had to happen sometime."

Rogue ignored the meaning behind that. "A month in jail is nothing in a tinker's life," he said lightly, and her shoulders twitched at his words.

His bandaged hand rested on his knee, and her eyes were on it.

"A knuckle driven in and thumb out of joint," he told her. Somehow, it pleased him to be frank with this lady. "Jamesy Coffey says it was awkwardness on my part."

"Is that your man that gave the remarkable evidence?"

"No, not my man, Mrs Trant. I am his man. Jamesy Coffey is boss, high-kicker, chieftain. I am in his care; he admonishes me during the day, and tucks me in at night."

Shamus Og laughed over his shoulder. "True for you," he said, "that ould fellow has to have his own way of it."

"And a good way."

"There I leave you."

"Is the lovely red-haired girl his daughter?" enquired the lady.

Shamus Og resumed his survey of the barred window, and the blood came up to his face.

"His wife's daughter," Rogue told her. "Maag Carty, an aloof queen, with strange power and vision out of old Egypt."

"The ould devil!" muttered Shamus Og.

Elspeth Trant's agitation, that had subdued itself in this preliminary talk, again asserted itself; she found it difficult to sit still, a foot tapped on the floor; her hands, coming together, twined and untwined; she looked quickly at Rogue and away. And that man, so strong and calm below his bruises, looked at her out of his half-shut eye and open eye, and waited.

"That advice you gave me!" She spoke at last in a low voice. "I have been thinking it over.

"Perhaps it was foolish advice," he said. "You might have noticed that I was not too sober at the time."

She was silent.

"I have known fear too," said Rogue, touching the core of her thought.

"That fear I do not want to know," she said.

She leant forward and her mouth quivered. "I don't know why I trouble you," she almost whispered, "but you have been through so much yourself that you might help me, lonely and unknowing, with your dearly bought wisdom. I want to be free—I would like to be clean—to live finely. Though you may not know, you have helped me greatly before now—and I needed help. There seemed—there seems—to be some tie between us. That is what I wanted to tell you. But will it hold?" She smiled wanly. "It is such a thin, drawn-out tie—and you are going out of my life. I may never see you again. Oh! No—No! I will not ask your help any more."

After all she was only a girl, a girl dowered dangerously in a half-strange land; not very wise, not at all sophisticated, and with a great urge in her to possess her own soul—and a great temptation drawing its net about her. He smiled at her with a clear and friendly confidence, placed an unbandaged finger-tip on her gloved hand and held it firmly there, and with that tie between them spoke with a fine assurance.

"This is all I know. My advice holds. Break with your present life, start from a fresh angle and go on—only for a few months, perhaps—until you get your feet and your mind cleared. Go abroad, anywhere, and let no one—no one in the world—know where you are going. After that," he lifted his finger and made a little pass in the air, "you'll be able to make and break your own life without being obsessed. Try it."

She drew in a deep breath. "But I have obligations."

"To yourself."

"But there is an old man—a man growing old—who has been kind always—who needs my help. It would be cowardly to run away."

"Do you want to run away?"

Her eyes were on the ground and her voice no more than a murmur. "If you were by to help me."

"In that case," said Rogan Stuart sombrely, "you will have to choose your own road to nowhere."

The door rattled and a civic guard looked round the corner.

"About train-time, ma'am."

She rose to her feet, and the two men rose with her. She did not look at either. The coldness of death was in her voice. "Good-bye! We may not meet again." And she went out without a glance backwards.

And still Rogan Stuart stood looking at the closed door. On what sad road was she now planning to set foot—to her fate and doom? What man would go that road with her? Must she go—must she go, then? And once again he felt for her a strange, keen, intense emotion —an emotion that was too intense to be impersonal. And he then knew that she had cried out to him for help, and that he had failed her.

"There goes a woman, by God!" said Shamus Og.

"By God—or the Devil!" said Rogue McCoy.

CHAPTER IV

I

PADDY JOE LONG's lime-washed, green-jalousied bungalow looked down on the deep, half-mile curve of the Ladies' Strand at Ballybwingan. On one hand, black and red cliffs lifted sheerly to sloping summits of sea-grass; on the other, a green-crowned promontory jutted out into the sea and carried an ancient Norman keep at its extreme point; and between, the blue-green floor of the sea flung out and up to a horizon that was laid down like a line between the high black portals of Loop Head and Kerry Head a dozen miles apart. The tired surf, leisurely breaking white along the golden-brown sands, sent up a sleepy sough; and the sun, rich and lazy in its fall haze, poured down its genial warmth.

The bungalow was fronted by a spread of green lawn with a big mound of rockery in the middle; and round this mound Paddy Joe's tall and lovely wife, Norrey, walked slowly, and resignedly contemplated the decay of autumn. She wore one of Paddy Joe's disreputable hats on her flaxen hair and carried a pointed weed extractor in a gauntleted left hand.

The green hand-gate from the beach road creaked open behind her, and the local postman shambled loose-footed across the lawn.

"Morning, Tade!"

"Good-morrow, ma'am! Isn't it the grand weather we're havin', glory be to God!—an' everything perishin' for a drop of rain. Devil a hen's egg has been laid in the village this week."

163

"And that reminds me, Tade. When you are passing Willie Carroll's, tell him to send up two dozen of his freshest eggs—and a few syphons of soda."

"To be sure, ma'am. Never fear he'll have a few laid aside for yourself."

At one side of the lawn, facing the sea, stood a detached sun-parlour, and through the half-open door of this came an urgent bellow.

"Get out! And don't tell him I said you were to have one pint of stout."

"Wan pint? Thank you, Paddy Joe! God spare you your health!" And thrusting a bundle of correspondence and a wrapped newspaper into Norrey's hand, Tade ambled quickly out of earshot.

Norrey strolled across the green and through the door of the sun-parlour; and her husband's feet clumped to the floor from their rest on the writing-desk.

"Woman!" he protested, "amn't I busy this morning?" He was engaged in filling his pipe, and in his lap rested a writing-pad on which no word had yet been scrawled.

Norrey looked at the jumble of letters in her hand. "Your usual fan mail," she said scathingly. "Mostly from a lot of foolish females. I'm afraid you're a mere woman's writer, Paddy Joe, darling."

"There was never a woman yet hadn't a soft corner for me," said Paddy Joe complacently.

She smacked him over the grey-flecked black head with a folded newspaper. "There's your *Kerryman*—I'll run through your correspondence."

Paddy Joe got his pipe going, Norrey sat on the corner of his desk and lit a cigarette, and for a time there was silence in the sunny room, broken only by the rip and rustle of paper.

And then Paddy Joe swore warmly. "Blur-an-agers! listen to this: 'At Castleinch Court to-day, before District

Justice McEnri, Rogue McCoy, giving his trade as tinker, and Shamus Og Coffey, travelling showman, were sentenced to one month and three months respectively for a breach of the peace at Castleinch Horse Fair—' I was afraid it would come to something like that between Shamus Og and Rogue—and I bet I know the red-head that was at the root of it—damn! 'From the evidence, mainly given by the well-known and popular roadman, Jamesy Coffey, father of one of the defendants, it appears that Mrs Elspeth Trant of Dounbeg——'"

"H-s-s-h!" Norrey silenced him, her hand impatient. She was deeply interested in the letter she was reading.

Paddy Joe read hurriedly through the column of court news. "Ha!" he exclaimed. "I was wrong. It wasn't Julie Brien at all. Bedam! I'd give an eye out of my head to be there."

Norrey finished the letter and looked up. "Go on," she requested quietly; "read it to me."

"It must have been one almighty good scrap," said Paddy Joe, his voice regretful for that he should have missed it. "You'll remember all I told you about Rogue McCoy—Rogan Stuart that was. Here it is then, headed 'THE FIGHTING TINKER—THE BLACK CAPTAIN MEETS HIS WATERLOO.'" And he went on to read a racy account of the court proceedings at Castleinch.

"'Captain Butler is still detained in the local hospital,'" he concluded, "'but is in no immediate danger.' That'll teach him—and the lesson overdue."

"The Justice was very severe," Norrey remarked.

"A month is the minimum for a tinker—right or wrong," said Paddy Joe easily, "and Shamus Og is an old offender."

Norrey raised the letter that had interested her. "Listen to this," she said, calmly serious. "It is addressed from 'Tinkers' Camp, Owenglass Bridge, Castleinch, the morning of the big fair—date unknown.' It is from your Rogue McCoy."

"The morning of the fair!" Paddy Joe sat up. "Go on, girl—read it, read it!"

" MY DEAR PADDY JOE LONG,—
The needle has been found in your bundle of hay, and I thought I had better inform you of the fact. Last evening it was. Shamus Og Coffey, who, by the way, has come down from Dublinwards to demonstrate to a certain one that he has turned over a new leaf—Shamus Og and I were engaged in conveying a fairish thirst to Mickeen's Bar when a certain young widow looked down from the porch of the Desmond Arms, and the light of recognition was unmistakable in her eye; and yet I have been accepted without question as a blooded tinker by some of the toughest tinkers on the road.

She was in bad company at the time, but, strangely enough, the bad company did not seem to recognise me——"

Paddy Joe struck the desk with a clenched fist. "That was Eudmon Butler. Go on, will you!"

" She said nothing then, but, later in the evening, very much later, she waylaid me on the road back to camp. She was alone and she was reasonable. We talked, and, being nicely lit up, I produced what I then considered a high level of wisdom, but this morning, being sober and sair-headed, I would class it, in Jamesy Coffey's language, as balderdash.

You will know what I should do next? But please, Mr Boss, do not seek to extract me like a periwinkle from this camp for yet a while. I fit rather cosily into my present shell, and Jamesy Coffey, while biting my ear, gives me a sort of self-satisfying impression that I carry the camp under my oxter.

I am grateful to you.

We are in a hurry this morning. Daheen, who is a jewel, and myself are going down to the fair to try and sell his *Copaleen Rua*. I'll post this on the way. We may run across the lady again, for *Copaleen Rua* is a nice colt and has 'leppin'' in him, and neither a splint, a spavin, nor a ringbone. We shall be here for one week and then go on to Tarbert Island,

166

where Jamesy has bought an old iron boat for scrapping.
I am yours to command.

It is a pity that she is in bad company. Yours aye,
ROGUE THE TINKER."

"And that's that," said Paddy Joe solemnly. He
sank deep into thought for a space, smoothing down his
lean cheeks with thumb and forefinger. Then he slowly
reached a hand for the letter and went over it word by
word. "We have it all here in our two fists," he growled.
"if we could tell what was in his mind. Not one word
that they said to each other."

"Of course not. That is the letter of a nice man."

"But I would like to know the things that were said—
might give us a lead to work on."

"You'll have time to think it out. Your Rogue—or
Rogan—is out of it for a month."

"That's the trouble. He is there under their thumb
if they want him for killing Trant."

"Not likely—not the least likely. And what about
poor Shamus Og and his new-turned leaf?"

"He'll have time to think if it was worth turning," said
Paddy Joe callously.

"And Julie Brien?"

"What's she got to do with this business?"

"You're losing your grip, husband. You haven't
begun to diagnose that letter. Don't you see that it
refers to her so indirectly that she must have been much
in the writer's mind?"

"Tuts! You women are all the same. Give me time
to think, will you!"

But his thoughts must have run slow and muddy, for
presently he looked up at his wife with frowning eyes.

"Haven't you a thought in your head, woman?"

She smiled at him. "You must do what you should
have done four months ago, Paddy Joe, and you know it."

167

"What the——"

"Talk to the woman. Shh! You behaved then like the sentimentalists that all men are. Because a woman was implicated you remained silent, and, having remained silent, it is now more essential than ever that none of you be drawn into the business."

He nodded agreement.

"See the woman, then. She is the only person that knows that Rogan Stuart was in the grounds that night. She merely guessed that you were poaching the river."

"It was a damn sound guess," said Paddy Joe.

"Don't you see? No matter what action she may contemplate, in the final issue she is only one against three—her word against yours. Very probably she intends taking no action at all—not after four months—but, if you want to make sure, talk to her, show her that you are ready to out-trump any card played."

"And what would I be saying to the poor girl?" asked Paddy Joe trustfully.

"You'll say plenty once you start," his wife mocked him gently. "There is that struggle at the boat-house, and the light feet you heard coming on the path—emphasise that if necessary."

Paddy Joe nodded gloomily, and his voice also was gloomy. "Yes, feet running lightly as a woman's!"

"And there your deduction was wrong, boy—and you so boastful of your sense of observation. Have you never noticed it?"

"Noticed what?"

"When I was on the stage—or off it in my dressing-room, with call-boys, scene-shifters, actors, chorus-girls running along the passages, I often noticed that an active man runs much more lightly than a woman."

Paddy Joe, for once, looked dumbly at his wife, his mind leaping in a fresh gambit.

"And another thing," went on this astounding wife, 'you'll notice how your friend says 'She was in bad company,' and again, 'It is a pity that she is in bad company.' You told me that she affected Rogan Stuart strangely at Dounbeg. She is in bad company and she is worth saving. That is what he means, and that is what he set out to tell you. He is interested. Go away up to Dounbeg and find out things for me. I'm interested too."

"You are a dangerous woman," said Paddy Joe humbly, "a dangerous woman to be the wife of a weak, transparent man." He rose to his feet. "I'll go, matriarch." And then he grinned at her, standing close above her. "But mind you, you are doing a foolish thing to send me."

"Why, darling?"

"She is a mighty attractive young woman, that young woman, and you know the way I am with that sort?"

"I do. That is why I'm sending you. I like a spice of danger."

He clasped her round the shoulders, and kissed her with the warmth of a young lover.

"Stop it, silly!" she reprimanded softly. "Do you want your children to see you making a fool of yourself?"

"Why wouldn't they?" said Paddy Joe. "It wouldn't be the first time."

II

Paddy Joe motored to Dounbeg next morning, had lunch at the Harty Arms, and then walked out on the pier to hold converse with Tom Whelan, the harbour-master.

The two tramped to the end of the resounding platform and stood gazing down the length of the bay, rippling green and silver under the whip of the shrewd

September breeze. All about them the tall, sun-hazed mountains looked at each other across the glens, and gathered in about the Narrows to hold austere commune

Paddy Joe came deftly to the subject. "Any late grilse about?"

"Are you thinking of having a go at one?" enquired the harbour-master. "The camping-place round the point is vacant and I have the tent handy."

"No," said Paddy Joe. "Another man might be killed on us."

"There's a man we could spare, maybe," rumbled the other.

"Nothing has come of that affair, I see," remarked Paddy Joe casually.

"Not a thing. The sergeant, for all his smartness, was kept backin' and fillin' in a head-wind."

"They're getting over it—up at the big house?"

"They are," said Tom Whelan a shade dryly. "The young widow, God be good to her, is out and about again. She was buying horses at Castleinch Fair the other day. And, by the hokey! did you see where a tinker off the road walloped hell out of the Black Captain?"

"I did. Is she home?"

"Yesterday."

"The Black Captain about?"

"Not with three busted ribs an' a flat nose. Good as that tinker was, he'd be better to my mind if he hit a taste harder."

"Butler the man you could spare?"

"Maybe so."

"Been here much?"

"Too much. People are beginning to talk—and they needn't."

"Would not Sir Jerome——?"

"What can he do?"

"What do you think?" enquired Paddy Joe guilelessly.

"He is doing what he can. Anywhere the Black Captain and herself are together, he is not far off. The old man is fond of that girl, I tell you."

"Fond?"

"Like a father. I'm tellin' you. Only——" He hesitated. "I suppose 'tis in the blood, but I wish he'd leave the drink alone. All the same, I wouldn't care to be Butler if——"

"You are an old prude, Thomas."

"What's that, you lubber?"

"Remember she is now an eligible young widow, and the Black Captain—he has no encumbrances, has he?"

"He'd make a damn bad husband."

"Do you know any man that is a good one?"

"Ask your wife that," suggested Tom Whelan.

"She has told me often without asking," laughed Paddy Joe.

"All the same," persisted the old man, "rather than see that young woman tied to him for life, I—I sometimes do be thinkin' it would be better for her to find out another way, God forgive me! It would give us an excuse——"

"Hush!" warned Paddy Joe. "If Sergeant McGrath heard you he'll suspect you of killing Ambrose Trant."

"You've the devil's own neck, Paddy Joe Long," said the harbour-master warmly.

III

Paddy Joe Long walked up the sweep of avenue to Dounbeg House, not with his accustomed easy-going slouch, but with a resolute solidity that bespoke some inflexible purpose; and his face was as grim as a hanging judge's. Yet, in truth, his mind was as flabby as a jelly-fish, and it was only sheer desperation that drove him on to get the interview over one way or another.

When he came in sight of the house round a curve of the drive he addressed it moodily. "You ugly brute! you'd make a man cut the legs off his own mother-in-law!"

The red walls, the cream astragals and cornices, stepped roofs and pepper-caster turrets looked out of place and baroque below the strong, stone-ribbed bulk of the mountains, and the big sandstone porch jutting from the façade spoiled whatever symmetry the building might have had. The fine spread of lawn, now clumped with softly-flaming masses of chrysanthemum, and the tall deciduous trees, rich in autumn tints, relieved but did not atone the ugliness.

Paddy Joe, striding round to the front, took his bearings with practised eye. Down there to the right was the path to the fatal boat-house; away beyond the lawn and shrubbery would be the pool that Alastair and he had poached; and well to the rear was the long slated roof of the stables, with the high wall of the kitchen garden just behind. The keeper's cottage and the kennels would be somewhere back there. A couple of gardeners were at work among the flower-beds, and another was heaping a barrow with fallen leaves. Paddy Joe could smell the faint, cold touch of decay as he went by, and had that first twinge of loneliness that comes with the dying of the year.

An antique bell-pull hung by the jamb of the open door, and the dull clang of a cow-bell reverberated somewhere deep in the house. "There'll be a butler, or maybe a footman," thought Paddy Joe, but, close on his thought, a maid in black and white tripped high-heeled across the parquetry floor.

She would be seeing if Mrs Trant was at home—what name would she say?

"Say Paddy Joe Long, my dear, and if she gives you a shilling for me, well and good."

But the maid smiled wisely to his melancholic smile and ushered him into the inner hall to wait.

After the sunlight outside it was cool and darkish and remotely quiet in there. A grandfather clock ticked with eternal patience somewhere out of sight, many bronze figures gloomed sombrely to themselves, and tall green plants stood out of brazen jars.

Within two minutes the maid was back. Would Mr Long come this way? She led him down a wing of hall, up a few steps, through an arch, and so into a medium-sized high room, looking out on the lawn. No lady's withdrawing room or boudoir this! This was a working woman's room. A roll-top desk, definitely in use, stood at mid-floor; an estate plan on a six-inch scale covered half a wall; and a series of oaken shelves carried heavy-looking japanned boxes. Of course! Was not the lady owner of a large Irish estate, and, doubtless, sometimes played at looking over her agent's accounts. A cased fishing-rod leant in a corner, and a vase of bronze chrysanthemums stood on a small table.

Elspeth Trant rose from a round-armed leather chair at the desk and came a few steps to meet her visitor.

"I am glad you called, Mr Long." Her voice was low and pleasant, and a faint, half-wistful, sideways smile dimpled one cheek. "You are the wise man of the three."

"God between us and harm!" murmured Paddy Joe deprecatingly.

She gave him her hand frankly, and there leaped into his mind the knowledge that she was glad to see him; and with that a wave of ease swept over his perplexed mood.

"Will you sit over here, Mr Long?"

He sat in a straight-backed chair at the corner of the desk and dropped his crumpled tweed hat at his side.

Elspeth Trant, whose image had been clean-etched in his mind, was a surprise to Paddy Joe. He had visualised her as rather a tall slip of a girl in riding-habit, long in the leg, a trace tomboyish, with dusky colour in her cheeks, and a healthy tan over all. But this young widow, in some sort of flowered afternoon dress, was not so tall, and was, somehow, at once slender and curved like a young goddess; and her black hair had a cultivated wave about her ears. A rare and delicate bit of humanity—a twister of the hearts of men. Ah! but her mouth had still that down-droop that went not with the light heart, and her dark-blue eyes looked out at the world too seriously.

She slipped sideways into her own chair, leant back, placed elbows on the high arm-rests, tapped her finger-tips gently together, and looked at Paddy Joe. And Paddy Joe sought hurriedly through the cells of his mind for an opening sentence. She took the initiative while he still groped.

"You know that your friend got into trouble at Castle-inch Fair, Mr Long?"

"I do, ma'am—saw it in the paper—and you were there yourself, I saw too." Now he had got his opening. He placed an elbow on the desk and leant to her a little eagerly. "Did you see the fight, Mrs Trant?"

She smiled whimsically to his assumed eagerness and nodded. "As the famous Jamesy Coffey said, every peg and belt."

"You were lucky."

She opened her eyes. "Do men fight like that in Ireland—so terribly?"

"Not often."

174

"Of course I've seen fisticuffs in the States—men hitting each other angrily, cowboys or visitors—and I have seen professionals in the ring. But tiger and panther——!"

"And a trace of gorilla," added Paddy Joe complacently. "A man wouldn't have time to observe any nicety of rules, and he occupied in making Eudmon Butler stay put—as you say in the West." He grinned at her engagingly. "I haven't spoken to any one who saw the fight, except yourself—maybe you would run over it for me, rally by rally, as it were?"

She shook her head and frowned thoughtfully. "No, it was too elemental. The impression I got from the beginning was that your friend was indestructible and the end merely a matter of time."

"Good!" said Paddy Joe to himself. With an impression like that she was playing no favourites.

"Yes, ma'am," he said aloud. "You never saw Rogan Stuart play international rugby? He was just the same, and I used curse him up and down the pitch. You see, he played for Scotland."

There was a small pause, and she looked at Paddy Joe, her head bent a little sideways, half-quizzically.

"I suppose he let you know that I recognised him at Castleinch?"

"He wrote me the morning of the Fair," said Paddy Joe, dissembling his surprise at the shrewd hit.

"And so you have come up to look me over?" There was a touch of satire in her cool voice. "I gather it was you that hid your friend under a tinker's garb and a tinker's life?"

"Like a needle in a bundle of hay, ma'am——"

"And the needle has been found!"

"At the first look."

"And your friend being laid by the heels for a month,

175

you are afraid for his safety, and want to ensure it—and possibly your own. I have been expecting you, Mr Long. By the way, what threats do you propose to use?"

She was giving Paddy Joe more than he bargained for. "Young lady," said he warmly, "if anything, you are worse than my wife Norrey. Divil the thing I ever had in my mind but she took it out on the point of her tongue." And then and suddenly his voice hardened. "But let me get this clear, Mrs Trant. When a man makes a friend of a man like Rogan Stuart he will not stop at threats to help him. That is the way between men. I would pull this house apart, brick by ugly red brick, and sacrifice every one in it to save the hurting of Rogan Stuart's little finger. He has been hurt enough already. Leave it at that, my lady, threat or no threat."

She looked down at her finger-tips, still gently tapping, and nodded her head slowly, calmness on her like a cloak.

"Yes, men are like that—some men," she said musingly. "They can be so unwaveringly loyal to each other."

"Or to a cause—or to a woman," added Paddy Joe softly.

"Some women are lucky." She looked at him. "There is no need for threats, Mr Long. Your friend is safe as far as I am concerned. You see, I know he is guiltless."

The lightning question, How do you know? leaped into his mind, but he did not put it into words.

"He said so himself," she said, as if in answer.

"You took his word——"

"Why not? He is a man whose word one would take." She smiled that sideways smile. "But I fear he would not take my word—he did not ask for it."

"When it comes to the pass that a woman's word has to be taken," said Paddy Joe, "no man asks for it."

"A Delphic utterance, Mr Long. Very well!" Her

176

blue eyes flashed suddenly, proudly between black lashes. "Let no word be asked—or given."

"Where no word is needed."

Her mood changed again, and she turned to him directly. "I wonder, could you satisfy my woman's curiosity, Mr Long?"

Paddy Joe smiled. "It has been tried, ma'am—same as extracting the square root of two."

"I would like very much to know what you think—what you know happened here that night last June?"

"Did not Rogan——?"

"Mr Stuart can be brutally silent when he likes."

Paddy Joe considered for a moment. Why not, after all?"

"Some of us saw very little, Mrs Trant," he said, and his voice grew apologetic. "The three of us were trying a little experiment up the river—you guessed that; and some day, with the help o' God, I'll be asking you to confirm your invitation to take a fish in daylight. Mind you, we were up to no harm—nothing like gelignite or roach lime. Just a bit of a net round the neck of a pool —about that length."

"Or a bit longer. Go on, Mr Long."

"Well, two of us went up in the coracle, and Rogan Stuart got off at the boat-house below there to patrol the grounds and guard our flank, as it were. In doing so he looked in at an open window and saw two men having a drink, and one man was reprimanding the other; and when you stepped down on the lawn your shawl nearly touched his sleeve. In his progress later you surprised him with an ancient song at a summer-house in the grounds, and ye talked there for a while—until your husband came out and called your name. You may remember that he called twice and after that was silent; and Rogan thought it was time to give us the agreed signal and work his way back to the boat-house. Ambrose Trant, apparently looking round for you, was there before him, but Rogan did not find that out till too late."

Paddy Joe paused for a moment and then went on, his hand explanatory. "See the position now? Ambrose Trant at the boat-house, Rogan coming silently along the path behind him, and we approaching from the river. Probably your husband heard us coming—we were in a hurry. Anyhow, when we scraped round the boat-house there was a dark figure leaning against the corner and looking down at us. We thought it was our scout, but when he spoke we knew better. He told us pungently what we were and urged us to come up and take what was coming to us, but we naturally declined—silently. Whereupon he informed us that he would soon round us up, and with that intention disappeared. By this time Rogan, who had also been surprised, was crouching at the side of the path a few yards away, and, before he could dodge clear, your husband fell right on top of him and grappled. That's how it happened."

"They fought?"

"Hardly that. Rogan Stuart, Mrs Trant, used only what force was necessary to win clear—one or two low tackles that had a winding effect. My friend, who had jumped on to the bank, saw it all. The moment your husband's grip relaxed and before he got his wind back, the two tumbled into the coracle on top of me."

Paddy Joe's voice slowed impressively and his eyes held hers. "As we sat there in the boat we heard feet running on the gravel—feet running very lightly and very fast—and, as they stopped where Ambrose Trant lay, we pushed off silently, let the current take us, and rowed across to camp. That is all we know. But whoever stopped at Ambrose Trant's side left him to lie there till morning."

Her eyes did not leave his. She took him up at once.

"And you decided that the feet that ran so lightly were a woman's feet—my feet? You saw nothing?"

"Nothing. Just a theory we built up—three wise fools. We judged that you were not content, happy—that your marriage was a failure—your husband drinking and jealous too." Her shoulders winced at that. "Actually we put ourselves in your place, saw you finding him, helping him to his feet, imagined his mad resentment and suspicion, heard the ugly words he used, saw you choke them in his throat—what a high-spirited, hot-tempered woman would do. He was rotten to the core. After his manhandling—a finger-snap might be enough to kill him. You would not know. That is the sort of theory we built up. We were so sure that it was a woman who ran—and you were in the grounds. But lately, Mrs Trant, I have discovered that a man runs more lightly than any woman."

Her eyes left his then and looked down at the edge of the desk before her; her head bent forward slowly, and her face became strangely immobile and strangely sad; and after a time she sighed deeply.

"I suppose I should be grateful that you remained silent," she murmured.

"We should be grateful too, my lady, when you come to think of it. You never reported seeing any one in the grounds."

"I was too frightened," she whispered, "and—and what was the use?"

IV

Paddy Joe leant for his old tweed hat and rose to his feet; and she looked up quickly.

"Oh, but you are not going yet, Mr Long?"

179

"I have been trouble enough to you, Mrs Trant, and I am sorry for it."

"But you must have some tea—or a whiskey-and-soda perhaps. Do stay."

She was almost eager, and he realised that there was something on her mind he had not yet touched on.

"My wife has been getting me into the habit of after-noon tea," he said. "I'll take a cup with you gladly, Mrs Trant."

He sat down again, and her finger pressed a bell-push on the desk. Her maid must have been prepared for that signal, for almost immediately she came in with the tray of tea-things.

And Paddy Joe, sitting cross-kneed, with the small cup of thin china in his long brown hands, decided to lighten the conversation.

"I saw you were buying a horse at Castleinch, Mrs Trant," he said. "You didn't clinch that bargain?"

"As a matter of fact, I did," she smiled. "He was a nice colt, and I went up to Coffey's camp the evening of the court and bought him."

"And had a pleasant rough-and-tumble bargain with Jamesy Coffey."

"Why, no! I offered him two hundred and fifty dollars—fifty pounds rather—and he accepted."

"Just like that?"

"Just like that."

"Thunder! What was wrong with Jamesy—or rather, what was wrong with the colt—spavined in every leg?"

"No! Quite sound, except for a touch of shoulder-wrench, hardly noticeable and getting well."

"You have tried him out?"

She hesitated, and the colour came slowly to her face and kept coming. Paddy Joe looked away.

"No. He is still in Coffey's camp," she explained.

"It was inconvenient to take him at the time, and Coffey promised to drop him here on his usual route some time this fall."

And that would not be till after Rogue McCoy got out of jail, considered Paddy Joe. Was that why you blushed, my lady? Are you wanting another look at my tinker's curate? Faith! there was virtue in a cup of tea after all. We will pursue this, black-haired darling!

Elspeth Trant was hurriedly making small talk. "There was a handsome, dark-skinned lad in camp, who wept whole-heartedly when what he called his *Copaleen Rua* was sold on him, and he had to be consoled by a striking young woman with wonderful hair."

"Daheen Coffey and Julie Brien. Shamus Og turned over a new leaf for that red hair—and blotted it badly."

"Poor fellow! I wish him luck. But he should have a rival or two?" She spoke smoothly casual.

"Divil a doubt of it," agreed Paddy Joe, sipping his tea, "or where do men keep their eyes? By the way, I'll be seeing Jamesy some of these days, and could get him to hurry up with the colt."

"No hurry!" she said quickly. "He is quite honest, I suppose."

"His own notion of honesty. The colt is as safe as in your stables. That old hero——"

And, launched into the congenial subject of Jamesy Coffey, Paddy Joe was hard to stop. The lady did not try. She was interested, and her resilient spirit, that needed only happiness for burgeoning, soon lifted head. In a little while he had her eyes asparkle and happy little chuckles breaking from her lips. The life, the outlook, the original methods appealed to every chord in her. Somehow her reaction made Paddy Joe's heart ache.

"Oh!' she cried, throwing her hands up as one throws off a yoke, "that is the life—and that is the kind of life

I lived for years with my father in a country of wider horizons and keener air." And then her shoulders sank and her voice deepened. "But all that is gone forever."

"Who knows, my dear lady?" comforted Paddy Joe. "God is good, and there is a physician of the spirit for every one of us."

She got his drift at once.

"Was that why you sent Rogan Stuart—or Rogue McCoy, as he calls himself—to Jamesy Coffey?"

"The main reason, surely."

"He must have found his physician of the spirit. On the two occasions I spoke to him at Castleinch he gave me the advice a wise man gave him: to change my life absolutely."

"It was not bad advice," said Paddy Joe solidly, his mind busy.

"If one could take it. One has obligations." She looked at him quaintly. "Could you find a physician of the spirit for me, Mr Long?"

"Why wouldn't I?" said Paddy Joe. "Give me time."

He drank off his second cup of tea. By the powders of war! they would win this darling woman into their own company yet.

v

Paddy Joe Long walked down the sweep of avenue, his shoulders swinging to his long stride, his lips whistling a soft tune, and his face serious with the weight of his thoughts. After a time he stopped whistling and his voice lifted in the quaint words wedded to the old tune:

> The old days were fine days,
> Oh, fine days were they !
> Fine days were the old days,
> 'Tis that that I do say.
> Oh ! do you mind those fine days
> From June right round to May ?
> Fine days and fine days and fine days all the way !

He stopped there, for the badly-silenced spit and crackle of a motor engine came to him round the bend of the drive. He moved into the side of the road and looked ahead with interest. The thought of Eudmon Butler came to his mind, but when the car came in sight round the curve a hundred yards away, he saw at a glance that the driver and only occupant was Sir Jerome Trant. The car was an old touring two-seater of serviceable model, probably useful for bucketing over the hilly roads of the estate.

Sir Jerome Trant was within twenty yards when Paddy Joe made up his mind; if he had had longer time to think he probably would have hesitated. He took one pace forward and thrust up an urgent, halting hand, every finger extended. The engine roared briefly on a free clutch, the wheels grated on the packed gravel, and the car slid to a stop two lengths past him. He walked back slowly to the left side of the car.

"Excuse me, Sir Jerome," he said, above the sound of the engine. "I wanted to speak to you."

"Well, sir? Oh, you're Mr Long, who was camping across the bay last summer?" He smiled. "Wanting some late fishing?"

Paddy Joe shook his head very definitely. "Much more serious business than fishing, Sir Jerome." And his tone proclaimed how serious the business was.

The baronet switched off the power, and the engine sighed twice into silence.

"Serious, Mr Long?' he queried quietly.

"Very, sir."

Paddy Joe placed a foot on the running-board and leant an arm on the closed door, and his eyes took in the elder man keenly.

A short, broad-shouldered figure, with strong square hands resting on the wheel—hands that might crush and kill. His face was aquiline and strongly lined, and his profuse iron-grey hair had a fine leonine sweep. No weak man this! But there was too much suffusion of blood in his face, his eye-sockets were deeply wrinkled, and the whites of his brown eyes showed veinings of red.

Paddy Joe tightened his hardihood before he spoke.

"Last June, Sir Jerome, the night your son was killed, three men were within the policies of this house."

The baronet cleared his throat after some habit he had acquired in the diplomatic service, but gave no other sign.

"Three men?"

"Three strange men. They were near the boat-house when your son was killed."

Sir Jerome was steady as a rock. "Did they do the killing?"

"No."

"Why have they remained silent, then? The police would have welcomed any evidence they might have had."

"They remained silent," said Paddy Joe steadily, "because they did not want to implicate a woman."

"A woman, Mr Long?" Paddy Joe saw the hands slowly clench on the wheel rim.

"Any woman, Sir Jerome, but especially one."

"You'll have to be more explicit, I fear."

"I will," said Paddy Joe, and in his own mind he asked forgiveness for the half-truth he was about to tell.

"They, the three friends, were up the river here that night, and, coming back, pulled in at the side of the boat-house. As they lay there they heard the sounds of struggle on the path, and a heavy fall, and then the sound of feet running."

"Did they see who ran away?" The baronet had taken the half-truth.

Paddy Joe did not answer that question. "We will implicate no one directly," he said. "The feet that ran ran very lightly and very fast."

"A woman's feet, you would suggest?" The voice sterned. "A man is not easily killed by a woman's hands, sir."

"No. But Ambrose Trant's body was found there next morning—and a touch might have killed him, as you know."

Sir Jerome frowned puzzledly. "But why do you act now—after months?"

"Because one of the three men was in the grounds for a while that night, and that fact is known—by whom I will not say. But there is now some risk that that man will be held for enquiry. If he is his two friends will safeguard him at all costs."

"By divulging all they know."

"Exactly."

"Why speak to me, Mr Long?"

"Because the three men are still firm in their desire to hurt no one. They will remain silent—if this house remains silent."

The baronet was prompt—too prompt with his reply. "I see your point. I can give you that assurance, Mr Long."

"You speak only for yourself, Sir Jerome?"

"You can leave the woman—any woman out of it."

Paddy Joe looked him steadily in the eye and slowly, obdurately shook his head. "I wish we could, but, when a friend is in danger, I will take no risk on God's earth."

The elder man smiled sadly into Paddy Joe's face.

"But this woman you will leave out of it, Mr Long," he said, quietly insistent. "You see, it was I killed my son Ambrose—and I run very lightly still."

Paddy Joe said nothing. He gazed down at his foot on the running-board and still said nothing. He said nothing for so long that the baronet, watching him half-furtively, frowned, and broke into speech almost eager—and so fluently that the speech seemed rehearsed.

"You can hardly doubt my word on that, sir. My evidence is there if you insist. The whole thing was unfortunate—accidental. My son and I were not on the best of terms because—well, because of his way of life. Take that night! There had been some poaching on the river, and we decided to pull up to the higher pool about midnight and there lie in wait. Before setting out we had a drink in my office and quarrelled—rather badly—and the quarrel broke out again on our way down to the boat-house. There he said something—something that made me see red—and I promptly tried to choke the words in his throat. I am very strong in the hands, I may tell you, and he sank under my grip. I just threw him from me. And I ran away for two reasons. I had an uncontrollable desire to stamp on his face, and I heard your boat scrape the wall of the boat-house. I did not want any one to know of our quarrel. As you suggested just now, he was easily killed—his heart rotten, I suppose. I did not know he was dead till next morning." Sir Jerome paused and finished quietly. "You can take my assurance, if you still wish to implicate no one, Mr Long."

"We will implicate no one," said Paddy Joe in a low voice. He did not raise his eyes as he stepped back from the car. There followed a pause, queerly drawn out, then the self-starter purred metallically, the engine roared, and he was alone in the middle of the road.

He lifted his eyes and watched the car disappear round the curve.   Sadly he shook his head.

"You lie neatly, strong man," he murmured, "but that time you lied too damn neatly.   Thunder! but haven't I plenty to tell that Norrey of mine."

CHAPTER V

I

THE chief warder, a thin black-haired man with a student's face, walked across the paved outer yard of the prison with Rogue McCoy, who walked with his head down. Rogue's hair-cut was a week old, his chin smooth after recent shaving; and there was no bandage on his right hand nor sticking-plaster on brow or cheek.

"Glad to be going out, McCoy?" the chief warder enquired.

"I suppose I am, chief," replied Rogue dully.

"Not too hard on you, were we?"

"You were very decent."

"We knew why you were in, of course. The man that licked the Black Captain could not be a bad man—in any way. This your first spell?"

"It is, chief."

"Make it your last. I don't know anything about you —or why you hide your identity in that of a tinker—but we've had men like you in here before, mostly political prisoners, and their minds suffered more than their bodies. Minds too active, I suppose. The ordinary thug hasn't a mind to suffer. I heard you slept hardly at all?"

"About as usual."

"Sorry for you, then. Keep outside if you can."

"Thanks, chief! I'll remember. By the way, could you tell me when Shamus Og Coffey gets out—the exact date."

"Three months, wasn't it—yes! The day before

Christmas Eve, then—the same hour. Shamus Og is all right, and will probably settle down, like his father before him."

They came under the gloom of the arch, and their footsteps echoed from the roof and from the iron-bolted gate in front of them. The chief nodded to the gate warder, and the huge key clicked smoothly in the wards.

"Well, good-bye and good luck!" The two men shook hands. "Hope we don't meet again, in here."

Rogue stepped through the narrow wicket into freedom, and the door clanged behind him. He took two steps forward and stopped.

It was eight o'clock of a late October morning, and a fine morning for that season of the year. Sharp and clear, with a high thin sky. The trees, tall above a high wall up the road, had lost little of their foliage, and shimmered ruddy and golden in the early sun; the walls of the prison cast a shadow across the wide street, but the long, two-storied public-house at the other side was in the full morning light, and its plate windows and varnished doors glistened brightly.

It was the sunlight beyond the shadow that made Rogue McCoy lonesome. It was so serene and unconcerned, in so remote a dimension from himself. And why not? What did he matter—what did the sun matter? And if it came to that, he did not care a hoot for the sun or for himself. Yet he was lonesome—lonesome.

He looked up and down the street, and the street was empty. Then a milk-cart clattered across a side entry lower down, and again the street was empty—empty as Rogue McCoy. He thrust his hands deep into his pockets and looked down at the cold stones. What was he to do now? What in all grey life was he to do now?

"Give him time—give him time!" Some entity that was himself implored an entity that was himself. "He will be able to carry on—if you give him a little time."

And there an upbraiding voice spoke behind him.

"Couldn't he bid a friend good-morrow?"

Rogue McCoy, almost with the gesture of a woman, put his hand over his breast and turned round—not too fast.

Jamesy Coffey, squat, blue-jowled, bowler-hatted, propped a shoulder close beside the wicket-gate. He had been there all the time, and he was scowling savagely.

"Divil such hours ye keep! I'been stuck here above two hours—and you at your ham and eggs."

Rogue stepped close to him, caught him by the lapels of his coat, drew him away from the gate, and shook him softly back and forth. He dared not try to speak.

"Take your jail-bird hands off me," warned Jamesy, but he made no effort to free himself. He was shrewdly examining his man, his charge, his ladeen. He read behind the wanness of those grey eyes, deep-set under brow; he noted the pinched cheeks below the stubborn strength of cheek-bones; he knew the desperate resoluteness of that mouth hiding so much pain. He thrust a hand into breast-pocket.

"The pub beyond won't be open for hours," he said, "but try a pull at this."

"This" was a flat noggin of whiskey. "There, 'tis for you." He spoke with the cork in his teeth. "An' lave a small sup at the bottom."

Rogue threw back his head and the liquor gurgled.

"Oh murther!" lamented Jamesy.

Rogue reached him the bottle and Jamesy held it up to the light. "The —— fool I was! But, sure, I always was. An' why didn't I take me own share first?"

"Good morning to you, strange man!" said Rogue,

finding his voice at last. "You remind me of one Jamesy Coffey I used to know."

Jamesy Coffey made no retort. His head was back and he looked coldly at Rogue down his nose. He took but a single mouthful, slapped the cork home, and thrust the bottle into breast-pocket. "Couldn't take more on an empty stomach, and we'll keep a sup for Maag Carty —she's wake, the crathur, in the mornin's." He caught Rogue roughly by the sleeve. "Come along with you! My breakfast is waitin', an' we have a good step of a walk before us."

The two turned side by side and walked up the lifting road. The road led away from the town and curved between high walls, with trees making an arch overhead. Jamesy walked slowly.

"No doubt the pins'll be a bit awkward under you," he said.

For answer Rogue strode ahead at a great rate and beckoned Jamesy on, but that stolid man kept his own pace.

"Where's the camp?" Rogue enquired, "and how are you all—Maag Carty and Julie Brien and Daheen?"

"The camp's round by Ballyard. An' what would be wrong with any one, barrin' myself? Hard they were to manage, but I kept a tight hold on 'em, I tell you."

"And belted Daheen to his fifth reader."

"Wisha! the poor little devil had plenty to teach him. Tell me, did you see Shamus Og at all?"

"To be sure. Jail is no worse than a hotel to him. Shared a packet of fags with me last week—and that reminds me—I'll smoke four straight pipes of your tobacco as soon as Maag Carty feeds me."

"Will you so? The first thing I did this mornin' was to hide me morsel o' plug."

"With Daheen watching you! That'll be all right. Say, have we *Copaleen Rua* still on our hands?"

Jamesy hesitated, and then: "I sold him."

"Twenty pounds?"

"I got fifty," said Jamesy quietly, without boastfulness.

Rogue lifted his face to the sky and laughed a great unbelieving laugh.

"The devil choke you!" Jamesy cursed him. "Pity the quod didn't silence the roarin' gullet of you. I tell you I got fifty."

"Whom did you cheat?"

"No one—a good judge of a horse. Fifty was offered and fifty I took; and could I refuse? I ask you that, now—could I refuse it?" He shook a fist fervently.

"Never mind. I know your purchaser. You're a dishonest old shark, but the money will come in handy for a couple of youngsters up at Limerick Junction."

"You'll buy nawthin' with that money," said Jamesy firmly. "There's the camp below there."

The road had come to the top of the hill, and turned sharply to the right; and they were in open country. The high wall, backed by trees, was still on one hand, but, on the other, a great spread of country swept up to the mountains. Just beneath them a short slope dipped to the bottom of a verdant valley, and, beyond, the long stretch of thorn-hedged, house-dotted pasture lands ran up into the breasts of the great hills of Kerry; tall, round-topped, deep-brown hills folded with purple valleys: Slievemish, Caherconree, Baurtregaum, all the way out to the far peak of Brandon above the green waters of the Atlantic Sea; and, over all, the high fragile sky, with the young sun casting long shadows.

Rogue drew in a deep breath. "And I so sorrowful a little time ago."

"'Tis the whiskey stirring."

A hundred yards down the road an open gate led into a small paddock, and the stove-pipe of the van showed beyond over the hawthorn hedge. In the open gateway Daheen stood sentinel, and the moment he saw Jamesy and Rogue appear, he leaped a foot into the air and shouted across the field. But he did not run to meet them. Suddenly he was smitten with a shyness, shouldered the wooden post of the gateway, and rubbed a broken boot-toe into the clay.

Rogue walked forward soberly and halted before him. "Put it there, Daheen Coffey," he greeted, offering open hand. "Glad am I to see you."

Daheen looked up at him with serious eyes, and saw a man on his own level greeting him seriously. They shook hands ceremoniously. "Good mornin', Rogue McCoy!"

"We'll have a lot to talk about," said Rogue, "but it will keep. Have you a bite of breakfast waiting for me?"

"A pound of rashers an' a pan of eggs—wait till I hurry it up for you." And he lifted up his light young feet and galloped across the field, the two men following slowly.

And now Julie Brien and the lurcher dog came running, the girl's voice as high and clear as the welcoming bark of the dog, her hair leaping like a ruddy flame, and her amber eyes glistening and warm.

The dog arrived first and leaped to Rogue's welcoming "Oh-ho, Tomboy!"

Julie pushed the dog aside and caught Rogue's two hands in hers. "Oh, Rogue, Rogue! You'll be weak as a rush."

"Not so weak, red-top—see!" He swung her playfully, and she threw her lithe body backwards and swung him in turn.

"Stop that, the two of ye!" shouted Jamesy Coffey.

"Sure, I had a grand time, Julie," Rogue told her.

"Shamus Og and myself used be smoking a fag on the quiet and we breaking stones. He sent a message to you, Julie Brien."

She at once sobered. "A lie you're telling now, Rogue McCoy?"

"I am not." He gave her red head a gentle pull. "'You'll be going out in four days,' said he. 'I will,' said I, 'and will I carry the message in your eyes?' 'Carry any message you can read,' said he, and——"

"Keep your folly to yourself, Rogue—come on to your breakfast."

But, though her face did not colour, he could see the pulse beating in her neck.

They arrived at the angle of the paddock, where a runnel of clear water gushed into the ditch from a field drain. And there was Maag Carty, the provider, sitting on her heels and presiding like a sombre priestess over the fire blazing within the rough but cunningly-built hearth. A lidded pan was propped over the flame, and the big kettle steamed.

"Our little clutch is here again," came her bell voice, but her eyes did not lift to the homing member of the brood.

He came and crouched at her side, and placed both hands on her knee in fealty. "I am glad to be home, dark mother."

Her long fine hand came to the back of his neck where the hair was crisp, and the great black eyes met the too-steady ones. He felt the soothing balm of her fingers and the soothing beat of her voice.

"Heart's darling! I will make you sleep yet."

"And change my dreams too, O mother," he whispered, "rolling waters, and the wind that makes no sound—and the eyes beseeching me, and I tied."

"God will do that for us, childeen."

Rogue stood upright and looked round the camp. There it all was: the gaily-painted van, the patched tilt, the old white horse—now without hobbles—the dainty jennet nibbling in the hedge bottom, and—could he believe his eyes? He blinked and looked again.

"Where is Jamesy Coffey?" he roared.

"I am here, where I have a right to be," said Jamesy boldly, but with a doubt in his eye.

Rogue strode at him and shook a fist under his nose. "You ancient, shameless, profligate purveyor of terminological inexactitudes——"

"Japus!" exclaimed Daheen delightedly. "He is the same as always."

"Fair play!" demanded Jamesy hotly. "Give me fair play, you jail-bird!"

"Did you tell me you sold *Copaleen Rua*?"

"I did, too."

"What chestnut horse is that, then, tethered behind the tilt?"

"That's *Copaleen Rua*."

"Whom did you sell him to?"

"The young widow Trant of Dounbeg. She wasn't ready to take him for a piece yet."

Rogue contemplated that.

"What did you say you got for the colt?" he enquired then, carelessly.

"Fifty pounds—an' got it."

"You poor done collector of lame dogs!"

"What do you mane?"

"Bah!" A stiff arm pushed him away, as if contemptuously. "You are no good any more. You have lost your punch. There is nothing but soggy porridge under your hat. Why in thunder did you not leave the sale to Daheen? He would have held out for sixty—and got it. Wouldn't you, Daheen?"

"I would try, anyway," agreed Daheen.

Jamesy Coffey's mouth opened; he lifted his bowler hat, and, with a smack, rammed it back again; a sheer dismay loosened all his features.

"Tare-an'-agers!" he cried. "An' isn't it true for him? I'm done. That finishes me. That's the end of Jamesy Coffey." His voice grew earnest. "Maag— Maag Carty," he implored, "when me few days are past, all I ask of you is to give me a dacent wake, with three half-tierces of porter, an' brass handles on me coffin."

"And 'tis full time we had a decent wake over the old Turk," said a quiet voice behind them.

II

Paddy Joe Long had come across the paddock without being seen, and slouched easily into their midst.

"*Thanaman Dhiaoul!*" exploded Jamesy. "Look who's here—like a bad ha'penny!" He strode at Paddy Joe and shook fist under his nose. "Did you hear what the robber said to me?"

"Things I would stand from no man, Jamesy."

"An' that's the sort of fellow you saddled on me, you thief o' the world." Jamesy frowned suspiciously. "Maybe you're here to take him off me hands?"

"If you want to pitch him out on his ear?"

"No," said Jamesy firmly. "I never threw a man on the roadside yet. The *boctan*—the poor fellow—is welcome to his bite an' sup." He looked over his shoulder towards Maag Carty. "An' when are we gettin' our bite o' food, I'd like to know?"

"'Tis ready now, kind man," said his wife.

Paddy Joe walked across to Rogue McCoy, and their hands met firmly. Paddy Joe's eyes took his man in.

"Home again, tinker!" he greeted. "Glad to see you keep the rough side of your tongue in practice."

"I have to," said Rogue.

"The divil melt the pair of ye!" said Jamesy.

Paddy Joe greeted Julie Brien and Daheen with a wave of hand and strolled across to the fireside. He placed a finger on Maag Carty's shoulder.

"Have you a bite o' breakfast for me under that lid, woman-o'-the-house?"

"I have, long darling. In the night I saw you coming —and you welcome." She lifted her softly-ringing voice. "Come away, children, or the eggs will be like the stones of the road."

"Sit down here, Mr Long," piped Daheen, "an' I'll carry the plates."

"Some one has been putting manners into you, young fellow," said Paddy Joe.

"The beltin's I do be givin' him," suggested Jamesy complacently.

"You couldn't belt a herrin' off a tongs," his son derided, and dodged clear.

III

The little camp partook of breakfast—and a good breakfast—and, thanks to Rogue McCoy and Paddy Joe, the proper atmosphere had been nourished and was maintained. Julie Brien and Paddy Joe sat comfortably at the head of the van steps, Jamesy Coffey sat on his soap-box at the bottom, and Rogue and Daheen close together on the ground at his feet; Maag Carty remained as ever at her own place by the fire.

Rogue McCoy drank strong tea out of an enamelled mug, and Daheen took the empty mug to his step-mother to be replenished. Rogue smiled a little grimly, noting that the subject of his time in jail had been carefully avoided. Did they intend to avoid that episode lest they hurt him, lest he feel degraded? But he was far outside any sense of hurt or degradation, and he must make that clear.

"Were you ever in jail, Paddy Joe Long?" he enquired casually.

"Once," said Paddy Joe carelessly. "Fourteen days in the Tombs Prison, New York, for keeping a fighting-dog."

"You got off light," remarked Jamesy. "Let me see, now. The last time I was there—yes—twelve—fifteen years ago, for batin' the head of a black-an'-tan in the Main Guard at Clonmel. But I was respectable that time—I was what they call a political prisoner in Cork Jail."

"Give me Stranleigh Jail every time," said Rogue.

"Faith, you'll have your choice of jails, me bucko, if you keep the road you're on," commented Jamesy.

"And Stranleigh will be my choice. Shamus Og and myself had a great time. I have a story or two for you, Jamesy, when we get under the tilt to-night."

"An' for me too," said Daheen.

"Oho! Are you promoted to the man's place?"

"Time for me. I'll sleep in the middle."

"An' there'll be none of Shamus Og's stories aither," said Jamesy.

"Not a word. Mind you, but for Shamus Og I should have had a tough time. He knows all the dodges and would go out of his way any day to help a friend. I was let off picking oakum because of my thumb, and he showed me the only proper way to break stones. You don't use a ten-pound hammer and wallop the stone from your heel up. No, sir! A three-ounce head, with a white-thorn shaft that carries no jar to your hands, and you look for the fault that's in every stone, and that you hit in a certain way—you know—with a flick and hold of the wrist that brings the hammer up of itself. There's a great art in it. And when the warder is looking the other way you take a pull at a fag and tap tap away with your left hand, and talk to your pal out of the side of your mouth. That way! See, Daheen? Listen, boyeen! Do you know where our da hid away his plug of 'bacca this morning?"

Daheen's eyes danced. He winked knowingly, rapped his outer jacket pocket, and nodded backward towards his father. Rogue drained his mug and turned cautiously towards the old man, who was talking over his shoulder to Paddy Joe.

Rogue looked at the plug of tobacco in the palm of his hand, a four-ounce bar of Bendigo that had not been touched yet by knife, and he nodded his head slowly and many times, and a whimsical, queerly tender smile lightened his strong face.

Jamesy turned and cleared his throat. "Well, well! I think I'll be havin' a smoke to myself; an' if there's any one can't afford the price of a smoke, that's his look-out."

He thrust his hand into the wide-flapped pocket of his old-fashioned half-morning-coat, and felt hurriedly.

"Blood an' turf!" he yelped. "What robber have we with us? Daheen, you—! did you have your hand in me pocket?"

"Maybe there's a hole in it," suggested Rogue.

"You thief! What's that hidin' in the heel of your fist, Rogue McCoy. Let me have a look at it!"

"Oh well! There's your old plug. It would poison a pup."

He thrust it into Jamesy's hand, and Jamesy, after one look, held it up and swore. "The devil melt you! A whole sound plug it was a minute ago, and already he has nicked the half of it." He turned furiously to Rogue. "There! Have that half with the other half, an' may it scorch the tongue off you. And Jamesy Coffey isn't so foolish to keep all his eggs in one basket: he has a bit in his other pocket as well."

Paddy Joe arched back his long throat and laughed, and his laughter was a pleasant thing to hear. He could thank God with all his heart then. Once again was Rogue McCoy a man amongst men, simple men, kindly men, men who could be terrible, men who used strong language as a matter of course, but always men who could never hide their decent hearts. Whatever else he might have done in life, he had done well in apprenticing Rogan Stuart to Jamesy Coffey.

"What's the *bosthoon* laughing at?" Jamesy wanted to know.

"At one Jamesy Coffey, of course," Rogue told him.

"The divil choke him."

"And at one Rogue McCoy too," said Paddy Joe.

"That's no great harm," said Jamesy.

Rogue puffed slowly and ruminatively at his pipe. There was one problem that called aloud for a solution, and how to tackle it effectively puzzled him; but he would make a tentative beginning right now.

"Daheen, this is a good place for a camp."

"Yes so," agreed Daheen heartily. "I heard a cock pheasant beyond in the wood early this morning."

"A likely place. And a mountain hare across there, I bet you. You and I might do worse than settle down here till about the first of the New Year."

"You'll sleep in the bottom of the hedge, then," said Jamesy sourly. "This very day I'll be makin' tracks out of this hole for Shannonside."

"You heartless old Turk! Listen, Daheen! This

morning, when I came out of the jail gate, I was terrible lonesome—till a friend met me, and then I wasn't lonesome. Look now, if you put that mountain on top of me—that big fellow—it would be no heavier than the weight of loneliness on me—till I heard a friend's voice; and after that, I could hold up that mountain and the one next it in that hand and that hand. I could so."

"I know what ye're drivin' at," said Jamesy Coffey, a stubborn note in his voice. "Dam' well I know! But let me tell you, Shamus Og had a pocketful of silver the last time I saw him, and it will buy him a ticket to Limerick—where he wants to be."

"Do you hear that, Daheen? Shamus Og is where he is for helping an old rogue to sell a horse—for helping us all, and will no one——"

Julie Brien, her eyes stormy and troubled, slid quickly down from the head of the steps, gathered up a few plates, went across to the drain-spout, and, her back turned, began busily rinsing.

Rogue McCoy watched her lowered red head and went on ruthlessly.

"The dark of the year it will be, and raw Christmas weather. Eight o'clock in the morning and the dawn breaking; the wind cold and the rain slanting. Stranleigh town in December, and even the ducks weary of rain. Have we no heart in us at all? And mind you, this was a fine sunny morning—and I was ready to cry——"

Jamesy Coffey watched Julie Brien too. "No use you talking, Rogue McCoy. All December we'll be up at Tarbert Island, thirty miles from here. There's a bit of an iron boat there I bought, an' I'll have men scrappin' her for Cardiff. An' that's all there is about it."

"Very well so," said Rogue resignedly. "The whole world knows you are a terrible tyrant and not happy unless you get your own way. But, let me tell you, and I don't care who hears me, Shamus Og deserves better treatment. Maybe he left your camp in a tantrum—and maybe he had cause—but remember that he has made good and—is—tied—to—no one." He spaced the words slowly. "He has got together a nice show, and down he comes to see his own and be near his own, and he has no one to look to but his own—and will there be no one there to give him the friendly hand and the helping word——"

The bell voice of Maag Carty broke in on his eloquence.

"Be not trying too much, white darling. You may be drawing down unhappiness for a brief joy."

"I may surely," said Rogue gloomily. "But do you know, dark mother?"

"That future is hidden. I am afraid."

"I am not," said Rogue firmly.

And Julie Brien turned and smiled at him.

Here Paddy Joe spoke to Jamesy Coffey.

"I have a message for you, Jamesy."

"Who sent it?"

"Young Mrs Trant of Dounbeg. She would like that colt she bought from you at Castleinch. Could you drop him at Dounbeg before making Tarbert Island?"

"I could—and charge her the price of his keep. We'll take a turn round that way, anyway."

"In your own time," said Paddy Joe, and came down the steps to the ground. He nodded a head sideways to Rogue McCoy, and the two men walked up the paddock towards the road.

IV

Paddy Joe leant a shoulder against one of the gateposts and slowly filled his pipe. Rogue McCoy stood in the middle of the gap and smoked leisurely.

"You fit in here nicely," remarked Paddy Joe. "I thought you would. I'm told that Jamesy haunted the jail gates for the past week, afraid you might slip away on him unbeknownst. Do you propose to stay on in the camp?"

"Unless you think I ought not to," said Rogue after a pause. "There are a couple of things I want to do—and one of them is not so easy. You got my letter? Do you think I should clear out?"

"There is no need any longer, in my opinion. I got your letter, and, next morning, my wife packed me straight off to Dounbeg to beard the lioness in her den. I did more than that—but wait till I tell you."

Paddy Joe told him very fully of the double interview, and, as Rogan listened, his face grew stern.

"What do you think?" Paddy Joe enquired at the end.

"The man was lying, almost certainly."

"Why?"

"To shield the woman. He has a very great affection for her, and probably knows—or is afraid—that she is guilty of her husband's death."

"A very great affection that would be!" said his friend, a little cynically.

"And a great understanding. Remember that theory of yours as to how Trant's death may have come about?"

"Theories like that are not always sound, thank the Lord! Suppose neither of them is guilty—who is?"

"There is—but did he need to kill?"

"Captain Eudmon Butler? Who knows? Remember that he was following Elspeth Trant into the room that night at Dounbeg and then slipped back into the dark! Why—and where did he go? Might he not have slipped into the grounds by another door? That would be exactly in his character."

"I saw or heard nothing of him."

"Yet, where was he? That is something unexplained in the whole bad business."

Rogue McCoy threw his hands wide. "It is none of my business," he said wearily.

"It should be some one's business," gave back Paddy Joe firmly, "and somehow we keep coming into it—despite us. Look here, Rogue! In your letter you made two references to Elspeth Trant, from which I gathered that she is worthy of a better fate than to fall into Eudmon Butler's clutches."

"Any woman is."

"Probably. Here are the considerations briefly: If she is guilty, as we theorised, she, in a mental state of despairing fatalism, might easily fall a victim, unless, well—unless she finds something to live for. Secondly, if Butler is guilty, how disastrous for her to become his wife. Something should be done. I don't know how; but you are going up there with the colt, and——"

And there Rogue stopped him.

"No. I am not going up there."

"No?"

"No."

Paddy Joe looked at him curiously. Rogue stood wide-legged, looking down at the little camp, his face set and gloomy, and his smokeless pipe clenched in his teeth. Paddy Joe looked down there too. Julie Brien walked between van and tilt, looked up at them and waved her hand lightly. She flaunted the lovely lines of youth and maturity, and the low sun made an oriflamme of her hair. Could Rogue McCoy be in camp with her all these months and not feel a stirring of the blood? Would such a stirring harden him against all others? Was it some strange form of self-torture or self-sacrifice that was making him plead Shamus Og's cause? . . .

Rogue was speaking half-musingly. "No, I cannot go,

Paddy Joe. I will not go. Already I have given her your advice—the very wine of it—and I will have nothing more to do with Elspeth Trant. I will have nothing more to do with any woman." He turned to his friend and smiled a smile that mocked himself. "Before God, I am afraid to go, Paddy Joe."

Paddy Joe's pulse stirred, yet his voice was cool.

"What will you do?"

"There is some business that I have to attend to in Dublin—long neglected. I will run up there for a couple of weeks and, later, join up with the camp at Tarbert Island—to do what I can for a friend."

"I see," said Paddy Joe. He leant heavily against the gate-post and looked down at the ground, his head moving sadly, heavily. "It can't be helped. Yet if a woman can be saved a man should be found to save her, despite all pain. What are men for anyway?"

"Don't ask me, Paddy Joe," besought Rogue McCoy. "I am not able—I am not of the men that count."

"I will not ask, brother. Go your own road, for I know it will not be a road on which you will be ashamed to look back."

PART III: THE END OF THE ROAD

CHAPTER I

I

THE green-orange-and-white-painted van with the high-set, red-curtained windows swayed behind the white horse down the long, winding street of Dounbeg, where lodging-houses with pretentious names like Atlantic Prospect and Ocean View turned their stuccoed fronts resolutely from the sea. Daheen held reins and switch under the jut-over, and tall Maag Carty sat at his side, jet ear-rings dangling to her shoulders, short pipe in mouth, eyes looking at nothing out of aquiline face.

Behind the van lumbered the ancient tilt-cart drawn by the dainty-footed jennet. Julie Brien loosely held the reins on the driving bench, her shoulders lissome to the sway of the cart and her red hair showing below a black knitted cap.

Jamesy Coffey, as ever, sat on the tail of the tilt, brown boots dangling, bowler hat on back hair, unbelievably short pipe jutting over blue jowl. He gloomily contemplated the fine legs of a tall, nicely-coupled chestnut colt that walked soberly, but without the least trace of limp, to a short leading-rein. Sometimes the colt's black muzzle almost touched the old man's knee. Tomboy, the lurcher, trotted under the axle, his sharp nose a bare inch from the jennet's lively heels.

Rogue McCoy? Alas! Rogue McCoy was not here. Rogue had left the camp ten days before on business of his own, with a promise to rejoin it again at Tarbert Island.

The van swayed past a big modern hotel fronted by a

spread of tennis lawn, and, as it went by, the curtain of one of the side windows of the bar moved an inch aside, as if some one were covertly watching. Neither Daheen, Julie, nor Jamesy saw that moving curtain, but Maag Carty turned a slow head, gazed quiet-faced at the window, and lifted a hand in a small gesture that might be of pity or welcome.

"When one is driven one comes, my jewel," she murmured.

"What is it, Ma?" enquired Daheen.

"Good news for you, ladeen."

"What news?"

"To-morrow you will know."

"Is it a drame you had? Maybe 'twould be Rogue McCoy coming home?"

"That would be good news!"

"The best in a month o' Sundays." Daheen loved Rogue McCoy better than he would ever love god or woman.

The van swung right, round a green-summited rocky mound, and the keen breeze of late fall blew about them up the length of the bay. It was October weather, and, though the sun was behind clouds, the atmosphere was wonderfully clear, so that the white horses could be seen racing the breeze on the blue-steel surface of the sea all the way down to Corullish Narrows, and the mountains, brown and purple and limestone grey, stood apart in one far-flung clean perspective.

Beyond the mound, in the angle of the brae, was a small green common, and on to this Daheen guided the van. In a sheltered corner, behind the rocky ribs of the mound, were the scars of old camp fires. Jamesy scrambled and kicked himself down from the tail of the tilt, and grunted dolorously in the process.

"Here we are, now," he grumbled, "an' 'tisn't much

good it will do us. What the divil are ye all doin' an' dinner-time on us?"

He ambled forward and began fussily to unhitch the jennet; already Daheen was at the traces of the white horse. Julie Brien with deft hands was building up the hearth of rough stones and methodically laying the fire of bog-pine and peat; Maag Carty was gathering her utensils and provisions out of the van. The camp was run on a long-practised routine, and in a few minutes horse and jennet were hobbled and pegged out to graze the short herbage, the fire was alight, Julie Brien attending her mother at the blazing fire, Daheen gambolling with Tomboy, and Jamesy Coffey sitting on his soapbox.

Presently Daheen shoved the dog aside and went to fondle the chestnut colt. "Da!" he called, and his voice was uncertain, "are ye takin' me *Copaleen Rua* up to the big house to-day?"

"I amn't," growled Jamesy. "There's time enough." He rubbed his blue chin and looked out to sea and up at blue sky. "But all the same I might be up there before to-morrow morning. The wind will come up in the night and there'll be a good moon—'tisn't a chance we do be often getting."

"If the keeper catches you," warned Julie, "you'll get a month in jail."

"That fellow, Mullally! He'll be sound asleep in his bed—an' whether or no, he could not catch me, an' him a weasel."

"Take me with you, Da," besought Daheen eagerly.

"I will not, you thief. A small buck-rabbit would frighten the life out of you. I'll take Julie Brien—she might like a bit of a vacation in jail—she's not been there yet, an'—" he looked slyly at her—"an' she would be out at the same time as Shamus Og."

Julie turned away to the fire. "Oh! I'll come with you if you want me," she said gloomily.

"If Rogue McCoy was here he'd take me," protested Daheen.

"'Tis enough bad notions he's put in your head already," snapped his father, and his voice lifted in grievance. "An' isn't it a fine thing that an ould man like me has to be running the bloody chance of a month in jail to be puttin' food in the mouths of ye, an' me apprentice—me fine apprentice—Rogue McCoy, ramblin' round the streets o' Dublin an' lookin' in at every second pub from Mooney's up to Tom Neary's."

'Maybe he is not so far away as Dublin, darling man," said his wife over her shoulder.

"Isn't he so?" said Jamesy quickly. "Wait ye then, an' the minute I set eyes on him ye'll hear me use the rough side of me tongue."

Maag Carty's quiet hint seemed to put life in the old man. He sat up on his soap-box, felt for pipe and tobacco, and began briskly slicing plug. "Woman," he cried, "will ye hurry up with my dinner an' me wantin' to go up town on a bit of a message?"

"Don't go near the town to-day, my light," advised Maag Carty quietly.

"I will if I like," proclaimed Jamesy.

II

Jamesy Coffey and Julie Brien leant against the tall iron gates and looked through the bars.

"The house is a long way up the drive," Jamesy whispered.

Julie turned the heavy knob and pressed forward with her knee.

"H-s-sh!" warned Jamesy. "Don't you see the light

in the lodge window? Do you want them to hear us? Come on."

They turned from the gates and slipped below the demesne wall on the grass edging of the road. In the afternoon Jamesy had been down from the camp at the mound to prospect the ground, and had noted where the mortar had fallen from between two badly-set stones. He had lined the spot from the bulky ruins of a magpie's nest in a hawthorn on the opposite side of the road, and was now looking out for his marks.

"'Tis a night poor honest fellows would be thankin' God for," he remarked with unusual cheerfulness.

A blowing night in October with a full moon. Every half-hour or so the cloud-rack blew up over the mountains, shrouded the faint stars, and scattered a spit of rain from the mouth of the wind; and the woods, spreading back from the demesne wall, soughed lonesomely, and the soughing ran away and died in the distance as the squalls came and went. And when the soughing of the wind died down, there arose the sough and thud of the waves on the gravelly shore of the bay.

"We're near it now," Jamesy whispered presently, his eye across the road and his hands feeling at the wall. "Yes—here is the crack. Could you give me a push up?"

"All of you?"

"Wait, then! You go first. Give me a hould of you."

He fitted her toe in the gap between the stones, got his thick shoulder under, and she swung lithely on to the crown of the wall as if it were a saddle.

"Silly!" she hissed, looking down at him. "You nearly threw me over it. Give me your hand."

"Drop this on the other side," he whispered, and reached her his poaching engine. It was no more than a short-stocked, muzzle-loading, percussion-cap, double-barrelled shot-gun, the barrels of which had been cut down to a mere nine inches. At the moment it was loaded in each barrel with a pinch of diamond-grain black powder and three pellets of number four shot, enough to kill a bird at a range of, say, a dozen feet, and the sound of the explosion would carry no farther than the snapping of a twig.

Jamesy's fingers hooked on Julie's, and, slowly, he gave her his weight to hold. Resiliently she yielded a few inches and recovered, and, with a kick and a scramble and a grunt, he got a hand over the coping and scrambled to her side.

The ground-level inside the wall was barely four feet from the top; and they let themselves down into a mass of dead leaves, and recovered the sawed-off shot-gun.

"Let me see," considered Jamesy, with a look at the sky for his bearings, "the pheasant covers are over there beyond the house. Take a grip of my sleeve, girl—we haven't the week before us."

She laid a hand on his arm and they faced into the woods. The trees, except for an occasional live-oak and copper-beech, had lost much of their foliage, and, in the light of the moon, the trespassers easily avoided the trunks and clumps of undergrowth. The sodden dead leaves rustled faintly under their feet, in the moonlight the tree-trunks cast ghostly shadows, and, now and then, a twig broke with a soft crunch.

As they went Jamesy felt Julie's arm tremble on his arm, and he sharply tapped her fingers. "It's all right," he growled. "What's frightenin' you?"

"Nothing. I—I was just thinkin' of the ugly thing that happened here."

"You poor *ownshuch*! You'll meet no ghost uglier than yourself." Julie Brien had often accompanied her step-father on expeditions like this, and had always been game as a pebble, a good scout, with a keen eye for a quarry, and full of cool resource in tight places. To-night she was not really frightened, but, rather, felt some queer psychic tension of nerves.

In time they came out on the carriage-drive and slipped along the grass edging just outside the avenue of limes, until they came in sight of a gable of the big house. There they halted behind a tree-trunk and talked in whispers.

"There it is," said Jamesy. "The keeper's house is over beyond the stables."

"And the dogs?"

"The kennels? Beyond that still. They'll never smell us with the wind behind our backs. Come on! We'll take a peep at the keeper."

Julie made no demur, for she knew the poacher's rule: "Always look for the enemy lest he be looking for you."

They made a wide detour round the stables and into the shadow below the high wall of the kitchen garden. There they slipped along in the dark to the far corner, and, from that shelter, peered out at the white walls of the keeper's cottage, not more than fifty yards away across open ground. It was fronted by a vegetable patch inside a wooden paling.

Jamesy, his head snaking from the dark corner, looked, foot by foot, over the moonlit ground before him. Then he turned to Julie.

"You stay where you are," he directed her, "and, if you see me coming on the hop, don't wait for me."

"Where are you going?"

"Don't you see that light in the left-hand window—turned full up? That might be a trick of Mullally's—an' he in ambush near the pheasants' roosts."

He went in one crouching trot across the grass and flattened out below the hand-gate in the railings. Julie, watching and listening, saw the gate slowly open, but she heard no sound, and then Jamesy slid out of sight amongst currant bushes.

She waited and listened anxiously, but, before she had time to grow restless, he came crouching out of the gate and across the grass, but not on the hop.

"Just as well you did not come up for a peep," he whispered, grinning into her face. "Hardly a stitch on him, his galluses trailin', his bare feet on the hob, an' him readin' *Hell open to Christians*! Where is that larch-wood from here?"

"Up the hill to the left, isn't it?"

"Up we go, then, in God's name."

They turned the corner and moved quietly along the wall to the next angle, and from there faced up a long slope of grass towards a dark band of trees. There they climbed over a sod-fence and brushed through a fringe of undergrowth, to find themselves amongst the open aisles of the larches. The soft carpet of dead needles made no rustle to their steps, and the high, lacy tops of the trees swung and soughed above them.

"There'll be a few cocks in here," whispered Jamesy, "unless them thiefs of Corullish poachers have been before us. Keep your eyes open."

He extracted his sawed - off muzzle - loader from poacher's skirt pocket, clicked it to half-cock, and carefully fitted on a brace of percussion caps.

They drifted cautiously into the heart of the wood, her hand occasionally touching his arm, and every time she touched him he felt her tremble, and, though her head moved restlessly and her eyes darted everywhere, he knew it was not a quarry she was looking for. For some reason she was a bundle of nerves to-night; if anything frightened her now she would scream and lose all power of movement. Jamesy had his cure for that already in his mind. At the first opportunity he would administer a small harmless shock that would rouse her tinker's fighting blood.

At that moment he saw their first cock-pheasant. They were below a larch with a long arm shooting off ten feet from the ground, and his practised eye made out the bird aroost, head under wing, half-way out. He knew it was a cock by the high set of it and the sweep of tail. Julie had not yet picked it out, was not even looking that way, and there and then he decided to give her that requisite little shock. He took her by the arm, led her directly under the sleeping bird, and stopped her suddenly with a tightening hand.

"Hss-h—down!" He pressed her urgently to the ground. "Down! Keep your head down."

And she crouched coweringly against his knee, her head gathered into her shoulders and her eyes desperately shut.

Thereupon he clicked one hammer to full cock, raised muzzle to within a couple of feet of the pheasant and pulled trigger. The shot went off with a smoking puff, and the bird fell clump, straight between the girl's tremoring shoulder-blades.

She released a small strangled yelp and fell forward on her hands.

And there was Jamesy crouching at her side with the dead bird thrust under her nose.

"There you are. Your to-morrow's dinner for you."

He snorted through his nostrils, he wheezed, he drew in his breath with a whoop. She looked at the bird; she looked at him.

"What are you laughing at?" she demanded dangerously.

Unable to speak, he pointed at herself.

"Did you do that to me?"

He nodded. Her growing indignation only made his head sway helplessly from side to side.

"I wouldn't doubt the black Coffey blood!"

He smacked her firmly on the back. "You needed that, chicken-heart. Shut up, or I'll give you more of it."

She controlled herself at once. "You will not. I'm all right now."

Five minutes later she herself brought down their second bird.

"Load up again!" she urged him.

"There you go!" reprimanded Jamesy, stuffing the pheasant in poacher's pocket. "Enough is as good as a feast. You remind me of your ould grandfather, Jimmy Brien. Wan night like this he bagged ten cocks in a bit of a plantation, and that didn't satisfy him, so he up and tried another, got jumped on be the keeper, an' spent the best part of a year in Cork Jail. Two will fill Maag Carty's pot, and we know where to get more if we want them. Let's be movin'."

They worked their way to the edge of the wood and found themselves well to windwards of the keeper's cottage. Below them it glimmered, a white speck against the bulk of the stables and the big turreted mansion.

"The dogs might scent us any nearer than this," said Jamesy. "We'll work round by the front of the house—'tis as safe a way as any."

"Very well," Julie agreed.

They kept within the margin of the wood, skirted round towards the house and, in time, came out of the larches and in amongst great sycamores that showed their ragged trunks in the moonlight above scattered clumps of rhododendron. The wind was dying down and their feet crunched rather loudly on the dead refuse of the wood. Once or twice Julie thought she heard the snapping of a twig amongst the trees behind them, but her quick and nervous eyes could distinguish no movement amongst the clumps of rhododendron.

And then, and with startling suddenness, a dog barked savagely, not behind, but in front of them. Luckily, at that moment, they were edging round a bush of evergreen, and, as one figure, they ducked close into its shelter. There, grasping each other, they held breath and waited. Again the dog barked, but came no nearer. Evidently it was in leash.

There was a movement amongst the trees a long gunshot away, just something darker than the half-darkness, and next instant a big voice bellowed out.

"I see you. I got you covered. Come out now, my fine fellow, or I'll blow the head off you!"

Julie whispered, "That's Mullally."

"He fooled me," said Jamesy shortly. "Keep still, he's only guessin'."

The dog again started barking—the full resonant bark of a red setter—but stopped short under the repression of a kick.

"Do you hear me, you ——?" roared the keeper. "Come out or I'll pepper you full of shot."

Jamesy thrust a shoulder in front of Julie, but made no other movement. There was a pause of perhaps half a minute, and then they heard the keeper speak sharply.

"Go on, Springer—root him out, boy!"

Jamesy, tough man of war, clamped his teeth, gripped his gun by the barrel ends, and moved Julie further behind him. Jamesy was afraid of no dogs—nor of their owners.

The dog came straight for them, not even growling, but, when a bare half-dozen bounds away, suddenly checked and stopped dead in its tracks. And what had stopped it was a quick clicking of thumb and finger that came from the fringe of shrubbery not five yards behind the poachers. Jamesy and Julie crouched still as mice, looking nowhere but at the dog: a thoroughbred red setter, standing two feet at the shoulder, with a great domed head, and a feathered flag of tail. He pointed dead ahead, one foot up and the others braced. And at that moment there again sounded the sharp click of thumb and middle finger and, added to it, a soft whistle.

That was enough. The setter whimpered and went bounding by the poachers, flag waving. He bundled into the shrubbery behind them, and there was a quickened flurry of leaves and branches. They heard an urgent whisper: "Down, Springer! Down!" and there was quiet, except for the rhythmic swish that told of a wagging tail. Again they heard the quick, urgent whisper.

"Back, lad, back! Go on! Quick—quick!"

The finely-trained dog obeyed at once. He turned out of the clump, trotted a few yards, looked over shoulder, heard a directing hiss, and went off towards the black shadow of the keeper.

And as he went there arose behind them a weird and anguished cry. It began low and desolate on a deep contralto note, pulsed a slow beat, lifted up and up, dropped tearingly to three short sobs, lifted again and kept on lifting, to end in a whimper of sheer madness. The veritable, broken, sobbing, whimpering, awesome note of the *Banshee*—the Woman of Death. It made Jamesy's hair lift and sent a cold shiver down his spine. Julie Brien fell against him, and he knew by the quivering intake of her breath that she was about to scream. He threw a strong arm about her, and spoke fiercely in her ear.

"Remember your blood, girl! Whatever is here is here to help us."

She sighed deeply and put her head on his trusty shoulder.

217

That awful wail had full effect on dog and man. The setter yelped frantically and bolted like a streak, tail between legs, for the keeper; and the keeper, seeing him come, yelled just as frantically and did not wait.

"Mother o' God protect me!" And man and dog burst through the undergrowth and out on the open slope above the house; and there they receded into the distance like a couple of bounding cannon-balls. And the dogs in the kennels howled as they came.

And then a woman's voice spoke quietly above our poachers: "Come out and get acquainted!"

III

Jamesy Coffey came to his feet on the edge of the rhododendron, brought Julie with him, and turned face on the woman who had spoken. The sky had blown itself clear, and the full moon shone aslant through the branches of a sycamore; and Jamesy Coffey knew the woman at the first glance. Young Widow Trant of Dounbeg, purchaser of *Copaleen Rua*, owner of these policies—and himself had two of her cock pheasants in his poacher's pocket, and a sawed-off shot-gun in the heel of his fist. As nice a case of night-poaching as any irate proprietor could wish to handle! Ah well, sure! God was good, and himself with a tongue in his head. Wonder if she knew him in the moonlight?

Elspeth Trant wore a rain-slicker, belted at the waist, and a close-fitting cloth helmet over her hair; and in the wan light of the moon her face was very white and her eyes very dark. These dark eyes made no mistake.

"Oh!" she said in some surprise, "you are Jamesy Coffey?" She glanced at the girl at his side. "And— Miss Julie Brien?"

As well as the surprise there was something in her

voice, half relief and half disappointment. Could it be that, in the dim light under the trees, she had mistaken him for another and was disappointed that he was not that other, and, at the same time, not displeased that it was not that other who was moving through the woods with this attractive girl?

"Yes, ma'am," said Jamesy brightly. "We were bringing you up your colt."

"Is he here with you?" Her smile could be seen. "Are you two alone?" She glanced round at the near-by clumps with some interest.

"The colt is not far away, ma'am," said Jamesy.

"You mean back at your camp with your—what do you call him—your curate?"

"No, ma'am! Me curate, Rogue McCoy, is gone off to Dublin on me."

"Oh indeed?" said the lady, a little blankly.

There followed a curiously empty pause, and Jamesy shifted his fowling-piece to a less obvious position. The next query was too much to the point for him.

"What are you doing here, might I ask?"

"'Tis the way myself and Julie Brien here was takin' a stroll by moonlight," he told her mildly, and added: "'Tis a habit of ours, ma'am."

"So I gather," she said dryly. "I also sometimes take a stroll on a windy night when there's a good moon— and am sometimes guilty of poaching one of my own pheasants."

"A fine, pleasant pastime, and no risk to it," agreed Jamesy brightly.

"Yes, it is the risk that counts," she murmured. "What do you intend doing now?"

"If it would be no harm to you, ma'am, we might be making for home. I'll bring the colt up in the morning."

"Very good! I'll accompany you part of the way—down here by the front of the house."

Jamesy hesitated. But where was the use? She knew him, and no crude bluff would extricate them at this juncture. Better go where she led and trust to luck.

"Whatever you say, ma'am," he agreed.

They worked their way down the slope, Elspeth Trant a little in the lead. Julie Brien had not spoken a word, for, like her mother, she was dowered of silence. And now Elspeth Trant was silent too, thinking her own thoughts. But Jamesy did not remain silent for long. He knew that it was not a good policy to let a woman brood, and he searched his mind for a subject that might lighten the issue.

"Do you know what I'd do if I were you, ma'am?" he put to her.

"Well?"

"I'd kick Mullally's backbone through the top of his head."

"A tall contract! Why?"

"He hasn't a hap'orth o' guts for one thing, and for another, that was no way to treat a fine dog. In another shake of a lamb's tail I'd be after breaking a front leg on him, and I'd be sorry to do that to your dog."

"I should be glad I saved Springer."

"You might well be, ma'am, and it was a pleasant act for us as well as the dog—an' a better-mannered dog I never seen."

"I hope I didn't frighten either of you?"

"Not what you could call frighten, just. I've been seein' an' listenin' to ghosts all me life, an' there's no harm in the crathurs, God rest them! Did you ever hear tell of the wan me gran'mother saw the night of the big wind?"

"Everybody's aunt seen a ghost," Elspeth Trant quoted Mr Dooley.

"Faith an' that's a fact."

And Jamesy went on to relate his grandmother's experience. He did it well, so well that Julie pressed close to him, and even the young woman of the world hung back to be nearer to him.

"It is given up to me," said Jamesy complacently, "to be the best teller of a ghost story in all Kerry. Paddy Joe Long is good, an' Rogue McCoy, me curate, is dam' good, but give me two pints an' I'll make your eyes crooked an' you tryin' to look through the back of your head."

"I'd hate to give you two pints," said the lady feelingly. "Well, here we are!"

She had brought them through the trees and shrubberies by the river-side, past the conical-shaped summer-house where she had talked with Rogue McCoy that summer night, and so to the margin of the green lawn fronting the house. There she stopped, and they stopped with her.

The big bulk of the house towered over there, the upper floor in darkness, but a lighted window here and there along the ground floor. A lamp glimmered in the front hall inside the big porch, and the French window on the right glowed brightly. That window, last June, had been wide open; now it was shut but not blinded, and the light, splaying out across the lawn, turned the grass a metallic green.

"We part here," said Elspeth Trant briefly. "See you to-morrow. Good night!"

"Thank you kindly, me lady," said Jamesy, much relieved, but after his own peculiar nature, not completely relieved; for how could a fellow know what would be in a woman's mind?

He laid hand on Julie Brien's arm and, before turning away, gave a last glance across at the house; and what he saw made him stiffen in his tracks, and exploded warm words from his lips.

"Pokers o' hell! How'd he get here?"

Close in to the house the figure of a man had stepped into the path of light from the French window, and had there halted, looking inwards.

"Who is it?" said Elspeth Trant in a startled whisper.

"'Tis himself, ma'am," Jamesy told her inadequately. "An' what the blazes is he up to?"

"Wait!" And the hand she laid on his arm trembled.

The figure was a dark silhouette close to the window, the silhouette of a middle-sized, bare-headed, strong-shouldered man. He stood there absolutely still for a full minute—more than a minute—looking into the room, and the three at the edge of the lawn watched with bated breath. And then he moved, not quickly, but with a prompt certainty of purpose. He rose on the shallow steps, a hand reached for the handle, and he entered the opening doorway.

"Be the powers!" exclaimed Jamesy.

Elspeth Trant, shocked into stillness for an instant, came to life with a snap.

"Come—come! He will kill him this time—he is in the house. Oh! my God!"

Jamesy had not time to enquire who would kill whom, for she dragged him forward across the lawn, with Julie clinging behind. In another moment he was hurrying as fast as she was; if any one was going to be killed he would see that one man got fair play.

As they got closer in they could see the intruder's back inside the open doorway. He certainly seemed in no killing mood, for he slouched easily, shoulders forward and one hand carelessly thrust in trouser-pocket.

Elspeth Trant lost her urgency. "Wait—wait a moment!" she whispered, and drew them aside behind the cedar treelet close to the window. They looked aslant into the room and listened.

"Japus!" said Jamesy Coffey to himself. "'Tis a pleasant night."

IV

Rogue McCoy went up to Dublin, donned the douce attire of suburbia, and tried to become Rogan Stuart, respectable man of business. And he found that he no longer fitted inside that skin. He was astounded at himself. He that had been broken out of anchorage and had gone drifting towards some tragic lee-shore, had, unknown to himself, come to moorings in an obscure but satisfying small haven. Somehow, without his knowing how it had happened, life, that had reached forward desolately from a tragic event, had taken a fresh slant, a new orientation, a different outlook. No longer was he the soul-weary Rogan Stuart with feet dourly aplod on the road to nowhere; he was Rogue McCoy, foot-loose on a careless twisting road that might lead anywhere or nowhere, a man of the sun and the wind and the warm south-west rain. "The rain shall wet him, and the sun dry him, and he not heeding the wetting or the drying." Rogue McCoy, the tinker, the travelling man, firm on his own feet, wary in life, wise in experience, clear-eyed to good fortune or mishap, no longer vulnerable to an abasing despair. What was such a man doing in Dublin town?

Within a day he suffered from nostalgia—plain homesickness for his roadman's camp. He thought of it during the day when his mind should have concentrated on business; it underlay all his dreams—and these nights he slept. It was home. The road reaching away in front and the rooks lazily flying; Jamesy Coffey's brown boots easily wagging from the tail of the tilt; Maag Carty presiding like a priestess at the fire; Julie Brien with the tell-tale pulse beating below her skin of old ivory; Daheen boasting of the two rabbits Tomboy took the scuts off. It was of Daheen he thought most, Daheen, the loyal small hero-worshipper, whose lips had quivered at the parting. There was good stuff in Daheen—heart and head. He would make a man of Daheen—if he had time—if he took time. . . . That would not be a half-bad mission in life. . . . And there he thought of another mission, and his mind shied away from it. But not for long. His friend, Paddy Joe Long, had pointed a finger, and Rogan Stuart had turned his back. Not Rogue Mc-Coy—Rogue McCoy need not turn his back on anything. Then why be afraid? No, he had better not go into that. . . . And yet, it was the world's own pity that nothing would be done when something might be done! Something—something—something!

Within a day or two he found himself holding grimly by reasons for staying by his business, and there were many; in another day he was looking for excuse to take the road and not finding any. Yet the very next dawn, though no clear-cut decision had been made, he slipped into his old and comfortable roadman's clothes, and the lift of sun found him moving loose-footed out of Dublin by the Great South Road: that wide old road of the days of the four-in-hand, that lifts across the clean curve of the Curragh common, swoops and loops over the great central plain to where the Devil's Bit and the Keeper Mountain lord it over Tipperary, and slants away westward to where noble Shannon River widens to the sea.

He did not know where he was going, but of one thing he was certain: Dounbeg was not at the end of the road. He just drifted southward, on the loose, accepting an occasional lift in a lorry, slanting off on a bus ride here and there. So he came to Limerick and found himself on the west road out of it. Late that night he was in Listowel, and next morning he walked the ten miles to Ballybwingan, where Paddy Joe Long was still in residence. He was actually in sight of the bungalow before he found he could not face Paddy Joe.

He turned back then, crossed the shoulder of Knockanore Hill, and came by dusty roads to the rendezvous at Tarbert Island. Jamesy Coffey had not yet arrived, and, somewhere deep down, he was glad of that. He crossed the two-mile width of the Shannon by the motor ferry and went northwards by the coast of Clare.

It was at this point that he really loosed all control of his drifting feet. . . . On the forenoon of the tenth day he peeped round the curtain on the window of the bar of the Harty Arms and saw his people go by.

v

The fire in the hearthstones had long gone out, the moon shone wanly over the grey common, and the wind, squall on squall, swished mournfully through the bearded grass on the summit of the mound. In their sheltered nook behind the van the animals quietly champed, Tomboy, the lurcher, whimpered in a dream from his box under the tilt, and, between the wind squalls, the breaking of the sea against the piles of the pier lifted with a muffled crash.

There was a comfortable red glow through the blinds of the high-set windows of the van. In there Maag Carty sat on a low stool before the black stove and solemnly watched the tin kettle coming to the boil. The small chamber was tidied and scrupulously clean and had a tonic savour of peat. The light from the tin-reflector lamp made brighter the bright chintz curtains on windows and bunks, and gleamed back from the arabesque decorations on the roof; and a small ruby night-light burned—as it burned in day or dark—before an ikon of the Sacred Heart.

Maag Carty turned a listening ear to the closed door. Out in the night Tomboy growled and then gave a short welcoming bark. The wise woman smiled, and her jet ear-rings clicked to the slow shake of her head. She turned to the fire and poked it to a flame under the kettle.

Then came a soft step on the ladder and a familiar tapping scratch on the door.

"Come!" Her voice was the single rubbing stroke of a bell.

The lower half of the door opened and Rogue McCoy, the wandered one, ducked in. Maag Carty never looked over shoulder at him.

"You are welcome home, childeen."

He came to her side and his fingers touched her shoulder in sign of fealty.

"It is good to be home, dark mother."

"And good that you are home, darling son. Sit here near me and I will draw you a cup of tea against the chill of the night."

He pulled in another stool and sat by her, and reached his hands to the pleasant glow of the turf fire. Oh! But good it was to be home and sitting here by this quiet, strange woman, who said so little and knew below the surface of speech or silence.

"You are very quiet here to-night, woman-of-the-house. Where are they all?"

"Daheen, the little lad, is keeping your corner warm for you. Jamesy Coffey and Julie are out—he had his bit of a gun with him."

"The old ruffian! In the demesne up by, I suppose?"

She inclined her hand and reached for the brown tea-pot. "They will not be back for an hour yet."

He brought out the cups from the corner cupboard and they had tea together, a strong hot beverage with a kick of its own. They said little to each other, but a bond was between them.

Thereafter he brought out his pipe and tapped it on the bar of the grate; but he did not fill it. He smoothed the bowl between his palms and looked into the heart of the fire.

"Hope they don't get into a tight corner," he muttered.

"They have their own way of getting out of it," she said with calm philosophy.

He put away his pipe, rubbed his brown chin after the very manner of his chief, and came slowly to his feet—just as if some force lifted him against his own inertia.

"It might be a good thing," he said, "if I went up the road to meet them?"

"It would be a good thing, son. I will have the tea hot for—whoever comes."

He went out under the half-door and down the steps. The waiting lurcher twisted round his knees and was quieted with a firm patting. Man and dog moved across to the tilt, and the dog lifted his ears; when his two masters got together a lively game was often afoot. But Rogue only leant into the tail of the cart to listen to the quiet breathing of the little lad, and a carefully quiet hand felt to make sure that the covering had not been kicked off. Sleep on, boyeen! There's a man here who will put his hands under your feet.

Rogue backed away, clicked the disappointed lurcher back to bed, and made his way out of the common.

The road curved round an inlet of the bay, where the backwash of the sea made a castanet rattle on the gravel, went on half a mile, and crossed the Dunmore River on a high-arched bridge. Rogue leant over the parapet and looked down on the water that flowed dark and coldly, with a roily gleam, under the moon. He called to mind that night in June when three men in a coracle flitted up there close under the trees to a fateful adventure—an adventure that kept drawing on and on, undeviating as fate, to this very hour, this very instant in which he sighed so deeply, so resignedly.

The road ran straight now for a quarter of a mile to where, in a deep curve, the tall wrought gates of Dounbeg cast a tracery of shadow on the drive within. There he cautiously turned the huge iron knob of the lock and pressed vainly with his shoulder. He leant so for a space, looking at the lodge through the bars, and then moved along below the wall on the grass edging. But he did not go far—not more than two hundred yards—before he halted and looked at the wall lifting eight feet above him.

An eight-foot wall was no obstacle to Rogue McCoy. His strong fingers felt for a projecting edge and clung leech-wise, his body pressed close and lifted to the draw of those tense fingers, an arm flung itself to the coping, and he slung himself over with superb ease of muscle. He landed in a bed of dead leaves, waded clear, and, without hesitation, slanted in amongst the trees, until he came out on the avenue a quarter of a mile beyond the lodge. Nor did he hesitate there, but went on under the shadow of the limes until he came in sight of the big house. There at last he halted.

He looked at the house of Dounbeg from a new angle. In the moonlight the stepped gables and pepper-caster turrets stood out clearly against the faint grey bulk of the hill behind; but he could not see the front of the house —only the bulge of the big porch, with a light reflecting dimly from the centre hall.

Did Rogue McCoy come this way to reconnoitre for his pair of poachers? If so, his proper road was to the rear behind the stables. But that road he did not take. Instead he kept to the main avenue, and he no longer moved cautiously under the trees. He strolled up the middle of the drive, his hands thrust deep in his pockets, as easily and boldly as an owner coming to his house after a pleasant walk.

The drive curved round to the big gravel spread in front of the porch, and to the very front of the porch Rogue came. The upper floor was dark, but some of the ground-floor windows were lighted behind blinds, and the French window farther up sent a strong splay of light across the lawn.

Rogue McCoy walked on slowly by the side of the house, stepped, with strange unconcern, into the cone of light, and looked through the unblinded window. For a moment he had a queer premonition that he would look on Ambrose Trant sitting in his red chair at the other side of the desk.

Whatever he saw, he stood there watching for a full minute. Then he placed foot on the step, turned the knob, and entered the room.

VI

Sir Jerome Trant's favourite room was his own office. He worked there during the day on the estate affairs that his daughter-in-law had delegated to him; and in the night, when the household and its guests were abed, he used slip down there for a last slow drink, a glance at his paper, a withdrawn cogitation with himself over a final pipe. From there, too, he could slip out into the grounds and wander about in the quiet dark.

Approaching midnight he sat forward over the square flat-topped desk opposite the French window, his shining linen reflected in the polished wood, and idly turned over some estate papers, pausing to read here and there; occasionally he relit his briar and dropped the match into a silver tray near his hand; and on each of these occasions he lifted a short-stemmed glass of amber liquid and took a brief sip.

There came a sharp tap on the door in the corner behind him, and on the tap, the door opened to admit Captain Eudmon Butler. He was in evening-dress, and the black and white of that garb went well with his height, his slim waist, his spread of shoulder. His face had still that clean pallor below the black curls, but the symmetry of his features now suffered from a nose that had been badly broken and not too well set. The strong arch had been flattened and one nostril was slightly askew, and the whole effect, while it did not detract much from the dare-devil beauty of the man, somehow gave one an impression of an underlying coarseness.

"You are a devil for work, Trant," he said in his pleasant tenor brogue.

Sir Jerome frowned. "Oh, just fooling! Care for a drink?"

"A small one."

"Help yourself."

Butler jerked one of the leather chairs to the side of the desk, sat down carelessly, and poured himself a reasonable whiskey. He could drink, and—on occasion—drink with the best or the worst, but drink was not one of his vices.

"*Slainthe!*" he toasted, and sipped his liquor.

Sir Jerome put down his pipe, lay back in his chair,

and looked at the other man out of critical, contemplative brown eyes; his lined face seemed to acquire a sternness as he looked, and, when he spoke, his voice was detachedly matter-of-fact.

"I thought that that Castleinch tinker might have held you on your back a bit longer."

Butler frowned. "You wouldn't mind?"

"Do you know, he rather spoiled your beauty?"

"You're damn'd rude, Sir Jerome!"

"Of course I always knew you were not a gentleman," went on the other equably, "but now the fact shows in your face."

A spark leaped in Butler's black eyes, but he only laughed shortly. "We must let you have the free use of your tongue, Trant."

"Meaning that is the only thing I may have."

"That or anything you dare."

"Let me be frank, then. I'm glad you looked in. To-night happens to be as opportune an occasion as I could wish. What brought you back to Dounbeg to-day?"

"Do you not remember?—Elspeth and you invited me for a few days among the pheasants."

"Or you invited yourself—it does not matter. Do you still want to marry Elspeth?"

"I do. You ought to see that, and be more reasonable." His voice grew serious. "She is the only woman I ever wanted to marry—the only one I will marry."

"Are you not afraid I may tell her the hound you are —that you are holding my son's death over us in order to keep me silent——?"

"That is not so," Butler stopped him. "I hold nothing over you. All I ask is that you forget all the scandal-mongering. Let the slate be wiped clean, and all I ask

231

is a fair field and no favour." He gazed speculatively at the elder man and smiled half-sneeringly. "Would you prefer that I go to Elspeth and say, 'Else, I know you killed Ambrose. I saw you and know that it was an unfortunate mishap, and that you are guiltless of any crime. Look! I share this secret with you, let me share my life too with you.' What would she say, what would she do?"

Sir Jerome did not reply, but an added shade of gloom went over his strong face.

Butler's hand slapped the table. "Dammit, man! Do you not see that I am seeking no advantage—that I want to do the honest thing by Elspeth Trant?"

"According to your lights. And yet, the only thing I am certain of is that the worst thing that could befall her is to become your wife. I know your kind, Butler. Your kind never changes. A son of mine made her unhappy enough, but, thank God, she is young. In this house I stand to her as guardian and parent, and I will not let her life be ruined if I can help it—and I can."

"What can you do?" the other questioned curiously.

"You'll find out—and now. You know, for a long time I doubted if you had told me the truth about Ambrose's death. I would never take your word where a woman was concerned. And I hoped that the police would discover that death had come in another way. That is why I have not acted before now. But in this past month I have learned something, and I fear that it was as you said. I have had a month to think it out, and I see only one way out. My mind is made up."

"To what?"

"To deal with you. I have here a document that is completely adequate." Trant reached a hand forward, slowly pulled open the middle drawer of the desk, and tapped a sealed envelope with forefinger. "This is a

igned confession that I killed my son Ambrose exactly
n the circumstances that you have described to me."

Eudmon Butler, in complete surprise, stared at him,
ınd then a slow contempt replaced the surprise.

"That document deals very adequately with yourself
ınly," he said.

"It clears Elspeth."

"Don't be a damned fool. What would she——?"

"Wait! You do not understand." The voice became
trangely smooth. "The last sentence in this confession
uns as follows: 'The only way out is death by my own
ıand.' But before I kill myself I kill you, Eudmon
Butler. Don't move!"

Trant's strong square hand lay along the surface of the
lesk, and the muzzle of the steel-blue automatic was
vithin four feet of Butler's white shirt-front.

"Or do move if you wish, Captain," the silky voice
vent on. "You will make it easier."

"You are mad," said Eudmon Butler. But he did not
nove. His finger-tips were pressed on the desk edge,
ust as they had pressed when he was on the point of
aunching his body forward; his face was no paler than
ısual; his black eyes were watchful—calculating his risk.
The man was no coward. In the calm face before him,
vith the eyes that had turned from brown to amber, he
aw inflexible determination, yet, on the brink of death,
ıis brain was busy and alert.

"Excuse the melodrama," besought the cool voice.
'There is no other way, I fear. You see, I am very fond
ıf Elspeth—yes! as you think, I may be too fond of her.
But that fine young life shall not be wasted on you or on
ne—and she has been good to me—and to Ambrose
ıntil—but never mind! Queer, isn't it? but I do not
vant to die, for I do not feel old, and of late my imagina-
ion has dwelt rather longingly on a small place I have

233

in the Mautopas—sun and wind and the white beach below palms. Only a dream before death! Any last thing you'd care to say, Captain?"

"There is," said Eudmon Butler. "If you would listen——"

And then a quiet voice spoke from the French window, quoting the memorable words of Specimen Jones:

"Don't let anybody hurt nobody!"

VII

The two men half-turned.

The man who had spoken so quietly stood inside the French window. A bare-headed man of the roads, rough-coated, with red kerchief hard-knotted about his throat. But his strong-boned lean face, and eyes, deep-set under brows, dominated the room.

Sir Jerome Trant had a good memory for faces. This man he knew. This was the tinker of Castleinch. Slowly his hand moved, and the automatic disappeared into the open drawer; but his fingers remained firmly on the butt.

Rogue McCoy took a single pace forward and addressed himself to the baronet.

"No need to waste lead on him, Sir Jerome Trant," he said. "He is as good as dead already."

And he faced Butler.

"The game is up, Black Captain. I am giving you an hour to leave this house and twenty-four hours to leave the country—if Sir Jerome does not mind."

Butler drew his feet under him.

"Don't move," warned Rogue McCoy deeply.

And again Butler obeyed that warning.

Rogue leant easily, almost lazily, on one foot, left hand carelessly thrust in trouser-pocket, but the other foot

234

rested on the ball of the toe, and his shoulders had the least trace of forward hunch.

"That's better. No woman to cry 'enough' to-night, and if your hands touch me, you die. Listen to me!"

For the first time something quenched at the back of Eudmon Butler's eyes.

Rogue McCoy's mask of face ridged into a smile of queer wonder. "There must be a God after all," he said. "I was driven here to-night, and in this room are all things prepared. Let us make a finish."

"What do you mean, Stuart?" There was a trace of bluster in Butler's voice.

"What I said. Clear out. I was here the night that Ambrose Trant was killed. You killed him."

Eudmon Butler came to his feet, and his chair slithered and crashed.

"The dastard!" cried Jerome Trant.

But before any one could act, in the very curve-over of action, there came a fresh interruption. Elspeth Trant, like a cold wind, was in the room, brushing past Rogue McCoy, facing Eudmon Butler.

"You killed Ambrose? Why?" She was unnaturally calm.

Butler pulled himself together, looked from her to Rogue, to Jerome Trant.

"Go on!" rasped Trant's voice. "Tell Elspeth why you killed her husband."

Butler turned to her and threw his hands forward. "I did not mean to. It was just—it was just bad luck."

"How did it happen?"

He concentrated on her then; his eyes held hers, his hands were expressive; he gathered all his forces to his aid.

"Before God, Elspeth, my hands are clean. It was for you I did what I did. Listen! You remember that night? You were out there on the lawn, and after a while I went out too. I heard you speaking to some one at the rustic shed, and thought it was Ambrose." He paused then and looked at Rogue McCoy, and wrenched his mind away from a staggering thought. "Later I heard him call your name, and then I saw you go into the house by the front door. I walked up the drive a little way, and it was then I heard Ambrose shout—more a shriek than a shout, as if he were in some kind of fit. He shrieked again and I ran to his assistance—down towards the boat-house. I found him scrabbling on the path and helped him to his feet. It was some sort of fit—he was stark mad. He struck me across the face, but I did not mind that. And then he made a vile insinuation about—about you, Elspeth—and I choked the words in his throat. I used no force—just shook him —but he grew limp under my hands, and I threw him from me and left him. That is all that happened—I swear it. I didn't know that he was dead till next morning—how could I know he was so rotten?"

Butler drew in a quick breath and went on before any one could interpose, making a final effort to hold his slipping world, careless of who heard him, forgetful of the whole damning case against him. He leant towards her possessively.

"Look, Elspeth! It was for your sake. I would do anything for your sake. Can you not see that? Never mind these people who do not understand. We—you and I—were made for each other. Why should we waste ourselves in this miserable, spiteful-minded little island? Come with me, and let us live our own lives where there is space to be free. Come—come now—this instant!"

His eyes blazed their summons and their force. In another moment he would have caught her in his arms and swept her from the room. But before he could move, she turned calmly on her heel and faced Rogue McCoy.

"You were silent too long, Mr. Stuart," she said coldly. "Why?"

But Rogue was as cool as she was, and no woman could stampede him with a sharp query. He reached forth a slow arm, grasped her by the elbow and, as if she were a small girl needing admonition, swung her round in front of him so that he stood between her and Eudmon Butler. His back was to his enemy.

"Do not be asking me any questions, girl, but listen to me." He used his soft Irish-Highland drawl. "Twice already I warned you, and I am giving you a final warning now. Get out of here, and get out by yourself. There is something sib between your breed and mine, and, since fate has pitched me neck and crop into this, I will see that in this one instance you do not make a fool of yourself. Do you hear me? There is something in you that will not be wasted on Eudmon Butler, even though I have to tear him apart to prevent it."

He held her at arm's length for a moment, and the pressure of his fingers, the jut of his jaw, the gleam in his deep eye made certain to her that he meant what he said. Then he released her and stepped aside.

Elspeth Trant had been still under his hand, but now she looked the three men over with some slow consideration of her own. And then, with startling suddenness, she flung up her head and laughed, a ringing laugh that had in it a merriness, a mocking, a joy that no man might understand. Her face had lost all colour, her eyes had an imperious light, every black hair on her head had a life of its own. She placed a hand on her breast.

"Am I the pawn that you men use in this game you play? No. I am no pawn in any game. Look at me!

237

I am Ailish Conroy, daughter of kings, and I play my own game in my own way. The game is set, gentlemen."

And she turned and walked, shoulders back and head up, into the night.

VIII

But out in the night, behind the young cedar, Elspeth Trant—or Ailish Conroy—was no longer queen on the board. She was merely excited now, and afraid. She caught Jamesy Coffey in a tense grip and dragged him across the grass out of the splay of light. Julie pushed him from behind, because he did not want to go. Out in the middle of the lawn he planted feet against them, and Elspeth caught the lapels of his coat and shook him.

"What am I to do? What am I to do?"

"For a small bit of a woman," said Jamesy warmly, "you are doin' bloody well."

"But I'm afraid—I'm afraid." Her voice was urgent. "I must get away from that ugly house. Look! you can help me. Will you—oh! will you hide me away for a little while—as you hid Rogue McCoy?"

"Blood an' turf!" said Jamesy, blank astonishment on him for once in his life.

"Only for a few days," she urged eagerly, "until I have time to think. I shall be no trouble to you—no trouble in the world. I am used to outdoor life and—and I would understand. Please—oh please!"

Jamesy Coffey grated his blue chin. It was Julie Brien that spoke and acted. Her voice, that used to be low and softly husky, took on the bell-like quality of her mother's.

"My darling lady!" Her arms went protectingly round the trembling woman. "Come with me to my mother—she will know. Come now!"

238

IX

When Elspeth Trant walked out of the door a dead silence came down upon the room. No man looked at the other, and each man thought his own thoughts. And on one thing their thoughts dwelt in common: the ruthlessness of a woman.

The oldest man moved first. He snapped shut the top drawer of the desk, leant back in his chair, and ran his hands through his hair.

"Yes," he said, "our game is played, and you have lost, Butler."

Eudmon Butler did not reply. His mind had not had time to recover balance. He ran a finger back and fore between his neck and collar as if the linen band had grown too tight for comfort. Then he looked down at the desk and his eye rested on his glass. It was more than half-full of whiskey. Slowly he reached out his hand and lifted it, and looked across the rim at Rogue McCoy. And Rogue watched him, every nerve alert. Surely the man was not going to drink?

Suddenly a spasm of fury twisted his face. "You dog!" he snarled, hurled the glass full at his enemy's face, and in the same motion hurtled himself forward, arms aswing.

But Rogue McCoy was ready and the one necessary shade quicker. All in one swift move he was under glass and arms; the glass shattered on the wall, and the Black Captain, struck with a terrific right drive on the breast-bone, crashed into a corner near the door.

"Now you'll die, Butler," said Rogan Stuart.

But before Eudmon Butler could gather himself away from the wall, before Rogan Stuart could close in, a sharp ringing command came from the French window.

"Aisy! Aisy now! I got ye covered."

It was a night of surprises.

Jamesy Coffey's wide shoulders filled the jambs, one cheek cuddled the stock of the cut-down poaching gun, one hand was thrown out under the short barrels, and the muzzle held unwaveringly to the centre of Butler's shirt-front. He wore now the fighting face of the Coffeys: black brows drawn down, and the whites of the eyes showing below the ice-blue.

"Say the word, Rogue," he urged, "and I'll blow his gizzard through his backbone."

Rogue McCoy inhaled and exhaled a deep breath and loosed taut muscles and taut nerves. It only needed Jamesy Coffey's presence and Jamesy Coffey's own style of tongue to resolve all ugly humours—the purple-streaked darkness in his mind, the tempting of sullen devils.

"No, Jamesy!" he said. "He is only a dead man on his feet. Let him be."

How often had he thought of himself as a dead man walking?

Eudmon Butler sagged against the wall. That terrible blow had winded him. He was done. There was no more good in him, or in life. What was the use? . . . The game was played.

Rogue McCoy dealt with him now as with one that did not count. He walked straight up to him, opened the door at his side, caught him, not roughly, by the shoulder, and thrust him into the dark passage.

"Find your own peace, dead man—if God lets you," he said, shut the door on him, turned round and strode across to Jamesy in the open window.

"Like a bad shilling—but you turn up," he said softly.

Jamesy grinned at him and looked down at his sawed-off gun. "Be the pipers!" said he, "I didn't remember till this minute that it wasn't loaded."

"To the muzzle with fate," said Rogue.

He looked Jamesy up and down. The long tail feather of a cock pheasant slanted across his breast from skirt pocket. Rogue tucked the feather carefully out of sight, buttoned the jacket across, and thrust a gentle fist into the broad chest.

"You should be ashamed of yourself, you old thief." he murmured.

"An' a nice *behunac* [1] to be talking about shame. I— I've a bloody good mind to be givin' you a small belt with the end o' this."

Rogue drew him up the room, and turned to Sir Jerome, who was now on his feet at the desk.

"This is my friend, Jamesy Coffey, Sir Jerome," he introduced. "Please excuse him."

The old diplomat bowed. "I have heard of your friend," he said, "and I have seen you in action—before to-night, Mr—McCoy."

"Divil the much you saw, sir," said Jamesy.

"We are sorry to have intruded like this," Rogue continued, "but it just happened. We will go now, if you don't mind."

"I owe you my gratitude, sir.' He paused and went on. "You came very opportunely and resolved a— very ugly business." He looked intently at Rogue. "I am sure that Else—Mrs Trant will be all right now."

Jamesy replied for his curate. "That wan! Didn't she have all her own way? She'll be all right, never you fear—an' do harm some fine day."

The baronet gestured a hand towards the silver tray.

"Will you gentlemen take a drink with me before you go?"

[1] Thief.

"Certainly, sir," accepted Rogue. "To be sure," agreed Jamesy.

The host poured out the drinks and lifted his own glass.

"A good deal of this business has been a puzzle to me," he said. "It seems to go back—and forward. I know who you are, of course, Mr McCoy, but—No! we need not go into things now. Instead, I will give you a toast. To Elspeth Trant!"

He tossed off his drink, and as he reached his hand towards the tray some intense surge of feeling reacted on his fingers, for the short shank of the glass snapped and tinkled on the desk. He looked at the crystal shell and smiled.

"So was *the* Woman toasted in the old days," he said, and, with a jerk of the arm, flung the bowl into the fireplace.

"*Slainthe gu' saol fada aici!* Health and long life to her," gave back Jamesy Coffey, and swallowed deeply.

But Rogue McCoy, that dour quiet man, finished his drink silently and laid his glass carefully on the tray.

CHAPTER II

I

IT was early afternoon of the big November fair at the town of Listowel, and most of the cattle had been already sold. From earliest dawn the fine old square—with its ivied Protestant Church in the middle—had been close-crowded with clumps of cattle, each guarded by two or three country lads—lean, shrill-voiced fellows, armed with ash-plants that they used mercilessly on beasts that tried to break away or trespass—but now all the best cattle had been sold and railed; the polled-Angus crosses, the shorthorns, white-fronted Herefords, blue-and-white Frisians; and there were left only scattered remnants of throw-outs, long-horns, frenchies. Here and there a felt-hatted dealer still moved from group to group, and high voices decried ridiculous offers or protestingly accepted equally ridiculous ones; but for all practical purposes the sale was over.

The public-houses—and there are fourscore in that town—were reaping their brief harvest; for the breeders, having been paid for their cattle, were engaged in soothing long throats strained from hard bargaining, and no farmer would care to leave Listowel with, as they say, the curse of the town on him. Before each and every public-house was a row of red-painted, springless country carts harnessed to donkeys, jennets, or short-coupled horses with remarkably clean legs; and the hum of the high-pitched Kerry voices came out from the bars like the song of bees swarming.

There had been heavy rain earlier in the day, and

then a blustering wind had blown up from the Atlantic, swept the clouds from the colourless winter sky, and dried most of the mire on the pavements. The wind had now died down, the clouds were again piling out of the west, and, presently, the rain would recommence and fall persistently till next morning.

Three people of the road picked their way across the mired square. One was a lithe slip of a girl with a green knitted cap pulled aside over black curls, and a green and black plaid shawl across her breast below an old raincoat; the second was a sturdy, lean-faced man, with brown hair tossing free, and a strong neck confined by a knotted silk kerchief; and between the two strode a dusky lad of twelve, copying the man's walk and bearing to perfection.

"Could you absorb a drink, Rogue?" enquired the young woman in a pleasant low-pitched voice.

"Could a duck swim?" Rogue wanted to know.

"Go and have one, then."

"And you?"

"Into one of those crowded bars? Certainly not."

"You for a tinker!" he taunted her.

"Very well," she changed her mind. "I'll come, tinker."

"No, you will not!"

"Och murther!" cried the lad of twelve. "An' me with my tongue out."

They came out of the square into the main street, and, a little way along, reached a wide cobbled elbow on the left. In this sheltered angle an old tattered street singer, with a sheaf of broadsheet ballads under his oxter, marched slowly up and down, and his singing voice soared high above all other sounds. A tall, thin old fellow with a tanned yellow face, a ragged yellow beard, and ragged yellow hair under a ruin of hat. To help himself to a high note he lifted up a long throat and hitched his pants dexterously with one hand, but, notwithstanding, his broken old voice never achieved that top note. People passed him by on the pavement, paused to listen, shook their heads and passed on; here and there a generous one tossed him a copper; but no one bought a broadsheet.

Our three people of the road paused too, and the old fellow came by, his head back and his washed-out but watchful blue eye aslant at them.

> At a fair or a wake I could twist my shillelagh
>   Or trip thro' the jig with my brogues bound with straw,
> And all the pretty colleens in village and valley
>   Loved the bold Phelim Brady, the Bard of Armagh.

"Lift it, Meehaul Bwee!" urged Rogue. "Lift it a taste!"

Meehaul Bwee—yellow Michael—stopped in front of them.

"Is it yourself, Rogue McCoy? And Ailish Conroy? How goes it?"

"Fine, Meehaul! Doing a roaring trade?"

"Trade!" cried Meehaul, and swore a strong oath. "Trade is it? The hobs o' hell before Listowel town for trade. Wishan! God be with the ould days when Cautheen Callaghan an' myself wor young an' we warblin' every second line—thrush and blackbird! In this very spot, too! An' we wouldn't have a verse out of us before the tanners and the bobs came rollin' in. I dunno what's come over the people at all—an' may the divil look sideways on them!"

"Stick to it, Meehaul," advised Rogue. "The day is young and yourself in good tune."

They moved on. "Poor old Meehaul Bwee!" said Rogue pityingly. "Once, I am told, he was the best ballad-singer in Munster; but his voice is gone and his trade with it—and he blames his audience."

"But would he sell if he could sing?" enquired Ailish, who was touched to compassion for the gallant old fellow who still persisted.

"I do believe he would. Give a Kerryman a deal that he can see and he'll play at any game."

She halted Rogue with a hand across Daheen. "Wait!" she cried and threw back her head and laughed, a gay mischievous light in her clear eyes.

"You're as full of fun as Patsy McCann's ass," said Rogue.

"Give me a shilling," she demanded with outstretched hand. "There, Daheen! run across to Spillane's and buy your sweets—and wait there. Come with me, Rogue!"

She caught his arm and turned him round, and, in accordance with the rule that had become implicit between them, he went with her without demur. It was her stunt.

They returned to the old ballad-singer and stopped before him.

"Let me see your ballads, Meehaul Bwee," demanded Ailish, plucked them forthwith from beneath his oxter, and inserted them under her own. She spoke decisively now, and pointed a finger. "Be off, Meehaul! over to that public-house for a pint, and tell them Rogue McCoy will pay for it."

"An' what'll you be doin' with me ballets?"

"You'll hear. Away with you!"

The old fellow still hesitated.

"Do what you're told, Meehaul Bwee!" ordered Rogue in a certain tone, "or I'll—I'll—go on, you old scarecrow!"

Whenever Rogue used that tone few men of the road dared gainsay him.

"The divil sweep the pair of ye!" cursed Meehaul, and shuffled hastily across the road.

Ailish unrolled the broadsheets and tossed over the first dog-eared leaves. She read hurriedly here and there and laughed. "Why, this is rich!" she cried. "I know some of these. My father used to sing them for me—'come-all-yous,' he called them. Listen to this bit.

> ' What brought you into my house, to my house, to my house?
> What brought you into my house?' said the mistress unto Dan.
> ' I've come to court your daughter, ma'am,
> I thought it no great harm, ma'am.'
> ' Oh, Dan, me dear, you're welcome here.'
> ' Thank you, ma'am,' says Dan."

"Going to sell them?" enquired Rogue.

"And sing them—those I know—with you to help. Your baritone is a bit of a bellow, but it will pass in the open. I'm going to test your Kerrymen to-day."

"We'll never sell that pile. You've got a nerve."

"Then you'd better root hard, fellow. You sell the last one or bust."

"And it's going to rain like blazes in half an hour."

"Root still harder."

"As soon as we get back to camp I'll get Jamesy Coffey to belt you."

"Belt me yourself, tinker."

Ailish had a fine clear flexible voice, and Rogue's rather rough baritone did not blend so badly; and, moreover, that elbow in the street had the useful acoustic property of making both voices resonant—a fact known to generations of ballad-singers. Ailish put her whole keen spirit into the work, and Rogue backed her up solidly.

In two minutes they sold their first broadsheet for six-pence and had the people halting as they came. Somewhere a rumour grew that these were no ordinary ballad-singers, but real opera stars out for a lark—from the Dublin Gaiety, from Covent Garden itself—and that rumour brought people to listen, and listening to admire. Soon they had an audience standing on both sides of the angle.

They tried all the time-honoured methods of the street singers: singing in unison, in harmony, in alternating verses, singing every second line, missing phrases to keep time with hand and foot. At a lively song Ailish would pull off her knitted cap, toss her black curls backward, swing her lithe shoulders as she marched, show her white teeth in gaiety. Her repertoire was wide and varied, for she sang only a verse or two of any song she knew in the broadsheet, songs her father taught her, gay sardonic songs like *Tatter Jack Walsh*, sad songs like *The Red-Haired Man's Wife*, country ballads like *The Rocks of Bawn*; and in the end she gave samples of cowboy songs—queer wailing songs with long cadences.

> There's b-lood on the saddle and b-lood all around,
> And a great big puddle of blood on the ground.

And at intervals Rogue went through the crowd and sold broadsheets. It is possible that the rapidity of the sale was as much due to Rogue's patter as to Ailish's singing, for he took the men into his confidence, made them partners with himself, showed them the humour and pathos of the undertaking. And many there, too, knew Rogue McCoy, knew him since the fair of Castle-inch, and any man that knew him was ready to buy a ballad sheet.

Young Daheen stood in the doorway of a shop munching sweets, and, when his mouth was not too full, put in a clear pipe in the choruses. Old Meehaul Bwee came occasionally to the door of the public-house, and gratification struggled with jealousy in his pale eyes. He was beginning to understand why his day was done.

More than three-fourths of the sheaf of ballads had been disposed of when the rain began and thinned the crowd. And as it fell, more and more people took refuge in the bars, until at last only a few enthusiasts were left, and most of these had already made a purchase.

"That will be enough, girl," urged the loyal Rogue. "You'll get your death."

She looked round. The enthusiasts were moving off and she had only one broadsheet left, the dog-eared one of the bunch.

"I'll sell it if it takes a year," she proclaimed obstinately, and blinked the rain off her long lashes. "There's a lad over there who has been absorbing ecstasy through his open mouth, and he has not yet moved hand towards pocket. Watch me!"

The lad indicated was a lank man sitting on the heel of a donkey's cart. He had the poet's eye and the long lantern jaw of the visionary; and he had listened with rapture to Ailish's singing, his cheeks atwitch and his Adam's-apple working. Now she walked across to him, and he gazed at her with diffident and adoring eyes.

"The last one for you, patient man," she said firmly, "and a song all for yourself into the bargain. Are you buying?"

"I would an' welcome, ma'am," he deprecated in a reedy voice, "but I can't sing."

"But you like singing?"

"Better'n my dinner. I—I'd folly a ballet-singer from here to Scartaglin, an' often did. Where are ye for next?"

"Ballyduff. And you can't sing a note?"

"Sure, sometimes I do be tryin' an odd stave to myself

an' no one listenin'. Do you know *The Three Say Captains?*"

"I know one as good—*The Fox in full chase and the Goose that he stole.* Listen to this note!" She sang a note in the upper register. "Try that one after me. Go on— you need not be shy. Listen again! No! that's a mile in the air for you. We'll drop an octave. . . . That's better—just a trifle sharp. Move over a little!"

He made room for her on the tail of the cart, and she hopped up lightly and faced him, a compelling light in her eye. "You'll sing before we're done, gallant man," she told him. "Listen, now! I am going to run up and down the scale and you will follow me, eyebrows and toe-nails. Are you ready? . . . Splendid. Let's try again. . . . Hit or miss."

The man's natural shyness was submerged in his secret ambition, and Ailish put her own enthusiastic spirit into him. Be the powers! he had more in him than he thought. Wasn't he getting a hoult of the thing already?

Ailish turned over the damp broadsheet. "Let me see! Yes! this one would be just within your compass. We'll try a verse of it. Hum it after me. Take it easy now—take it easy."

The town of Ballylongford by Carrig's lovely shore,
The strand of Ballybwingan, an' the hill of Knockanore;
'Twas there I spent my boyhood's prime—I told you once before,
And I'll tell you ten times more to-morrow morning.

"Bravo! You'll never again be too shy to sing—and honest men will take an axe to you. Come! one more try. . . ."

People looked laughingly, admiringly from doorways and windows, saw Ailish keeping time with her hand, the pupil with his head, heard the quavering half-tenor follow the clear contralto. They were alone in the street, and the rain poured slantwise on the three of them; for Rogue

McCoy stood to the windward of Ailish, and his broad shoulders kept the lash of the rain off her. Occasionally he helped the pupil with a difficult note, and the teacher hushed him with an impatient hand. At last she was satisfied.

"There are twenty-seven more verses——"

"We'll try them, begobs!" said the enthusiast.

"You can read?"

"Och, I pick out the words fine."

"Good! There's your ballad and pay me what you like for it."

"I will so, my darling princess," he crièd, and, fumbling deeply in a pocket that did not jingle, he brought forth a solitary florin. "There, ma'am, an' it would be more if I had it."

Rogue leant over and stopped the man's hand. "You've earned your ballad, heart o' corn. Put your money away and come with me."

He brought the man off the tail of the cart with one hand, lifted Ailish down with the other, and, using all his energy, ran the two across the street into the doorway of the public-house, where Meehaul Bwee stood waiting.

"Where's me fine ballets?" he wanted to know, and followed them round to the back bar, which was lined with thirsty customers; but room was readily made, and a man who knew Rogue called across, "You'll have this with me, Rogue boy?"

"No, Paddy! this is mine. What'll it be? A pint? Right!" And to the barman, "Tommy, two pints of stout, two large whiskies, and half a large glass of boiling water with two lumps of sugar and two cloves——" He felt a quick tug at his coat-tails—"Oh yes! and a large bottle of Nash's lemonade for Daheen Coffey." He looked along the bottle-garnished shelves inside the bar. "Fine old tawny—mostly logwood—Three-Star, Three-

Swallows, D.W.D., Paddy himself, Gorzalas and Byass—good enough—claret, Médoc, St Julien—St Julien, and good enough too. That black bottle, Tommy, and take the cork out."

He poured a generous measure of claret into the boiling water, pounded the sugar and cloves with the circular-topped mixer, and handed the glass to Ailish with, "Try that, tinker."

Ailish had been watching his compounding with interest. She had taken off her sodden cap, and was drying her face and curls with Rogue's handkerchief, which she had quietly extracted from his pocket. She looked at him with wide eyes, and her smile dimpled one cheek. "Will it make me drunk, Rogue?"

"No, but it may stave off a cold. Try it."

She warmed her cold little paws on the hot glass, tasted the contents gingerly, and smiled more broadly. "Why, this is lovely—this is good! Why was I not told about this? This is my tipple."

"Not by a jugful!" said Rogue, and turned with a fistful of silver and coppers to Meehaul Bwee.

"Dammit, Rogue! Dammit, man! Keep your own share—that'll be enough, I tell you!"

"You keep it for me, Meehaul—I'll ask for it." And he went on emptying his pocket.

Meehaul looked over Rogue's shoulder at Ailish. "My soul, girl! but 'tis yourself has the linnet's windpipe. You're good, but Rogue McCoy and a crow make a pair. Look now, if you'd join the road with me, in a week I'd have you learned all the grace-notes—an' we'd be bankin' our money. Och! but it's grand to be young!"

Daheen raised a speculative voice. "I wonder, would a drop of claret put life into this?"

"It will colour it, anyway," said Rogue, and poured a

little claret into Daheen's lemonade. Daheen still held out his glass, but Rogue put the bottle back firmly on the counter.

"A mane drop!" grumbled Daheen, and sampled it. "Ha! 'tisn't bad, aither." And he drank his mixture with the gusto of ten topers.

Ailish went deeper and deeper into her warm negus and disconsolately peered through the bottom of her glass.

Her pupil, the new singer, stood breast to the bar, not saying a word, lost in ambitious dreams. He had drunk half his whiskey, and maggots of inspiration were swarming in his brain. His visionary eyes were fixed unseeing on the cornice, a nerve twitched in his cheek, his Adam's-apple worked up and down. Then, without warning, sudden as an explosion, he threw up his head, and his voice soared up in an incredibly high note.

"The town of Ballylongford by Carrig's lovely shore——"

"We're sunk," cried Rogue. "In two minutes there'll be a lynching in this place." He caught at Ailish and Daheen. "Let us go while the going is good. Moreover, you must change out of these wet things."

"You're a brick, Rogue," said Ailish.

"To a brick-and-a-half like yourself," said Rogue.

And a warmth that was finer than the warmth of hot claret poured through Ailish Conroy.

II

But neither the warmth of praise nor the warmth of wine-negus saved the young woman, now called Ailish Conroy, from the chill that was due to her. In the night her overtaxed throat began to hurt, a throbbing started in her head, little cold shivers ran up and down her

253

back; the inside of the van, lit dimly by the red lamp below its holy picture, seemed to grow oppressive, and she threw her slim arms free of the coverlet; then her throat tickled, and she coughed a croupy, wheezy, small cough.

The far bunk creaked and Maag Carty's bell voice murmured: "The cold is rising on you, colleen."

Ailish's reply was a husky whisper. "All right in the morning, dark mother."

But dark mother was at once by her bunk side, feeling her hands, feeling her brow, smoothing her round neck.

"Only the cold, lovely darling. There'll be drouth on you?"

"A little, mother."

"A nice warm lemon drink I'll make for the two of us. Keep your hands in, treasureen."

She lighted a hand-lamp, got a small Primus-stove hissing, and set her tin kettle to boil. Julie Brien, in the deep sleep of youth, breathed quietly behind the chintz curtain of her bunk.

In two minutes there was a scratching at the door, and Maag Carty, pulling a shawl round her shoulders, opened the top half and peered out.

"Who is it?"

"Only Rogue. Is Ailish all right?"

"What'd be wrong with the hardy little trout?" she whispered down. "'Tis the way I couldn't sleep with the rain on the roof, and a cup o' tea is comforting. Go back to your bed, foolish son, or you'll get your death in your bare feet."

She heard him pad back to the tilt, and whispered to Ailish. "Like a hen with a clutch of chicks—you'd think he was your mother."

"And that only," said Ailish huskily.

"He is terrible fond of you, little one."

"And of you all."

"Of all of us surely, but—be quiet now, little one, and don't hurt your throat."

Rogue climbed back under the tilt, where Jamesy Coffey lay quietly on his back and Daheen slept the grand deep sleep of youth. In the dark of night under the tilt Jamesy was no longer querulous and abusive.

"Nothing wrong?" he enquired softly.

"No—just the light in the van."

"Do you ever sleep at all?"

"I have slept worse."

"Is Ailish all right?"

"Maag Carty says so—she's making a cup of tea."

"The delicate crathur!" He raised on an elbow. "A cup would be nice too."

Rogue sat up again. "Wait and I'll crave a mug for you."

Jamesy pressed him back. "No, boy! If I took tay this hour o' night I wouldn't sleep another wink. Sleep is a grand thing."

"It is," agreed Rogue. "It is a fine thing—though once I thought it a new torment stolen by Satan from God."

"Did you, now? You know, I had that sort of feelin' in my time too."

"Oh," exclaimed Rogue with interest, "I am sorry, Jamesy!"

"Well, you might. I mind the time well. I laid ten pounds on Amberwave to win the National, an' the bastard up an' fell at the second fence. I didn't get a sound sleep for a week—like me old friend John Walsh of Ballydonohue, who hasn't slep' a night since De Valera won the election. Was it a horse you backed?"

"They are usually coupled with horses," said Rogue evenly.

"To be sure—to be sure. Do you know what I'm thinkin' the last coupla days?"

"Not all of it."

"I was plannin' a trip for the spring days—when they come. You an' that girl beyant haven't seen the best of Ireland at all. We'll box *Copaleen Rua*, and send him to stable at Dounbeg, and then we'll slip down the coast to Coomakista, over the windy gap to Kenmare, and by the tunnel road to Glengariffe. Then we'll twist over the Pass of the Deer at Ceimaneigh, leavin' orange Bandon on one hand and strikin' for Macroom. After that we might make for Limerick and have a bit of a spree with Shamus Og, if he isn't in jail again—and then down by the Shannon, where the first run of white trout will be in on the Loghill Water; an' so, striking Ballybwingan by the middle of June, where Paddy Joe Long will be puttin' us through our catechism. Such a devil to talk you never met, the same Paddy Joe—an' him takin' notes on a scrap o' paper, an' puttin' them in books, so I'm told—an' foolish people buyin' them."

"We'll touch him for a royalty, Jamesy."

"What's that?"

"Blood money."

"No, be Jacus! Blood money I wouldn't never touch. Whisper! Me great-great-gran'mother's second cousin was a spy in black '47, an' we never got over it. Don't be mentionin' it to Daheen."

"Was that why Cracawley Sheridan called you an informer's melt at Ballinasloe Fair?" enquired the drowsy voice of Daheen.

"Bluranagers! I never liked that Cracawley anyway."

"He'd have belted you if it worn't for Shamus Og."

"Maybe he would. Be quiet, now, *gorsoons*, an' let us get our share o' sleep."

But in the morning—a clear winter morning after a night of rain, with a breeze swinging north from the damp south-west—when they tumbled out of the tilt and made clamour for breakfast, Maag Carty—Julie with her—came down from the van and spoke seriously.

"Ailish has a cold on her chest—she'll stay in bed to-day."

Rogue's mouth softened strangely and, again, firmed. He said no word, but strode straight to the steps and mounted into the van. Ailish's fevered eyes looked at him out of a flushed face, and she greeted him with her half-wistful, one-dimpled smile.

"Only a strained larynx, Rogue," she said huskily.

Her arm, bare to the elbow, lay outside the coverlet, and he circled her wrist with gentle fingers. Her pulse was fast but not racing. He felt her brow and found it hot and dry.

"What a lovely cool palm!" she whispered, and he smoothed back her tossed curls.

"Just a cold, old girl," he said confidently. "A day in bed and you'll be right as rain." And he went out with an easy swing of the shoulder.

But outside he went round to the back of the van and kicked a sod of turf so furiously that Tomboy, the lurcher, and his yelp barely got out from under. Whereat he cursed Tomboy in a furious whisper.

Jamesy came round the van after him and was caught forcefully by both shoulders. "Jamesy, will you be good enough to kick me into the Feale River below? Go on!"

"Let me go, you big gom! Sure, 'tis only a bit of a cold—but we could be gettin' the doctor to make sure. I'll send Julie Brien."

"I'll go. Where?"

"At the top o' William Street—you'll see his plate. An' do you know what I'll be doin', Rogue McCoy? I'll be makin' straight for Mick Lane's lodging-house, an' I'll take Meehaul Bwee an' drown him in the castle-pool—I will so. . . . What the divil are you lookin' for, Daheen?"

"I'm lookin'," said Daheen fiercely, "I'm lookin' for a lump of a stone an' a piece of rope for you."

"You b—— little murderer! I'll drown him me own way. Look now, Rogue——"

But Rogue was already up at the roadside. He came hurrying back in half an hour, and the doctor—a pleasant-faced, youngish man—was hurrying with him. The impression that Rogue had given the doctor was that there awaited him a case of double pneumonia with complications.

"Hullo, Jamesy!" greeted the doctor, and mounted into the van, where Julie Brien had made everything tidy; and Rogue stood at the head of the steps looking over the half-door, ready to relay the bad news to Jamesy and Daheen, who stood at the bottom.

The experienced man looked at the patient, nodded his head, and smiled.

"Nothing much wrong with you, young woman," he said, his hand on her pulse.

At the end of his examination he pocketed his stethoscope and chuckled. "Well—well! A nice feverish cold and a relaxed throat—and nothing more. Keep her in bed as long as you can."

"A month, doctor?" enquired Rogue.

"I am speaking to a wiser head, young fellow. Three days if she stays—lungs of leather and heart of teak. You don't need any medicine. Give her all the liquid she asks—oranges—soda and milk—you know, Maag Carty?"

"Time for me, Doctor Tim."

He patted the patient on the shoulder. "This your husband, young woman?" he asked, his eyes curious. He was wondering how a van-dweller came to wear silk for night attire. But he knew Jamesy Coffey, and Jamesy had strange acquaintances, and in many walks of life.

Rogue did not wait for Ailish's reply: he turned away so hastily that he took the steps at a tumble and a jump.

"Damn those steps!" he cursed warmly.

"What is it?" enquired Jamesy.

"Only a cold, as you said—three days in bed."

"The devil mend her, and the fright she's after givin' us. Would you mind if I gave you that kicking for a start?"

"Wait! Here comes the doctor."

"Doctor Tim," urged Jamesy, "will you be givin' her a good bitter bottle, like a good man?"

"Not this time, Jamesy. Get her a few throat pastilles when you're up town. Well, I'm off."

"Wait, man! We owe you something!"

The doctor winked at Jamesy. "For double pneumonia with complications I usually run to ten guineas —but for a feverish cold I generally curse a little. Let me know how she is." And he hurried off to his car on the crown of the road above him.

"Let him be," said Jamesy. "We'll drop a couple of lustre jugs in on him. We might need him yet for other things; they say he is a good woman's doctor. Do you hear me?"

"Go to blazes!" said Rogue McCoy.

IV

Jamesy and Daheen had gone up to town, professedly to drown Meehaul Bwee, Maag Carty was paying a visit to the chapel, and Julie Brien was foraging through the woods for dry sticks for her mother's fire. The camp was pitched amongst the wide-spaced trees below the wing parapets of the River Feale Bridge, and the river flowed strongly under its four tall arches, the swollen waters gleaming golden in the sheen of the sun. The blusteriness of November was temporarily gone, and a grateful, almost spring-like, warmth poured itself through the open door of the van.

Rogue McCoy, left nurse in charge, sat in the doorway and smoked a comfortable pipe. A gallant conquistador wasp hummed by and made him feel drowsy, but not lonesome, and a gentle waft of air brought the chuckling babble of running water. Yes! this was not such a bad life—a fellow could do with this kind of existence. One could sit here for long enough and contemplate things remotely, and go into an abstraction of thought where thought became less than a bodiless emanation, and one grew satisfied with the loneliness of life. And he realised then that this fatalistic comfortable feeling would go over the edge into lonesomeness but for the quiet presence of his companion, Ailish Conroy, behind him in her bunk. He stirred restlessly, and Ailish coughed her small cough. He looked over his shoulder at her.

Already she was getting her voice back. "I wish I could get out in the sun—it is so close in here."

"Grumbler!" He laid down his pipe and went across to the bunk side. She was still flushed and her brow felt hot under his palm. He turned her chin from side to side. "Did Maag Carty wash your face this morning?"

"What she called 'a Scotch lick.'"

"I am going to give you a cool sponge, then." He went to the square-foot of dressing-table below the red lamp and found her toilet sponge. The water was still lukewarm in the tin kettle, and he poured some into an enamelled basin, soaked the sponge, squeezed it and repeated the operation. Then he sponged her brow and cheeks and neck, and she closed her eyes with a sigh of ecstasy.

"You are so strong and gentle."

So he brusquely brushed her curls aside and dabbed at the pink shell of ear.

She snickered. "You're tickling me."

"Be still," he threatened, "or I'll stuff your mouth full of sponge. Turn your head!"

Then he carefully dried her face with the towel, and she twisted her features so like a child's that a strange stab of memory and affection went through him. After that he sponged her arms and hands and dried them briskly; and then pulled up Maag Carty's three-legged stool and sat down by the side of the bunk.

"Feel cooler now?"

"Lovely. Give me a lozenge to suck."

He shook one out on his palm, and she took it in her lips from his fingers with a playful snap.

Her arm was outside the coverlet, and he took her brown hand in his finger-tips and turned it over. It was a soft little palm with no calluses.

"What a useless little paw!" he murmured.

She clenched her fist. "See that? That is what smote you within a minute of our first meeting—and you had to hang on."

"No. It was the other fist."

They were silent for a long time.

"Do you know, girl, he said at last, "this life is too hard for you."

"An ordinary cold——"

"But you may get another. Tell me, Ailish, are

you—are you all right now? I mean—you're not unhappy?"

"I never was happier."

"But you cannot live this life indefinitely."

"Why not?—Oh! I suppose not. I think I will build a small cottage for myself at Dounbeg—right down by the bay—or away up the glen out of sight. . . . You might come and see me there some time?"

He did not answer, and she looked sideways at his strong profile.

"What about you? What will you do with yourself—after June?"

"Work, I suppose. I have a partner in Dublin swearing at me—and this present life has saddled me with responsibilities too."

"What are they?"

"Daheen is one. There is potential stuff in Daheen, and I'm not going to lose sight of him."

"Any others?"

"Yes. I've been neglecting one this past month, but I'm going to dig right in to it these coming three weeks."

"And that is all?"

He smiled playfully. "There is one, Ailish Conroy."

"That is only fair," she said seriously. "I feel that you are responsible for me." Her mouth quivered sensitively. "I—I don't know what might happen if you lost sight of me."

He touched her hand and his voice was firm. "I am not going to lose sight of you."

CHAPTER III

I

It was a dull December evening, with a lowering sky far out in the west beyond Scattery Island; and Jamesy Coffey, lowering as the sky, came up the slope from the pier. Behind him was the clang of sixteen-pound breaking hammers on ships' plating and the hissing flame of an oxyacetylene blow-lamp; before him, at the head of the green slope, the massive dressed-stone walls of the disused battery rose against the sky, with his own camp nestling cosily in the angle between the armoury and the fortified compound.

"Rogue McCoy!" he shouted in his own high tenor. "Where are you, Rogue the schamer?"

His voice boomed back from the walls, and that was the only reply he received.

"Where is every dam' one?" he yelled.

A head of black curls looked down at him over the battery wall.

"Is Rogue up there with you, woman of the Conroys?"

"No. He went down to the harbour after dinner."

"He did not, then. There's a sixteen-pound hammer waitin' for him below there—and he off with Daheen and the hound somewhere. Wait till I get hold o' him!"

He went through the big gateway in the walls, climbed up a sloping way, and came out on the summit of the gun park. Ailish Conroy, slender yet strong, alean against the rising breeze, was standing on one of the flagged gun platforms and gazing out towards Shannon Mouth.

"Come up here, loud man," she called to him.

He scrambled to her side, and she placed a hand on his arm. "Look!" she cried, her arm flung wide. "Is it not lovely and forlorn?"

"'Twill be the devil's own wet day to-morrow," said Jamesy gloomily.

Down below the tide was making across the wide sand-flat between the island and the village of Tarbert; and behind the village the grey-green winter landscape sloped upwards to a dim horizon. Through the gapped sides of the old iron hulk against the pier the blinding flame of a blow-lamp pierced and spat, in contrast to the soft glow of the blinded windows of the public-house on the quay. In front of them stretched the two-mile width of Shannon estuary, with the round-headed hills of Clare beyond, and the deep, curved current of Tarbert Race was a gleam of wan silver on the leaden blue of the great river. The white tower of the lighthouse on the point stood out sharply against the dim coast beyond; and away in the west the rain-clouds heaped themselves over Scattery, with one long stain of dulled orange broken across their faces. Out there under that low sky the sea ran forlornly and strangely, and, here and there, little whitecaps glimmered and ran before the freshening breeze.

"The winter is on us, Jamesy Coffey," said Ailish in her deepest voice.

"And we snug for it. Where's every one?"

"You are there and I am here, Maag Carty is gone up the causeway to the village to get Father Jerry O'Connor to say prayers for her pagan husband, Daheen and Tom-boy are in the woods over there after rabbits—Rogue is not with them. I haven't seen Julie Brien."

264

"Maybe the pair of them are together," suggested Jamesy dourly.

"Why not? They are young enough."

"You are young enough too."

"But wise, my father."

"I dunno—I dunno at all! 'Twas him sent you to me—out the window he sent you that night up yonder. Dammit! I'm not satisfied with this camp for the best part of a month. Whisperin' here and whisperin' there, and cross words and cross tempers."

"And you cross-tempered now for your tea. Well, come along, and I'll boil the kettle for a fly cup, and by then Maag Carty will be back with the sausages."

Ailish had to admit that the camp had not gone well for nearly a month. The first month had been perfect, right up to the famous fair at Listowel, but since coming to Tarbert Island some sort of tension had strained the camp. She felt disappointed, even a little disillusioned. Life, after all, was much the same everywhere, and perhaps she had not been overwise in trying to change it. But she would not dwell on that thought. She would give this life a fair trial, and, if it did pall, and go on palling, it would at least have given her a sane outlook by the time she returned to her normal existence. Her normal existence! And what was that to be? She would not dwell on that thought either. Better go on from day to day and let the future take care of itself. Her present job was to build a fire of sticks and peat, and boil a black kettle.

She did that task, and she and Jamesy were drinking tea companionably together when Maag Carty returned laden with sausages, baker's bread, and six bottles of stout. Next minute Daheen and the lurcher raced up the slope from the woods, but with no spoil from the afternoon's hunting.

"That place," he explained, "is as full of burrows as a bee's comb. Tomboy hadn't a fair run once, but faix, he took the scut off two all the same. Myself and Rogue will set a couple more snares to-night. Where is he?"

No one answered him. No one asked where Julie Brien was. Neither of them turned up for tea, nor did Maag Carty reserve part of the sausages for them. That dark mysterious woman maintained an aloof silence all the evening, and did not once reply to her husband's grumblings and insinuations—and he did grumble unhappily, vindictively, even slyly.

"Yes so! Ready enough some one was to put a stop to the whisperin's and colloguin's when Shamus Og was in it. But Rogue—! that's a horse of a different colour. Rogue, me darlin'! No harm in him. Hand on shoulder and carroty head down listenin', an' then close together along the beach. An' not a word from any one. . . . She is no daughter of mine, but be the powers if she was . . ."

With the fall of dark the woman left him sitting gloomily asmoke on his soap-box before the fire, and went up into the van. Presently the light of the ancient tin-reflector lamp glowed through the red curtains of the high-set windows, and Ailish's dark head appeared over the half-door. She looked down at Jamesy, crouched gloomily over the flame, and at Daheen sitting solemnly at his side on two sods of dry peat. Poor Daheen was subdued to-night. He was leaning forward, his hands between his knees and his fine dark eyes fixed on the glowing coals.

"Daheen," she whispered, "come here!"

Daheen started and looked up, and she beckoned him with a finger to the foot of the steps.

"What is it, Ailish?"

"The day's work must be finished, small man. Come away up!"

266

"Very well so," he agreed resignedly.

He mounted into the cosy small chamber of the van, with its bright chintz curtains, tidied bunks, painted decorations on walls and roof, and the small red lamp that burned night and day below a picture of the Sacred Heart. And there he had his nightly lesson. Daheen was bright—indeed brilliant; already he could work through the fifth reader and was beginning to grasp the rule of three. He did his lessons gravely, and Ailish smiled at him.

"What about a story to-night, Daheen?"

"Wisha! somehow I'm in no humour for it."

"It is not always good to be a hero worshipper, Daheen boy."

"But I do be liking your stories too, Ailish."

And that was the truth. She had grand stories—of Indians, and bears, and cowboys, and guns shooting, and horses galloping. Every bit as good as Rogue McCoy's—only somehow, now and then, she did not get the kick in the right place. But they were good stories, and he could listen for a year—but not to-night.

The night crept on slowly, but neither Rogue nor Julie returned to camp. At ten o'clock Jamesy, grumbling to himself, went to bed under the tilt, and Daheen went with him, disconsolately snuggling down in Rogue's place. When Rogue came—if he came—he would find his corner warm and slip in quietly to smooth a hand through his small friend's hair. The light across in the van went out after a time, and the bunks creaked.

The two women were very quiet. Maag Carty, who had not spoken a word all evening, now turned her face to the wall, and lay so still that Ailish could not tell whether she slept or waked. Ailish herself did not sleep for a long time. Her bunk was below the window, and she lifted a corner of the curtain and looked out. There was no moon, and the night was dead black; down at the pier the light in the public-house window was a red spark, and, across the wide stretch of sand-flat, the village lights twinkled yellow; and every ten seconds the wheel of the lighthouse lanthorn splayed a faint splash of radiance across the uplands on the Limerick border.

She lay down and listened. The rising wind cried forlornly, rustling through the withered grass on top of the wall, lifting to an eerie note in the notches of the parapet, sighing distantly in the bare woods; and from the beach below came the swish and hiss of the breakers and the sharp castanet rattle of rounded pebbles in the undertow. She lay down again and sighed, and thoughts not pleasant would no longer be ignored. She had to admit to herself that Jamesy Coffey was right, that it was the whisperings and colloguings that had put the camp out of tune, that had made her discontented and—yes! almost unhappy. Why? Was she jealous? No. Was this strange man, Rogue McCoy—or Rogan Stuart— becoming of importance in her life? She could not say— she could not be sure. But she realised that his presence in the camp added a savour to this new experience of life, indeed made it a worth-while experience in spite of all disillusionment.

She dozed and woke up, and lifted her head to listen. No sound but the wind and the tide—no sound of any one coming. She would be sorry now if any one came, for, at the back of her mind, she had an explanation for the whisperings between Rogue and Julie, and if the two returned home at this hour of the night that explanation would be blown into shreds; and she could not stand that. She knew then that Rogue McCoy was too important in her life.

She slept at last, and waked at dawn. And Rogue and Julie had not returned.

The chief warder passed across the paved prison yard with Shamus Og Coffey, who walked head up and with the old devil-me-care look in his eyes.

"Hope you'll not make a habit of this, Coffey?" said the chief warder.

"A bad habit sticks, chief," gave back Shamus Og lightly.

"As we know here. No doubt, you were unlucky last time—you couldn't let your friend down—but in future——"

"Who cares about my future?" Shamus Og interrupted bitterly.

"Depends on yourself. We have not so many guests these days that we cannot check up on their records. Yours is wild, but no more, Shamus Og, and you are a decent man's son——"

"Was he never wild?"

"Exactly! Wild in a wild crew, but he worked himself up and out of it. You can, too. A wife would do you a lot of good."

"Or a lot of harm?"

"Depends on you—and the wife."

"There's only one—never mind, chief! That one will take a better man. You'll not be seeing me this road again, I promise you."

"Watch the other roads too. Well, good-bye and good luck!"

The wards of the big lock clicked smoothly and Shamus Og stepped through the wicket-gate into freedom.

The desolate light of the dawn was in the wide empty street. A drear December morning. There had been rain in the night, and the pavement glistened coldly, and the water-splashes in the roadway were a wan silver; and the blown arms of the big trees up the slope tossed bare branches in a chill wind that sent brown leaves scurrying to lie soddenly in damp corners.

Shamus Og pulled the collar of his coat about his ears. "Dammit! What need had he to put the thought of her in my head?"

He walked out into the roadway and hesitated. What was he to do now? Go on up to Limerick where his show was? What else was there? And from Limerick to Thurles, and Thurles to Birr, and Birr to Mullingar, and Mullingar to Punchestown, and Punchestown to the Curragh—and the same road over again all his empty days, with an occasional wild burst as a protest against the emptiness. He shrugged his shoulders. Ah well! The train to Limerick was not due for two hours yet, and he must pass the time; and all he could do would be to get half-drunk in a Boherbwee shebeen. And why not?

He took half a dozen hesitant steps and stopped dead.

"Mother o' God!" he whispered.

A young woman, tall and slender and closely shawled, had come round the corner twenty yards away. That young woman had been at the other side of the corner for a quarter of an hour, gathering a courage hard to gather, and was driven forward now by a desperation that was not courage. Yet she came on resolutely, with a smile on her face and no flush of excitement in her smooth cheeks. Only her heart hurt her with its beating, and a pulse was stormy in her neck.

She walked directly and unhesitatingly to Shamus Og, who seemed solidly planted in mid-street, and reached him out her right hand.

"You are welcome out, Shamus Og," she said, and

270

her voice was low and softly husky; and in spite of herself there was a shy tremor in it.

It was that shy tremor that gave Shamus Og the power to carry off his great minute. He caught her right hand in his left, her left in his right, so that the shawl slipped down on her shoulders and showed her red hair. His grip was no gentle one; and his voice was no more gentle than his grip.

"You'll say more than that to me, Julie Brien."

"What will I say, Shamus Og?"

"What I would say to you. That you are the only one for me and that I cannot do without you—an' I know that now, an' I knew it all the time, an' I had to come back—an' here I am."

"I will say anything you like, Shamus Og," she whispered softly, and her amber eyes flashed on him and melted and looked down.

"You have said all I want, heart's treasure," said Shamus Og, and he placed a hand gently across her shoulder. "We will go back to my father's camp man and wife. Have you any friend in this town?"

"Two of your friends are here with me, Shamus Og," she whispered.

III

It was evening again and the rain had stopped. That rain had fallen almost without ceasing for two days, and the shoreward current of the Shannon ran brown and swollen. The sky was now a washed-out thin blue, and a few wisps of clouds came up out of the west and filmed and died; and the sun, a sullen yellow ball, above the hill of Knockanore, lit all that wide landscape to a sullen glory.

A big brazier of charcoal burned redly a few yards away from the steps of the van. Jamesy Coffey sat in front of this on his soap-box; across at the other side Maag Carty crouched and smoked and watched the big kettle coming to the boil; Daheen was under the van sitting unusually quiet, his arm round the neck of Tomboy, the lurcher; and at the head of the steps sat Ailish Conroy, deep in a book. That book was a gazetteer of Irish place-names, and only last night she had discovered that Daheen, son of the twisting Irish roads, knew more about it than she did.

"Will you be hurrying up that cup o' tay, Ma," urged Jamesy irritably.

"No hurry, darling! You'll get a good cup when the time comes."

"An' it four o'clock already! Daheen," Jamesy shouted, "come away from that dog—there was a flay at me last night—or I'll belt you!"

"You couldn't belt your grandmother," Ailish derided him from the head of the steps.

"There you are now—there you go—an' no man here to give me a hand with the three o' ye. But be the 'tarnal! if—if——"

Tomboy barked sharply under the van, and tried to break from Daheen's grip. All turned quickly, with a start of surprise and expectation, and looked down the slope of grass towards the harbour. A man was coming up towards them, but he was not the man they looked for. This was a short sturdy man, with iron-grey hair blown backwards and shoulders rolling to the swing of his light feet. Ailish looked at him intently for a moment or two, and then cried out in pleased surprise.

"Why, it is Sir Jerome—Sir Jerome Trant, you know!"

She slid down the steps and ran to meet him; and he halted to make sure who this light-footed girl of the roads was. And then she had his hands in hers and was shaking them impulsively.

"Why, Jerry—Dad—I am glad to see you. Wherever did you come from?—and how well you look!"

He laughed pleasantly, and his brown eyes, no longer veined with red, lightened to the warmth of affection in her deep blue ones.

"Now then, young gypsy woman, you must not rough-handle a respectable member of society." His hands pressed hers firmly.

"But how did you know where to find me?"

"Your friend Mr Long told me that—and several other things. Is he not here?"

"No," and she added, "not yet," for a quick, keen thought flashed in her mind.

"He dropped me word that this would be a convenient evening to come across." The voice sobered. "I am just here to say good-bye, Elspeth. I take the Panama boat next week."

"But is there need to go, Dad? You know——"

"Just a dream of mine, Else. I'm going to give it a trial."

There was a pause of hesitation and then she pulled at his hands.

"Come and let me introduce you to some wonderful people."

"Wait!" he said smilingly. "I want to look you over. You are rather surprising, you know."

He loosed his hands and stepped back, and she threw up her chin and smiled at him.

Her head was bare, and her hair, that used to be subdued in a cultivated wave, was now a mass of black curls; her face, innocent of cosmetics, had taken on a smooth tan above an underflush of clean blood; and the well-defined bones of her cheek and jaw gave her that touch of jauntiness and resolution that is not unusual in women of the road. A black and green knitted guernsey outlined her slim vigour, and her clean ankles rose from serviceable brogues.

"At least you are alive," he said inadequately, and then very seriously: "Tell me, Elspeth, are you happy?"

"I never was happier in my life." And as she spoke she knew she spoke the truth.

He nodded. "Yes, I can see that. That is all I wanted to know, my dear. Come, then, and introduce me to your wonderful people—with whom I have drunk your health already."

Sir Jerome was received in the camp with courtesy and decorum. "The noble gentleman is welcome," intoned Maag Carty from her place at the fire. Jamesy Coffey shook hands warmly, fanned a three-legged stool with his bowler hat, seated his guest, and sat down by him on his soap-box. Ailish smiled, knowing that no one was allowed to share that throne except Rogue McCoy; and a small pang went through her, remembering how the two used sit side by side smoking amicably. Daheen murmured his shy "How're you, sir?" from beneath the van, and poked Tomboy's head with his own.

The baronet glanced round the camp and then at Ailish interrogatively.

"Rogue McCoy is out of camp for a day or two," she told him easily, and turned to Maag Carty.

"Woman-o'-the-house, Jamesy wants his tea, and Sir Jerome will take a cup with us."

"Delighted," said the old diplomat.

"A great honour to us, surely," said the priestess at the fire.

"'Tis only an excuse I am all me days, your honour," said Jamesy.

They had tea agreeably together, and Sir Jerome admired the handy clean way these outdoor folks manipulated the heavy stoneware cups and the buttered scones.

He and Jamesy talked briskly of horses and hunting and fishing-waters; and Ailish noted the diplomatic deftness with which he swept away all shyness and restraint.

Tea was over and Daheen had collected and carried the utensils into the van, when the purr of a motor-car on the island road roused the camp to a fresh interest.

A big closed car came slipping along by the woods, across the causeway, and over the bridge below them, to disappear at the other side of the public-house on the pier. It did not reappear on the road beyond, and the people in camp watched with some hopeful interest for a space.

"Only a commercial traveller looking for orders from Mary O'Connor," grumbled Jamesy at last, and warmed his hands over the brazier.

IV

It was the lurcher that again apprised them that visitors were approaching. He pricked his ears, gave a short excited bark, wrenched free from Daheen, and tore down the slope. Two people were coming up shoulder to shoulder, and Tomboy charged them, sprang about them, made knots of himself. The two bent over him, and their heads were close together; and, seeing those two heads close together, something drained out of Ailish Conroy's breast, and her heart beat hollowly in her side.

"There they are now for you, Maag Carty," said Jamesy in a strangely subdued voice.

"It is youth's way to be playing games," murmured Maag Carty."

"And a game I don't like," he said heavily.

"Patience, darling man!"

Sir Jerome Trant looked on interestedly. He sensed

275

that the four people in camp were stirred deeply by the arrival of this man and girl.

Julie Brien and Rogue McCoy—yes, Rogue McCoy—walked into their midst. Julie's eyes were downcast to hide their shyness, but her smile gave that shyness away. Rogue was the bold villain, bold and calm; he looked at no one till he escorted Julie to the foot of the steps. "Sit there, *acara*," he said, and turned at Maag Carty's side.

"What's for supper, dark mother?" he enquired carelessly, and peered into a brown-paper parcel at her side. "Glory! I knew that you would have a feast for us—chops and sausages trimmed with onion and tomato—and shares to spare."

"And some one for them, too, son darling," she whispered up at him, her firm mouth just flickering to a faint smile.

"O wise one!" he murmured, and placed the palm of fealty on her shoulder. He looked across at Sir Jerome Trant and lifted a hand in easy salute. "Good evening, Sir Jerome, I was told that you were to be here."

He strode round the brazier to Jamesy on his soap-box. "Shove over!" he ordered casually. "Have I always to be telling you?"

Without a word Jamesy gave him half the box, and the two sat side by side.

"How goes the work, ganger?" enquired Rogue.

"Well you might ask, an' a sixteen-pound hammer gone rusty these two days."

"It won't be rusty this time to-morrow," said Rogue.

"Maybe it will an' maybe it won't," Jamesy mildly retorted.

Rogue for the first time looked up and across the quivering glow of the brazier at Ailish. She had taken her customary seat at the head of the steps, her book on her knees. Somehow his eyes had avoided her till now, and somehow, too, he felt a small touch of shame meeting her glance. The red glow of the coke lit her face to a queer blend of tenderness and strength, and her dark eyes and sensitive mouth smiled whimsically. That smile came out of splendid bravery.

"Hullo, Ailish! What's the book?"

She accepted that cue. She raised the book and held it to the last of the western light. "Could you give me," she questioned, "the exact location of Clounthanaghalkeen?"

"To be sure I could," he proclaimed boldly. "If you were to take the road from Inchageela to Gougane Barra——"

"Ho-ho-ho!" came Daheen's laughter from under the van. "'Tis at the back of the Stack Mountains, that place."

"Dash it, man! why didn't you give me time to get there?"

"'Tis the roundabout road you were takin'," jeered Jamesy.

"Bah, headmaster!" derided Ailish.

"Only two days away," lamented Rogue, "and Jamesy Coffey lets every one get out of hand. Come away out, young fellow, and get your belting."

But Daheen stayed shyly under the van. There was something here he did not understand. Rogue frowned into the brazier and cursed himself for this play-acting. But it would soon be over—and some people did deserve a little punishment for a month of suspicion. As if he, Rogan Stuart, would play any old direful game ever again!

The lurcher barked once more, and two tall men came round the corner of the armoury and strode in amongst them.

V

One was Shamus Og Coffey, gay and gallant, the other Paddy Joe Long, his lean features faintly humorous.

Ailish Conroy's heart leaped into her throat.

Paddy Joe leant against a corner of the out-jut, looked up at her, and smiled half-mockingly; he looked across at Sir Jerome Trant and nodded understandingly; he took no notice of any one else, though Jamesy fixed him with an intent eye.

But Shamus Og walked straight to where Julie Brien sat on the last tread of the steps, towered over her, and reached her a hand that spoke of nothing but all-possessiveness. And she came to her feet, her hand in his, and her head poised half shyly.

He led her across to his mother.

"Maag Carty, this is my wife, Julie Brien."

The mother ignored him and looked calmly up at her daughter.

"Before the altar rails, girl?"

"With Rogue McCoy and Paddy Joe Long to witness, mother."

"Have you your lines?"

Julie touched her breast and her marriage certificate crackled below her fingers.

"I have no more to say."

But Shamus Og had. He crouched down on his heels at her side, and placed his two hands on her knee; and the light from the brazier gleamed aside in his eyes and on the strong jut of his chin. "Mother, I will make you two promises, and I will keep them before God and man."

She nodded to him.

"No other woman will take your daughter's place.

278

That's one, and the other is that, though I have my father's tongue, and often the cross word and the angry word, I will never lift my hand to her, as God is my judge."

She placed her fine long hand across his for a moment. "God keep ye, children! You'll have your share of happiness. And now I will make the supper for all of ye."

Ailish Conroy came into action now. She sprang down the steps and faced Shamus Og.

"You silly play-actors of men!" she said devastatingly; and then she smiled her dimpled sideways smile and reached out a hand. "I am Ailish Conroy, Shamus Og. Let me be the first to congratulate you, and will you please present me to your wife?"

He grasped her hand warmly, lifted his cap, and bowed like a fine and gentle man. "To be sure, my lady! —Julie Brien, my wife."

Next instant Julie was caught close in Ailish's arms.

Ailish turned then to Rogue McCoy, sitting stolidly on the soap-box. "Must you always be compelled to do good by stealth, Rogue?" she questioned softly.

"Good?" He shook his head. "How do I know, Ailish girl?"

She shrugged her shoulders and went back to the van steps.

Maag Carty began arranging her mutton chops in the frying-pan and took no notice of any one. Rogue McCoy rose to his feet, his part played, moved round to the side of the van, and rested a shoulder against the wheel. Presently Daheen slipped from his shelter, sidled close to his hero, and nestled under the arm that came quietly round his shoulder.

"Man, Rogue!" he whispered up, "*Copaleen Rua* is a grand jumper. Ailish would fly the moon on him."

"That's a big lepp, Daheen."

"She would so. She let me take one weeshy jump over in O'Connor's field, an' I never fell off—only he bled me nose with his poll."

"And I'll bleed hers if you break your collar-bone."

Jamesy Coffey interrupted any further whisperings. He jumped to his feet and kicked the soap-box out of his way.

"I been watchin' ye," he said in a grim strange voice, "an' I been listenin' to ye, an' no one has been payin' no heed to me. But in my own camp I will be heeded. Don't you be in no hurry with our supper, Maag Carty. There is something to be done yet that was always done where a Coffey had the last word—and that's me this night. Wait ye!"

He hurried to the tilt-cart, scrambled inside, scrambled out again, and lifted a heavy leather bag to the ground. It was an ancient bag of a kind never seen nowadays, with stiff square ends, and a heavy curved bar across the top. It dragged down his shoulder as he brought it across between brazier and van where there was no draught. There he laid it down, fumbled at the catch, and thrust it open in a wide gape that showed the complete jumbled kit of the tinsman: the small anvil in its wooden block, the blunt-nosed vice on its stilt, the soldering irons, scissors, tweezers, pincers, long-nosed hammers, old-fashioned rods of solder, and half-empty bottles of spirits of salt.

Jamesy shook his head reminiscently at his tinker's budget. "God be with the ould days when my father used you in every townland in Munster and in Connaught as well. That ould tilt there was the first car he ever owned, and it will carry me to the grave; and this budget belonged to my grand-grandfather—and the use of it will go with me; but many a lively couple jumped it, with no priest to bless or curse before or after—and this night it will be jumped too, priest or no priest."

He fumbled in the bottom of the budget and brought out two dusty wax candles; next he propped the vice upright in the bag and fixed the candles close together in its jaws, took off his bowler hat, scraped a match alight on tightened pants, made the sign of the cross carefully with the flame and lighted the candles to a muttered Gaelic phrase—"*agus go gouirid Dia an rath*—and God send luck."

"Julie Brien Shamus Og Coffey—come here!" His voice had grown strangely deep and stern.

Julie looked at her mother, and her mother nodded. "Let not a law be made or broken," said the wise woman.

The two young people came to the old man's hands, and he placed them back to back by the side of the burning candles. "You will do what I tell you now!" he ordered. "Are ye ready?" He was as solemn as a vestmented celebrant, and his blue-jowled face, in the light of the brazier, had taken on an old dignity. The ritual was more ancient than his name, as ancient as fire worship, and was in a Gaelic of many obsolete words.

"*Brostuig agus gluisigid go mear*—haste ye and walk swiftly from the lightness of your youth." They obeyed and came face to face at the other side of the budget.

"*Iumpuig agus siubal ar ais*—turn and haste back again and welcome the clan not yet born."

"*Fill ar ais aris*—return again, and that is for the last meeting of all in Tir-nan-og—the land of youth."

The two were face to face now, and, with a motion of the hand, he directed them to turn to the lighted candles, shoulder to shoulder.

"*Leim, a Shiobain ni Briain!*—Jump, Julie Brien! to happiness or to sorrow, and let the flame tell you."

Julie gathered her skirts close about her slim legs, looked anxiously at the flaring candles, relaxed her knees, and bounded, like a fawn, safely over. The light flickered below her toes and flared again. Shamus Og drew a deep sigh of relief.

"*Leim Sheamus Oig Ui Cobhthaig!*—Jump, Shamus Og Coffey."

"*Suas e!*—Shamus Og!" cried that bold man, and jumped four feet into the air and over. The candle flame did not even flicker. He landed neatly at Julie's side, threw his arms round her, and kissed her full on the mouth before them all.

"Jacus! Paddy Joe Long!" cried Jamesy disgustedly, "wou-wouldn't they give you a pain in your belly?"

He bent down and put the candles out between thumb and finger. "So life goes without blow of breath to warn it." He finished the ritual. "*Ta sib posta, anois*—now ye are bound."

VI

Shamus Og and Julie moved back, and Jamesy, still solemn, lifted his hand for quiet. They all watched him. He stood staring down at the open budget and his hand smoothed over his blue jowl. He was in deep and serious thought and remained so for all of a minute. Then he spoke quietly, without lifting his head.

"Paddy Joe Long, come here!"

"Here I am, pagan chief," said Paddy Joe, just as quietly, and came forward to his side.

The two had little to say to each other. They understood. They looked at each other steadily, and Jamesy spoke in a low voice.

"Is the time come, Paddy Joe Long?"

"On God's earth, never a better time." And Paddy Joe stepped back to stand by Jerome Trant's side.

Using the same quiet yet dominant tone, Jamesy Coffey went on:

"Rogue McCoy, I will speak to you."

And without a word Rogue came across from where he leant with Daheen against the wheel of the van.

"Ailish Conroy, come here!"

"Goodness!" That little startled exclamation sprang out of sheer surprise, and the start she gave brought her to her feet at the foot of the steps. A flush came up to her very brow and a whirl of thought, half dismay, half excitement, made her dizzy. Yet she came light-footed to Jamesy's other hand.

The old man, looking out straight ahead over the darkening river, spoke slowly, and his words made a low boom from the walls of the fort.

"Rogue McCoy, you were sent to me by a man I trust, for a reason that was not given, and that man is here now to know how you and I have acted by each other. The thought of his coming has been on my mind this many a day, and heavy on it." The voice firmed. "But, this minute I know, before God and man, that you and I are not ashamed of the things we done by each other in this camp."

Rogue inhaled a deep breath, and a fine surge of pride went through him. The old man went on.

"You were son to me, you were father to me, sometimes you were God Almighty to me." He shook his head slowly. "But it is lonely to be God Almighty." And here he repeated an old Gaelic rune: *Eolas na Tigearna*—the Wisdom of the Lord God.

> The Lord knows, Oh ! He knows !
>   He knows all :
> What you think, what I think,
>   Why sparrows fall.
> If you knew what God knew,
>   Oh ! sorry hour !
> Hunger to lose, Wonder to lose,
>   And passion's power.

"And as you were sent to me you sent this woman at my side—out into the dark of the night you sent her into my two hands. It is so?"

Rogue steadied himself. He had not sent this woman; yet it must so stand. "It is so," he agreed, deep-voiced.

"And it is so. What she was to you is your own business, but what she is to you in this camp is mine. I saw you near kill a man at Castleinch Fair, and he would be a dead man if her voice had not stopped you in the very fall of the blow. Listen to me, now. Julie Brien is leaving me to-night for her own life, and I will be left with you two in this camp. But in this camp you cannot stay—one or both—unless you obey my law."

"And that law?"

"Jump the budget this night with Ailish Conroy."

"Marriage?"

"As I know it. Any other marriage ye can make or not make as ye like when mine is bound."

"Sir Jerome Trant and I will see to that," said Paddy Joe.

The baronet, on his feet, bowed assent. He had no thought of interfering in this strangely solemn ritual.

Jamesy Coffey stepped back, and Rogue and Ailish faced each other. Rogue's face was grim and unyielding, but his grey eyes were deeply lit. In Ailish's face there was no longer any colour, but her chin was up and her head thrown back gallantly. So they looked at each other in a silence that bound everything under the winter gloaming.

And then Rogue spoke in his sombre, tired voice:

"What is it that I can give, Ailish?"

"What I would hold against all hurt," she answered simply.

"You would have me?"

"Only you."

He threw his hands out in a gesture that was all resignation, surrender, surcease of struggle against the inevitable.

And he turned to his chief. "We are ready, Jamesy Coffey."

And so the little ceremony was repeated.

Ailish jumped the lighted candles with the ease of a roe, and turned to watch Rogue, anxiety in her eye; and Rogue, looking down at the pulsing flame, had a last queer impulse to kick the candles over as he leaped, but in the very act of jumping he changed his mind, pulled his feet up, and the flame sank, flickered, and drew up again.

Ailish drew a sigh of relief and faced him, her cheeks now aflush and her mouth ready for that whimsical sideways smile. And he took her right hand in his and bent his lips to it. And the quick warm pressure of her fingers made his heart stir.

"That's another way," said Jamesy, back in his old guise, "an' no worse than the next."

And at that Rogue's arms went over Ailish's shoulders, and he kissed her gently, softly, tenderly on the mouth.

"Well—well!" said Jamesy philosophically, "every man his own way. But divil the woman I ever seen I would kiss in daylight."